# Blackwood Manor

# BLACKWOOD MANOR

## ASHLEY BUNDY

Blackwood Manor

Copyright 12/01/2023, by Ashley Bundy.



Cover by Sleepy Fox Studio

Thanks to the creepy houses of childhood. Without you there would be no Blackwood Manor.

# <u>PART ONE</u>

## CHAPTER ONE—WINTER 1864

Blackwood Manor sat on Georgia's rolling hills. A magnificent building in her prime, she now sat cold and lonely. The war had changed her just as it changed those within. It had drawn every last ounce of hope and joy out of their souls until all that was left was little more than a shell shaking with dread and regret.

Now the building was a vessel for hate and greed. The grounds that once housed hundreds of souls were now empty except for four people: three living in the main house and one in the cottage out back.

Blackwood once stood majestically, with her brilliant white paint job and columns framing the wide brick front porch. The big windows looked out at the land, smiling at approaching visitors with such a joyous glow that the light from inside seemed to dance in their frames.

She had been in the family since 1802, when Gerald Blackwood built her for his new bride, Elizabeth. Family members may have passed, but their memories were said to live on behind the walls of the manor house. The memories of the slaves throughout the years were also said to linger on, roaming the house, the fields, and the surrounding woods. There were good memories too, but they were long put away and forgotten by the living. In turn, the memories that lashed out were negative, angry and bitter. *"Open your eyes. See me!"* they demanded. *"Did I never matter?"*

Now, as the war changed everything, the house changed as well. It no longer stared out with the appearance of dancing lights in the windows, but an eerie glow that would often send chills down the spines of anyone who dared to enter the property. Which didn't happen often. The woman of the house couldn't keep up with the repairs, so Blackwood Manor was slowly decaying.

It will never be known whether the grounds' atmosphere changed due to the war taking away everything, or to the people's changing attitudes and raving secrets.

Inside the main house, a servant girl named Josie was descending the staircase into the cellar while holding a tray of food in one hand and a lantern in the other. When she reached the bottom she turned and saw the frightened child huddled against one wall, shaking. The girl was two years old, though she was not much bigger than a fifteen-month-old.

Josie's breath caught in the back of her throat at the sight of her, as it always did. This poor child, so sweet and precious, had been banished down here when she was barely a year old. She was forced to sit in the dark, make no noise, and not ask questions. Any other behavior would earn her a beating. She couldn't say for herself when she was hungry, just hope that someone remembered to bring her food.

Josie snuck down whenever she could, usually after everyone was asleep, but it wasn't possible every night. Miss Margaret often had migraines and would be up late and sometimes she just sat in darkness in the parlor waiting, as though she suspected.

The little girl relaxed as Josie approached her and recognition flew across her face. Josie only ever treated the child with kindness.

"Here you go, sugar," Josie said sweetly, setting a tray down in front of the girl and smiling as she watched her eyes go wide as she began to eat.

Josie didn't know what she meant to this girl, the awe that filled her tiny heart whenever she saw her. She was short and slender but her bones and eyes didn't stick out so sharply. Her dark skin was smooth and clear of blemishes and always seemed to glow, especially when she laughed. When she laughed her chocolate brown eyes would dance and crinkle up at the edges just the tiniest bit. She was beautiful. She was an angel. She had no way of knowing that this child often dreamed of Josie taking her and running away together or that she imagined Josie was sent down straight from heaven itself to rescue her.

"I'm sorry it's so late. Miss Margaret has been in a state. She kept me running today," she sighed and ran her fingers through the girl's dirty hair. "Almost two days. Sometimes I think she wants you to die."

The girl looked up at her with those eyes that were much too big and spoke for the first time in almost a week. Her voice cracked from dryness. "Die?"

Josie hesitated a moment, unsure of how to answer. She had never been asked that question by someone quite as young. Finally, she took a deep breath and said, "To die is to not be a part of this world anymore. Instead, you must live with the spooks and will never be able to do anything good or talk to anyone you love."

"No die," she was firm, her small mouth set in a tight line.

"You won't, honey. Not for a long, long time." Josie smiled for the child's benefit, but her eyes still showed the worry that was always on her mind.

"She ought to at least give you a name."

The girl smiled and went back to her food, disregarding her fork and shoveling handfuls of food into her mouth until her cheeks puffed up.

The girl wore a tattered rag of a dress that was too baggy on her tiny frame. Her blonde hair was a tangled and dirty mess that hung down her face as she ate.

Josie studied her face and was instantly glad the child couldn't see the concern in her features.

She was so small that her eyes appeared much too large for her face, protruding from the sockets ever so slightly as though they might pop if she smacked her head against something. Those eyes sat over prominent dark circles that never went away.

Josie wondered if this poor child ever got a peaceful sleep. Probably not. The fear would not let her.

The girl swallowed and as the food left her mouth her cheeks sunk in so dramatically that her cheekbones and jawline sat out in sharp comparison.

"Gloria. I think I'll call you Gloria because you're such a happy child. Wonderful. No matter what she says."

"Gloria." The girl giggled and pushed the empty tray away from her. Josie picked up a rag and quickly wiped the girl's hands and face.

"Come now. Let's get you settled. She'll be coming to check that you're asleep soon. You'll be wanting to see that you are when she does."

Josie helped Gloria burrow between the musty blankets that covered one section of the floor against the wall, then picked up the empty tray, blew out the single candle lighting the room, and made her way back up the stairs.

She tried to shut the door to the cellar quietly, but it creaked anyway and she gasped when she turned around to find Margaret Blackwood standing in the doorway to the parlor, staring at her. She looked formidable with the darkness behind her, most of her face hidden in shadow behind the flickering candlelight. All that did nothing to hide the silhouette of Margaret's tall, thin form, the hair piled on her head in a tight bun. The dark clothing that she now insisted on wearing full-time only made her appear more shadowed and more….evil.

"Miss Margaret. I didn't know you were awake, madam."

"Clearly," she said icily, glancing at the empty tray in Josie's hands. "You've been on a goodwill stroll, I see."

"Madam, the child is hungry."

"Aren't we all? What did you give her?"

"Grits. A piece of bread, carrots, and some milk."

Margaret sighed, but her eyes never grew softer. "Josie, isn't food hard to come by these days?"

"Yes, madam."

"Aren't we all breaking our backs out in the fields every day just to scrape by?"

"Yes, madam."

"What is it going to take for you to see that we simply don't have any extra?"

"Madam, she hadn't eaten in two days. I couldn't bear to hear her cry anymore."

"That's my business."

"She's your daughter. Surely, you don't want her to–"

Josie was cut off by the open-handed slap across her right cheek. It stung hard, and she stumbled, dropped the tray, and raised her hand to her cheek. The sound of glass breaking echoed in the otherwise silent house like a deafening roar.

She looked up in surprise, in fear. Miss Margaret had never struck her before. Nor, had any of the others that had been on the property since she had been born here. They had always been treated very well. Once upon a time, she had been quite close with Miss Margaret. She'd felt more like a confidant and friend than a slave. Until now. Still, she hadn't expected to be struck. The terror it caused started at her toes and rolled up into her belly in a fiery and painful knot.

"I'm sorry," Margaret said through her tight-lipped frown and rubbed her hand against her dress. "I lost my temper. Josie, that girl is an accident of birth. Not my daughter. What happens with her is purely my discretion. Now, clean up this broken glass and get to bed. This house has had enough activity for one day."

With that, Margaret turned towards the staircase to the second floor and floated up, the train of her dress flowing behind her.

Josie knelt on the ground and swept the contents back onto the tray. When she was sure she was alone, she sat on the ground and wept. She continued to send glances towards the staircase, for any sign that Miss Margaret was returning.

She was worried. Worried for Gloria. Worried for herself. Conditions were getting worse by the day, and with the cruelty at a whole new level, it would only escalate. But what could she do? She knew deep down she needed to find some way to help that little girl.

## CHAPTER TWO -2009

Emma Price looked away from the steering wheel and grinned at her best friend. Claire Donahue, always care free and crazy sat on the edge of the seat of the big suburban taking photo after photo through the rolled-down window as they drove along.

God, they had been apart way too long. Attached at the hip as children, they had kept in contact when Emma first moved back to Georgia for college. They only saw each other a handful of times since then and even phone calls had been sparse for a while. Life got in the way. But Emma never stopped thinking about or missing Claire.

Now she couldn't help smiling at her friend's reactions to the area. As soon as they got into the car Claire dug out her camera and started shooting. She was completely captivated by the Georgia countryside. The rolling hills and several plantation houses they passed were so steeped in history that it sucked in her attention like a sponge. The photographer in her had never been able to pass by the majestic and sad beauty of old places without capturing it forever in film.

Her passion was one of the many things that Emma loved about Claire. When she set her sights on something she was like a dog with a bone. All that energy and dedication seemed to flow right through the camera and shine in the glossy photographs as a loving tribute every single time.

"You never told me it was so beautiful." Claire tossed her hair behind her shoulder and reached down into the bag by her feet to grab a new roll of film.

Emma glanced over again and chuckled at her wild appearance. "Beauty is in the eye of the beholder."

Claire was what some might call an unconventional beauty. She was tall and lanky but it was her long dirty blonde hair, hanging in messy curls every which way, that revealed the wildness within. The magnificent mop framed a square jawline. Freckles sporadically spotted her face and stood out noticeably against her pale white skin. The pale blue eyes may have been light against her washed-out-looking skin, but they stood alive with a fire that made them the windows to her soul.

For as long as either one of them could remember, Claire had been a firecracker. She hadn't been one to take any crap from any of the boys in the playground at school and could kick ass before anyone even noticed a fight had begun, which ironically, is what started their friendship.

Despite her family being well off, at least for their position in the neighborhood, Emma had been bullied relentlessly. Her seven-year-old self hadn't known what to do when she'd been cornered on the playground her first day, called every name under the sun, and told that *her* kind didn't belong in *their* school. The biggest of the boys, who had to have been in at least fourth grade, knocked her down and dragged her by her hair toward the street. Out of nowhere Claire jumped off the jungle gym, strolled right up to that little punk, and without a single word she'd socked him right in the nose. She reached down to help Emma up and then turned back to tell him he was the nasty one and maybe he should leave. Neither one of them could remember that little snot's name now, but it had been the start of a beautiful friendship that never wavered despite the time and distance.

That fight transferred into her love of film in a way that nothing else could.  From a young age, she could make the simplest shots look as though they belonged in a museum somewhere.  She started by photographing the religious relics around her parents' house with a cheap Polaroid camera she received for Christmas when she was seven.  Everyone had been amazed at how well the pictures turned out.

Now, the greenery of the hills spoke to her, pulling her almost as if by a magnetic force to look further off into the distance.

"Stop!" Claire cried out suddenly.

Emma slammed on the brakes and looked around frantically, trying to see the cause of urgency in her friend's voice.

"There!" Claire pointed off into the distance at a massive plantation house that sat far back in the hills. It was decrepit, even from their spot on the road, but Claire stared, unblinking. "What is that place?"

"Blackwood Manor?" Emma asked with some confusion. "It's been vacant ever since I've lived here."

"Why would a place this magnificent be vacant for so long?"

"Maybe because it would take a fortune to get it back up to code," Emma laughed. When Claire didn't return her laugh and continued to stare at the structure, unblinking, she felt a panic she could not explain deep in her gut. "Plus, it's got a terrible reputation."

This seemed to zap Claire out of her trance and her head snapped back toward Emma. "Bad reputation?" she asked with an excited inquisitive tone to her voice, and her eyebrow shot up in the way it did when she was on the verge of learning something particularly juicy.

"Supposedly, it can't keep occupants. Legend has it that the house and grounds are so severely haunted that people will tear out in the middle of the night." Emma shuddered and forced her gaze away from the house and looked at the road straight ahead.

"Ghost stories?" Claire laughed and nudged her playfully. "Why so glum, Em? I thought you were totally into ghost stories. Bloody Mary? Light as a feather, stiff as a board?"

Emma shrugged her shoulders. "Those were kids' games. There's something not right about that place." Her voice quavered with her nervousness and there was the slightest tremble in her hands.

"Come on!" Claire cried. "It's a beautiful building and it's steeped in an elaborate, fascinating history."

"A terrible history!" Emma turned and looked back at her, and finally raised her eyes in the direction of the house again. "It was a bustling Civil War plantation that was supposedly taken over by enemy troops who burned the crops and killed the women and children who lived there. It's full of hundreds of angry spirits looking for revenge for what was taken from them."

"Now, you're bringing me back to our childhood!" Claire laughed playfully, and flung the door open, hopping from the car, clutching her camera. She was running through the overgrown fields toward the tree-lined path in the direction of the house.

"Claire!" Emma called. She was answered by Claire's gleeful cackling laugh, and she turned to look out the windshield once more. She took a deep breath and leaned her head back against the headrest. She moved her gaze to the rearview mirror, made eye contact with herself, and breathed slowly to calm her anxiety. A buddy in a support group many years before suggested this technique and she discovered it always worked for her. The idea behind it was to stare yourself down when you fear you're being irrational. Confront those demons in the eye and take charge, by God.

Looking back from the mirror she took in her sleek black hair framing a heart-shaped face, big expressive brown eyes, and flawless umber skin that she had gotten plenty of attention for, both positive and negative, over the years. Her beauty was unquestionable but her reserved nature always guaranteed that Claire was the one in the spotlight, always. That was just fine with her. Just fine. As her breathing slowed she allowed herself to break eye contact and think about what Claire said.

It was true that they had played these games when they were younger. It had been all fun and games trying to scare the pants off each other. It stopped being fun that frightful night when they were ten years old and led to a terrifying summer. The fun had been dead and buried when Emma's grandmother visited her an hour after her father called to tell her she passed away. That had been her senior year of college. Strange things happened since then too, and Emma became much more careful of the supernatural. She followed all the superstitions and did her best to stay away from anything that may trigger an occurrence.

She thought back to the feel of the air in the room with the Ouija board between them, the candles burning all around, and the sweet vanilla scent that came from them. She thought of how the planchette moved under her fingers.

Claire assumed that Emma became dull after getting married and having children; that her disinterest in those games was a mere desire to keep her children away from it, but she was wrong.

It had been a long time since Emma had a brush with the paranormal; still, every time she passed

Blackwood Manor she was filled with a very overwhelming sense of foreboding. The air was heavy and she had difficulty breathing. The smell of rot and death seemed to come off the land like heat, making it more difficult for her to breathe. It was as if the entire structure and fields surrounding it were secreted in this bubble of its own world. You could never be truly safe until you were well outside the confines of the bubble. She never stayed in front of it for so long. She normally sped up just a little bit when passing. The sooner she put space between herself and Blackwood Manor, the better.

She could no longer hear Claire's laughter or see her wild mess of curls over the overgrown grass. She took another deep breath and bolted from the car without stopping and ran straight for the path before she could change her mind.

"Claire!" she called, looking frantically for her friend. As she ran farther down the path her chest began to feel tighter, as if a hand had wrapped around her heart, slowly squeezing it inch by miserable inch. Her heart beat rapidly and she could feel it pounding inside her head. She could feel the heat flushing into her cheeks. Her chest would surely explode at any second. She willed herself to stop running, but it was as if she was no longer in control of her own body. Her feet seemed to move faster than they ever had in her entire life, as if an invisible force with much longer legs than hers had taken over her body, and was willing her to go faster. She could not stop her legs but she could feel the burn and tightening of the muscles, angry from this sudden and brazen assault.

Finally, she collapsed into a heap on the ground. A mixture of red clay and weeds was inches from her face, and she gasped for breath, trying to ignore the shaking in her sore legs and pounding in her head.

She looked up and saw she had collapsed right at the broken brick steps leading up to the porch of Blackwood Manor. The massive house towered over her, the broken front windows seemingly smiling down at her in a twisted, ferocious grin.

Emma scrambled to her feet, shaking. This was the closest she had ever gotten to the manor house. The house was a whitewashed color that would have looked amazing at a different time, but was now grimy and peeling. The giant columns on the front steps framed the busted windows of the front and the splintered wood of the massive oak door in a way that made her see nothing but a sinister face.

It was not difficult to see how beautiful it had once been, but now, in its run-down state, it looked positively evil, staring at her with a mocking grin that seemed to say, *"Come inside, Emma. You know you want to. Join us."*

She backed away, first taking one small step, then another. She wanted to put as much space between her and Blackwood Manor as was humanly possible but she couldn't leave Claire.

Finally, she heard the familiar sounds of Claire's camera shutter and saw her friend creeping around from the side of the house towards the front, snapping picture after picture.

"Claire!" she called out in relief. She walked towards her friend slowly who gave her a bedazzled look of excitement. "Why didn't you answer me? I've been calling and calling you."

Claire laughed and threw back her head in another throaty laugh, her eyes dancing. "Em, I would have heard you if you'd called. Plus, I got out of the car less than five minutes ago."

That wasn't even possible. It had to have been at least ten. "Stop clowning around, Claire. It isn't funny. Bad things happen here. I was worried."

"What's going to get me all the way out here? The house?"

"What's *in* the house will," Emma said firmly.

Emma felt embarrassed as Claire's playful look of mischievousness disappeared when she finally took in Emma's appearance. She was sweaty, out of breath, and her skin was completely flushed as if she had just finished running a marathon. Her black hair had tangled, making her look slightly wild. Her cheeks and clothes were streaked from the dirt where she had fallen. What got to Claire though, were the tears in her eyes. "You really believe this, don't you?"

Emma didn't answer but turned swiftly on her heel. "I want to go back to the car now." She took no more than two steps when she tripped over something hidden in the tall weeds. Something big. She screamed and fell down a slight hill, clutching her leg.

"Em! Emma, you okay?" Claire ran towards her and helped her friend up. "What happened?"

Emma motioned towards the tall and wild weeds. "I tripped over something big."

They walked back over slowly, Claire helping to support Emma's weight as she limped on her injured leg. Claire brushed back the weeds and saw a stone structure with a rusted metal hoop attached to it.

"Wow," she murmured in awe, running her fingers over it lovingly.

"What is that?" Emma asked. It was the most ridiculous-looking thing she had ever seen.

"It's a carriage block," said Claire, surprised. When Emma's puzzled expression didn't subside, Claire sighed in frustration and gestured towards it again. "A carriage block! It's where horse-led buggies used to be tethered in the olden days."

"I thought all those had been removed."

"Some older towns still have them. This one is truly remarkable though. It shows that it's been a long time since anyone has bothered with the upkeep of this place. See the rust?"

Emma stared at Claire in disbelief. The old place was falling down, it was staring them down like a psychotic stalker, and she was worried about a little rust on an old carriage block?

"Such a shame," Claire whispered, oblivious to Emma's looks of discomfort as she ran her hands over the stone. She lifted her camera and began to take pictures.

"Um mm, Claire? I don't mean to interrupt your love affair with the carriage block, but I hurt my leg. I think I'd like to go now."

"Hmm," Claire looked up finally. "Oh, yes. Of course." She returned to Emma's side and assisted her down the path towards the car, fighting weeds down as they went. When they finally reached the road, Emma screamed.

All four doors plus the hatch to the trunk were wide open. Everything that had been inside the car was now out, sitting in neat little piles around the car but they had heard nothing.

Emma trembled as she saw everything, her children's car seats, toys, camping equipment that they hadn't bothered to take out yet, her purse with her phone neatly placed on top sitting directly in front of the car.

"I told you there was something wrong with this place," she muttered and started loading things back inside as fast as her injured leg would allow her.

"It's just kids," Claire shrugged her shoulders.

"It isn't. Not that fast. If it were kids or vandals they would've taken the valuables. I want to get out of here."

"That's going to have to wait. At least for a little while."

"And why is that?"

Claire pulled in a deep breath and motioned towards the tires. The two facing the women were both flat.

"No!" Emma dragged herself around to the other side to find that the other two tires were flat as well. She began to tremble. "Oh, God."

"It's a simple thing," Claire said, taking her shoulders firmly and steering her back towards the passenger side of the car. "We just have to call Triple-A."

Once she had Emma secured in the passenger seat, Claire pulled out her phone and began to dial Triple-A, circling the car as she spoke.

Inside the car, Emma was fighting the panicked tightness in her chest and the splitting headache once again. She looked up towards the house again with watering eyes. Did it wink at her? A powerful wave of nausea gripped her stomach and she just felt, she *knew* that Blackwood Manor did not want them to leave. They could call her crazy if they wanted, but Emma hardly felt that it was a good sign.

≈

Later that night, as they sat around the dining room table, Emma continued to feel the twisting of her stomach and a tightness in her chest. Since leaving Blackwood Manor she had no ease. That sense of foreboding sat on her, growing more and more insistent like a rotting tooth.

"Mom, are you okay?" said a soft voice that snapped her back to reality. Emma looked across the table at her thirteen-year-old daughter Bailey. Bailey was a perfect blend of Emma and Michael. She was more light-skinned than Emma but still owned her color like she'd never seen before, and she had Michael's electric blue eyes that made her gaze immediately noticeable. Right now, those eyes were narrowed in concern.

Emma had been pushing around her potatoes on her plate mindlessly. She smiled and took a bite, though the food tasted like chalk in her mouth. "I'm fine."

"Oh, she's just a little on edge," Claire said from the seat beside her. She gave Emma a playful clap on the back. "She twisted her ankle at Blackwood Manor today and is completely convinced that demons or ghosts or whatever are going to get us now."

Emma dropped her fork back down on her plate, shooting Claire an icy look. Claire didn't seem to notice. She just pushed her wild hair out of her face and went back to her food. The rest of the table seemed to explode in excitement.

"Blackwood Manor?" Bailey squealed. "That place is so spooky. It's so cool. Lexie Woods said her sister and two of her friends were dared to break in and spend the night there last year. They didn't last an hour. Something grabbed Sarah Cummings and dragged her by the hair down the staircase and tossed her out on the front porch. And Abby Marsh said like twenty years ago or something a bunch of kids went in for a party and they all died and one of the boys was never found."

Emma shifted uncomfortably in her seat.

"Bailey, that's enough," Emma's husband Michael said from his spot at the head of the table. He glanced briefly over at the couple's two youngest children. He didn't so much mind the girl's interest in the paranormal, it was ordinary enough for a teenager. He dabbled to an extent in his youth, if you counted watching "The Exorcist" and "Poltergeist" until the tapes wore out. The younger two though were particularly impressionable. Eight-year-old Richie didn't seem scared now. He leaned forward, taking in every word his older sister said. Tonight, though, he would likely have nightmares just like when he would talk his way into watching a scary movie with the rest of the family. Michael had a business meeting bright and early in the morning; he couldn't be draped over the foot of Richie's bed all night. Three-year-old Callie had her face scrunched up in confusion and a piece of chicken clamped in her tiny fist. She wasn't eating. She was watching Bailey. Her fascination mirrored how Richie's had started. Perfect.

"It was a demon, Dad," Bailey continued, ignoring her father. She put her face down close to Richie's and made her eyes go wide.

"You liar!" Richie said, putting his hand on her forehead and pushing her away. He was giggling and sent a grin across the table to Claire, who was laughing too.

"It wasn't a demon," Emma said softly. She wasn't sure where she found the voice to speak. She wasn't altogether sure what she just said was the truth. She felt it was important that she say it, though. "A demon wouldn't have wanted them to leave."

"It would if it thinks the house belongs to it," Bailey said, matter-of-fact, pinching a chunk off of her roll and dipping it in her mashed potatoes. "Demons are very territorial. That place was there long before the Civil War. All kinds of nasty things happened there. I wouldn't be surprised if all those places have demons. I heard the demon at Blackwood Manor is the worst one in the state. Unless you say a special poem when you go in. Then you're safe."

"Get out!" Richie squeaked in a near whisper. His eyes were dancing with interest. "Demons are bad. They won't leave you alone just because you say some stupid poem. Blackwood Manor probably doesn't even have any demons."

"Demons!" Callie yelled, then giggled and put her chicken in her mouth.

"Stop it," Michael said again, continuing to eat.

"Maybe not. If not demons, then mad ghosts. There's something bad about the place. Something that doesn't want anyone or anything there. How many owners did it go through? How long has it been empty? Use your brain, Dingus!"

"Ghosts!" Callie said.

"THAT'S ENOUGH!" Michael bellowed, bringing his fist down hard onto the table, making everyone jump. There was a moment of silence, then Claire spoke again.

"Well, we'll show you, kids, soon enough that there aren't any such things as ghosts or demons. Blackwood Manor is only an old, neglected building, in need of some tender loving care."

"How are you going to do that, Aunt Claire?" Bailey asked. She always called her Aunt Claire.

"Well, I spent the day making some phone calls," she said, her blue eyes sparkling with the excitement of finally making this announcement several hours in the making. "I found the current owner of Blackwood Manor. They've owned the place for thirty-five years but haven't lived there for thirty-four. It turns out that the owner's wife has a lot of medical issues requiring them to live further in the city. Her medical debt is sinking them. They're willing to take a payment well under value for the property. I'm going to buy it."

Emma's head snapped around. "You're going to what?"

"I'm going to buy it," Claire shrugged and winked at Bailey. "I'm thirty-eight. Who needs a savings account? I'm going to restore that place to the magnificence it deserves."

"Kids, go to your rooms," Emma said, without turning her head away from Claire.

"But we aren't done eating," Richie whined.

"Now!" she sharply repeated.

There was a scramble as Bailey and Richie got up from the table. Bailey pulled Callie out of her booster seat and the kids made their way down the hall toward their bedrooms. Once they heard the snap of their doors closing, Emma started in.

"Are you crazy? Claire, I told you what happened there. Families flee in the middle of the night. People that wander onto the property tend to get hurt. I wouldn't be surprised if Sarah Cummings was dragged out of that house by her hair."

"No one got hurt today," Claire shrugged.

"Hello," Emma swung her wrapped ankle out from under the table and pointed at it.

"Oh, Emma," Claire sighed and put her hand on her friend's shoulder as if to calm her. "I know you believe in that stuff, but I don't."

"You should. You know what happened when we were kids."

"I know we were a couple of ten-year-old kids who scared themselves senseless. It was fun, sure. But it wasn't real, Em. It's been nearly thirty years. It's time to let it go."

"Bullshit!" Emma was shaking with her anger. "It started as fun and games and what it escalated to was *not* fun. Please, don't do this."

"I would think you would be happy. We've been talking about me moving closer to you guys for years and now I'm going to do it. I don't see why you're being so uptight. Nothing is going on at Blackwood Manor except a bunch of speculation on why it's been empty for so long."

Emma turned to her husband, her eyes pleading. "Michael, help me! Tell her! Tell her about all the stories, even the ones I don't know! Please!"

Michael slowly swallowed the bite of food he had been chewing, and set his knife and fork down, carefully choosing his next words. "I agree that you shouldn't buy Blackwood Manor, Claire, but not because of ghost stories."

"Mich-" Emma began to interrupt, but he held up a hand, silencing her.

"I'm sorry, honey. Claire is absolutely right. That's all they are. Ghost stories. The place has been empty for so long and is so old with such a complex history that people created stories to pacify their wild imaginations. There's nothing there but dry rot and ruin."

Emma slammed back in her chair, her lips disappearing in a tight line, her brown eyes not leaving his as they swam with fury.

Michael ignored the furious stare and turned his attention to Claire. "However, I do agree that you shouldn't buy the place."

"Why the hell not?" Claire asked him, crossing her arms over her chest.

≈

He sighed, knowing he was going to have a hell of a night. Both women were looking at him with fury, arms crossed over their chests. No matter what he answered he was going to be in the hot seat. So he could only answer as honestly and sincerely as he felt and bear the consequences later. He wasn't looking forward to it. He was a bigger man, tall and thick, with a little bit of what he'd heard described as a "dad bod." His hair had once been thick and brown but began thinning and graying prematurely forcing him into shaving bald. That had given him no end of grief from the good old boys at the country club. His big stature didn't mean authority. The women in his life had him wrapped around their fingers. He'd loved Emma from the moment he had met her and he'd loved Claire like a sister from the jump. He would walk through fire for either of them and he didn't want to fight.

"It's seriously decrepit," he said, simply. "They may be offering you a bargain price for the house and land but have you thought about what it's going to take to restore the place? Building materials, labor, not to mention licenses to get everything up to code? It will have to be redone to 2009 standards, not 1909 standards. It could very well break you."

"That place is magnificent and historic. It should be a landmark like all the other plantations and I intend to get it there."

"Fine," Michael put his hands up in mock defeat. "It's your money. You're an adult. Do what you want. But I wouldn't be a friend if I didn't give you honest feedback."

There was another moment of awkward silence before Emma spoke again. "Would Brock let you do this?"

Claire slowly turned to glare at her, her eyes so dark they looked almost black. "Don't you say his name to me."

"Just because you ruined him does not mean you have to ruin yourself now."

Claire slammed her napkin on the table and got up, storming away towards the guest bedroom.

Emma put her head in her hands, trying to massage away the headache that had begun to form at her temples. She could only pray that she had gotten through. She glanced over at Michael, not bothering to hide the betrayal and hurt on her face.

"What?" he asked. "I told her not to buy it."

"You threw me under the bus."

"No, I didn't," he glanced up from his plate to look into her icy gaze and dropped his fork. "Emma, damn it, the place is falling in. It's going to cost her a fortune. I thought those were more important points than myths and urban legends."

There was a slight pause before she spoke again. "You said you believed me."

"I do," his voice was softer now. "I also believe her. Not everyone is as touched by these things as you are, honey. If she's unaffected what's the harm?"

"Blackwood Manor though?" her voice shook as tears began to flow down her face. "You know what they say about that place. I can't describe the way I feel when I pass it. What I went through today--"

Michael reached over, took her hand, and squeezed it gently.

"I can't lose her too."

"She's not Donna, honey," he said gently.

"She may as well be. I lost one sister but I gained another. If something happens to her…"

"It won't."

"Yeah," Emma pulled her hand from his grip and glided out of the room, leaving Michael alone at the table to realize that he was going to have a hard time at his meeting tomorrow morning no matter what.

## CHAPTER THREE

A month later, despite vigorous protests from Emma, Claire pulled up on the street in front of Blackwood Manor. The overgrown driveway proved impassable and moved to the top of her list. She hoped that she would still have tires the next time she came out. The guy from Triple-A last month had told her he made more money from breakdowns outside the manor than the rest of the county. Security cameras were at the top of the priority list as well. She was going to put a stop to that as soon as possible. The county's teens would learn not to screw with her property.

She dug the key that she had received just over an hour ago in the real estate office out of her purse and smirked at the feeling of accomplishment. She grabbed her purse and camera bag and began to make her way through the undergrowth up toward Blackwood Manor. *Her manor.*

She didn't recognize the change in the air, the silence when she crossed past the tree line as she got closer to the house. As she got closer and closer, the house looming larger and larger over her, she was only aware of the beauty that no longer was, of the energy that seemed to say, *"Welcome home, Claire. Come in. Kick off your shoes. Get comfortable. You'll stay here forever now."*

She walked up to the massive porch, careful of the broken, crumbling brick, and slipped the key into the keyhole on the massive oak door. She expected the lock to stick from years of neglect but it turned over smoothly with a musical *click*.

She pushed the door open and stepped over the threshold into an entrance hall that tantalized her despite the wear and tear. The floors were made up of the same oak as the front door and appeared to be in fair condition despite the dirt and grime. The stairway was ahead, sitting on the left with a wonderful oak banister and a faded and dirty red carpet trailing over the steps.

She couldn't hold back the gasp and the smile that came over her face as she took it all in. She had done a brief tour with the real estate agent before, very brief. The woman would only go between certain times of the day and had spent less than a minute in each room on the main floor, and skipped some rooms entirely on the second floor. Claire had appreciated the beauty then, but she hadn't had time to let it all soak in. Now, she could enjoy it. As she walked around the house and snapped pictures as she went, she began to envision it all. The work that would have to be done, the beauty that lay under the decay, and what she could do with this space.

The big parlor right off the entrance would be where she would shoot her "in-office" clients. There were two picture windows at the front of the house that, though now littered with broken glass and partially hidden underneath sagging, torn curtains, provided the best natural lighting and was an extremely spacious room. She could put her desk on one wall and set up backdrops on another large wall. She eyed the beautiful fireplace that sat in the corner.

Before buying Blackwood Manor she had never seen a corner fireplace before. It was extremely beautiful and she loved the effect it had. She may even be able to shoot some photos in that very spot. There was a large, ornate mirror hanging above the mantle, though the glass was now broken. She hoped she'd be able to find another one that looked as nice to put there. There were three corner fireplaces all backed up to connect in a circle from the adjoining rooms.

She quickly made her way toward the back of the house where the kitchen was. It had called to her since she briefly got to see it during the walkthrough. The real estate agent had barely let her peek inside. Now, she understood why. The kitchen was outdated with blue appliances from the 1950s and the door was hanging off the fridge.

The stench hit her in the face almost immediately and she grabbed the hem of her shirt, pulling it up to cover her mouth and nose. She approached the fridge and saw that it was still full of food from the previous inhabitants and saw maggots. She jerked the door back upright and jammed a bar stool up under the handle to keep it closed. Then a chill ran along her spine. The house had been vacant way too long. There *couldn't* still be food. She jerked the door open again. The stench was gone though there were still empty plates and containers inside. She closed the door again in an attempt to ignore what she just saw and continued her tour.

Along one wall was a massive shelf that stood from floor to ceiling. It was unnecessarily large and looked completely out of place. It would have to go.

The state of the kitchen did nothing to deter her. She knew she was buying As Is. Claire could picture the grand Chef's kitchen that it would become. She wanted to redo it in neutral grays with stainless steel appliances with a touch of blue in the curtains she would hang above the window. It would make for a marvelous photo shoot and she was already planning it. It didn't matter what it looked like now. This was *her* house. She had known it from the moment she saw it. There was a tall, shelf along one wall next to a door that led to a walk-in pantry.

She continued to walk through the lower floor. She glanced towards the door to the cellar but she didn't go down. She knew from the walkthrough that there wasn't a lightbulb down there currently and would be pitch black, so she would have to wait. But she decided that it would be her darkroom for developing photos. The absence of light would make it the perfect place.

She turned to mount the stairs to go out and survey the bedrooms. She hadn't even seen all of them in the walkthrough. The steps groaned under her weight and she stepped carefully just in case there were any warped boards.

When she reached the second-floor landing, Claire took in a small intake of breath as she saw the doors of the bedrooms leading down the hall. She counted six doors on each side of the hallway. Twelve rooms. What would she do with that much space?

She began to glide from room to room. Some rooms were bare, others crammed. One room was a small bathroom with a claw foot bathtub that someone renovated from one of the small bedrooms once upon a time.

Each room was extremely dirty, covered in broken glass, peeling wallpaper, and paint. At the end of the long hallway was a room that Claire instantly decided was hers. She adored the view out over the green hills and overgrown land. There was a perfect view of the small cottage out back, which the Realtor had told her had once been servant's quarters. Outside the door of her bedroom were two little narrow staircases; one leading up, one leading down.

Before exploring further, she became overwhelmed with emotion and had to sit down on the old, musty mattress that was sitting half off its bed frame. The beauty was incredible. She couldn't believe this was all hers now. Before she could push the thought away, she wondered what Brock would have thought of Blackwood Manor. She scowled almost immediately. He no doubt would have said that the place was a money pit and a stupid waste of time. He would have had the gall to *forbid* her from buying it. Well, they would just see who would have the last laugh here. Once this place was fixed up and restored to its former glory, she would have a landmark plantation home with more history in the floorboards than he had in what was left of the ginger hairs on his damn near bald head.

"Claire?" came Emma's voice from downstairs, yanking her thoughts back to the present. To the now.

"I'm up here!" she called and couldn't help grinning. She thought it would take her much longer to get Emma to come and see the house; but despite all her squawking, she knew that it would only be a matter of time before she'd come to help. Emma was not the type to let a close friend take on such a massive project on their own.

Her cell phone began to ring and Claire hurriedly pulled it from her jeans pocket and called down to Emma before answering. "I'll be down in a minute, Em! Phone! Might be an electrician!"

"Hello?" she answered. As soon as she had known what day she would be getting the keys she called a few electricians in town, but no one seemed to want to come to Blackwood Manor, claiming it to be too far out. She then placed ads online, searching for a freelancer, as well as a contractor. She wouldn't be able to move in officially until she had the place rewired and got the place back up to code. She would stay with Emma and Michael in the meantime.

"Yes, is this Claire Donahue?" asked a gruff male voice. From the sound of it, Claire estimated the owner of that voice to be at least in his fifties.

"Yes, it is."

"Yes, this is John Porter. I'm calling about the ad you placed for an electrician."

"Mr. Porter, thank you so much for calling. I just received the keys to a plantation home that has been vacant for quite some time. I need to get it rewired to code before I can move in. I've already tried a few electricians in town, but they all say it's too far out. I know it's a big project, but I'd be willing to pay you handsomely for the job."

"I know most of the plantation homes in the area. I don't know of any being so far out that anyone would be unwilling to go. Where is your place?"

"It's the old Blackwood Manor."

There was a moment of silence on the other end of the phone, and Claire could hear Porter taking a deep breath as if he were choosing his words carefully. "I'm afraid Blackwood Manor is too big a job for me to take on at this time. See, I already have other clients too and a project of that size would cause me to neglect them."

"I see," Claire sighed, disappointment evident in her voice. "Do you have any recommendations? I'm new to the area."

"I know a couple of independents like myself," he answered after a moment. "I'll pass your number around and see if anyone is willing to take it on."

"Thank you. I'd appreciate that very much."

"Say, your husband's there to help you take on some of the work, isn't he?"

"No, it's just me. I'm divorced."

There was a long moment of silence and then, "Heaven help you," and a click as Mr. Porter hung up the phone.

Claire stared at the phone in confused silence before returning it to her pocket just as she heard a creaky floorboard from downstairs.

"Hello?" a soft voice called up the stairs.

"Sorry!" Claire called, heading out of the bedroom and towards the staircase. "Em, I just had the weirdest phone conversation."

Claire stopped about halfway down the staircase. It was not Emma at the foot, but a woman in her mid-seventies that she had never seen before. She sported a baby blue business suit and bright red lipstick under heavy eyeliner and mascara. Her bleached blonde hair was piled in a messy bun at the crown of her head. She had a look that screamed unique, trying too hard to be normal. She wore a smile and held a pie out in front of her.

"I'm sorry," Claire chuckled and put a hand to her racing heart. "I thought you were my friend. She's roaming around here somewhere."

She descended the rest of the steps and extended her hand to the woman who warmly took it.

"That's quite alright," she released her hand and extended the pie. "I hope you like blueberry."

"Yes, very much," Claire took the pie. "How did you know I'd be here?"

"Your realtor called and told us we had a new neighbor at last. I'm Kate Wilkes. My family owns the neighboring plantation, Heaven's Estate."

"Oh yes, I remember seeing it. It's truly beautiful."

"Thank you. So is this place," Kate took a quick look around and blushed as she downcast her eyes. "Or it once was."

"And will be again," Claire smiled. "I'm Claire Donahue."

"Are you taking this place on all by yourself?" Kate followed Claire into the parlor and sat down on a dusty old sofa. She watched as Claire placed the pie on the mantelpiece and then strode back over to join her on the sofa.

"Well, yes and no. I'm buying the place alone. I just had a rough divorce and came out here to be closer to my best friend. She's practically like my sister and helped me through a lot over the past year. I'll be hiring a lot of people to help of course, and I'm sure my friend will help too."

"Well, that's very nice. Everyone should get a fresh start in rough circumstances."

"I think so."

"If it's not too over the line though, dear, I should probably tell you that you won't have a lot of help getting locals to work here."

"Why not?"

"Well," Kate took a deep breath and patted Claire's hand. "The place doesn't have the best reputation."

"You don't mean those silly ghost stories?" Claire rolled her eyes without realizing how rude it may come across. "You don't believe that do you?"

"No, I—I don't suppose I do," Kate's fingers were absentmindedly playing with the hem of her skirt. "Not in the way people tell it at least. I do believe there is something. But that's true of all these old places. They are too old with too much history."

"It's just a house. Beautiful and long neglected, but a house just the same."

"Yes, well," Kate rose to her feet. "I better get back. The place won't run itself."

Claire rose to her feet and shook Kate's hand. "One more thing. Do you know where I might find a freelance electrician willing to rewire the place for me?"

"I suppose Bradley Morse would do it. He may even be able to help with the other work as well. He's a bit of a chameleon. He's worked on a lot of renovations."

"He doesn't believe in the ghost stories?"

"Oh, he believes in them. They don't faze him, however. His grandmother raised him and she was a seer. I'll have him swing by."

"Thank you," Claire said as she followed Kate to the front door. "I appreciate it."

"You feel free to come by and visit anytime you want."

"I will. And you're welcome to come here and visit once everything is safer."

Kate smiled and said, "We'll see, dear," and swept her way out the front door.

Claire looked around, straining her ears for any sign of noise to give away Emma's location, then finally pulled out her phone in frustration to call.

"Hello?" Emma answered.

"Did you get lost?" Claire chuckled.

"What are you talking about?"

"You called out to me and I haven't seen you since."

"Claire, I told you that I'm not going out there until you can prove to me that it isn't dangerous."

Claire stood rooted to the spot, with her phone plastered to her ear.

≈

Later that afternoon, just before dusk, Claire was sitting on the dusty floor of the attic. She spent a good portion of the day up there, going through what was left, deciding what could stay and what was going.

While she was going through an ornate trunk, she decided it would be the last of it for the day. She was about to snap the lid of the trunk closed when she looked up and thought she saw a face looking at her from the other side of the room.

Claire rose slowly to her feet and began to approach it. "Hello. This is private property," she called out, sticking her hand straight out in front of her. Her fingers brushed a veil just in front of her face, and she yanked it down to reveal what she had been startled by.

It was a stack of oil paintings. No doubt portraits of a family that owned the place at one point. In front there was a small girl with blonde hair and piercing blue eyes. Behind her was a boy, a man, and then a formidable looking woman.

"Who were you?" Claire whispered as she ran her finger over the subtle lines of the little girl's face and suddenly rose to her feet. She tucked the portraits underneath one arm and descended the staircase back down to the second story.

## CHAPTER FOUR

Over the course of the next three weeks, Claire tried aimlessly to get a crew into the house and continued to fail. Everyone she spoke to, whether it be on the phone or in person, would always miraculously think of something they needed to do upon hearing where the project would be.

Except for Bradley, *"Just call me Brad,"* Morse, the electrician that Kate Wilkes recommended. Brad called her the morning after she had received the keys and met Kate. He didn't care that she bought *the* Blackwood Manor, or about the scale of the project, only that he had somewhere to spend his daytime hours, provided lunches, and a fat weekly paycheck.

He worked tirelessly at Blackwood Manor from sun up to sun down every single day, save for Sundays, for the past three weeks. He had a scruffy look that reminded Claire of the cowboys in the old westerns that she would sometimes watch with her dad until they had drifted apart and her parents all but ignored her.

He was short and stocky, wore dirty, well-worn jeans with a tucked-in white t-shirt almost every single day, had a scruffy beard peppered with gray hair, and messy graying hair behind a receding hairline that she could picture lying under a crisp white cowboy hat. He always wore a belt and despite being dressed down, he always looked nice. His eyes were a hazel green and extremely kind. She liked him instantly.

Brad quickly became a good friend, her best next to Emma, and since he was the only person that she spoke to some days, they had plenty to talk about. Brad often spoke of his wife Sylvia and their two daughters, ages six and ten, of his love for fixing things, and life in general. Despite seeing him as a friend, Claire didn't confide in him at quite the same level.

She told him of coming to be near Emma and her family following her divorce from Brock, but she didn't go into the details of the divorce or tell him that Emma was the closest thing that she had to a family, even as a child. The way that she answered Claire's call even when they hadn't spoken in so long proved that.

With round-the-clock work, Brad had the house's electrical system passable enough for her to move in. So Claire packed up her things and set up shop in the biggest bedroom upstairs, and did her best to clean day and night.

On one warm Monday morning, Claire was out in the cottage cleaning out the old junk that had been stuffed in there over the years. There was a knock on the door and Claire turned and smiled as Brad walked in. He held up two large IHOP bags. "Breakfast delivery."

"Great, I'm starving." She gestured to a milk crate that she cleaned and set up in the corner to use as a table.

Brad set the bags down and chuckled. "You must be. That's a lot of chow."

"It's for you too."

"Oh no. I—I couldn't. That wasn't part of our deal."

"Sit, eat. The next few days are going to be hell."

Her tone dripped with authority. She knelt on one side of the milk crate and he finally sank down on the other side.

Claire opened plastic containers of eggs, bacon, sausage, and pancakes and they began to eat.

"I'll tell ya'," Brad laughed as he loaded his fork with eggs and a bit of sausage. "That delivery kid was scared shitless. When I opened the door he was shaking in his boots and mumbling. Sounded like a rhyme."

"Apparently there's a myth at the school that if you say a special poem on Blackwood Manor you're safe from the demons," Claire sighed. "Did you hear what it was?"

"No. I couldn't understand him. When I opened the door he just shoved the bags at me and ran off so fast it looked like his feet were on fire."

"I just don't get it," Claire let out an exasperated grunt. "It's just a house. Beautiful, majestic, and full of history, absolutely, but still, just a house."

"Well, that history scares a lot of people that have lived here for generations. The stories are passed down from one generation to the next. I'm sure they get a little more convoluted and exaggerated with each generation. Still, those stories scare the bejeezus out of them."

"Not you." Claire took a sip of Dr. Pepper. "I think you're the only one I've met who hasn't been scared.

Emma's husband says he doesn't believe but I have my doubts. He doesn't like the kids talking about ghosts."

"He probably just doesn't want them getting as scared as everyone else and it doesn't help that their Mama is terrified."

"True-" Claire paused for a moment and then looked back up at him. "Why aren't you scared, Brad?"

"I've seen too much bad shit in this world. I believe in ghosts and the supernatural and I do believe there is something here. Those stories, though? Exaggerated through time. That's how I feel. The real evil lies in the living flesh. When I was doing time...well, I don't think we have enough time for me to explain the sadistic shit that I saw. Rapists and murderers running free and my sweet Caroline is battling leukemia at six years old. She could go anytime but I can't see her enough. I have to work to keep up with her medical costs so there's a chance we can save her. This world is fucked."

"You never told me why you did time."

Brad paused and looked up at her. His eyes appeared to be begging.

"No judgment here," she told him reassuringly. "Just idle curiosity. I feel like I've really gotten to know you over the past few weeks and you just don't strike me as a hardened criminal."

"In '78 I was walking home from work and I heard screaming. So I followed that screaming. In the alleyway behind the general store, a gang of four kids were attacking this colored girl. Poor thing couldn't have been more than fourteen."

Claire reached over and put a hand over his. "Brad," she began gently, "don't say 'colored.'"

"Hmm?" He looked at her with wrinkled eyebrows, confused.

"It's okay to say she was Black. Colored is considered offensive now."

"Oh, I don't mean nothing by it. Please don't fire me."

"I know you didn't mean it maliciously, Brad. I understand you're from a different generation and you were taught differently. I just wanted to tell you before others join us on the project. Michael would skin you alive if he heard you say that. I'm definitely not going to fire you. Just wanted to make you aware."

"Thank you, ma'am."

"It's alright. Go on with your story."

"Well, anyway. She was down on the ground and bloody just trying to cover her face with her arms and they were kicking and hitting her with things. So, I walked up and told them to go on--get. One of them turned around and clocked me on the jaw. I hit the ground and they start coming after me. Next thing I know my gun was out and I got off a shot."

Claire lowered her fork but nodded, urging him to go on.

"No one got killed. I just got one of 'em in the shoulder. The others managed to disarm me and contain me until cops showed up though. That poor girl was lying on the ground, bruised and bloody and I went to jail for shooting this punk. Defending a colored--sorry, a Black girl wasn't reason enough I guess," he scoffed with disgust. "I don't care about none of that shit. Color is only skin deep, and Black or not that child didn't deserve to be beaten like that behind a dumpster like a piece of trash. If I hadn't done something they woulda killed her."

Claire nodded. She understood. She'd seen discrimination thrown at Emma, and by association, she'd experienced it herself a fair few times. Though never to the extent Brad did. "Why'd they finally let you out?"

"Because it was discovered that same punk killed four Black girls from '78 to '80. Guess they believed me then," he hung his head down. "I don't regret helping her. Not for a minute. But people do look at me funny and I can't get steady work. Have to do shit under the table. I have all my licenses and everything but no one wants to work with an ex-con. No one ever cares to know why. They just judge."

Claire covered one of his hands with hers. "I will never judge you. You are a good man, Brad. Look at it this way, you'll be working on Blackwood for at least a year. So you are definitely steadily employed. When we get to the end of the project I will give you glowing recommendations."

He smiled at her and clapped the back of her hand with his other one.

"And Brad," she said, her voice growing softer still, "if you need to take time off for Caroline, just tell me. You won't lose your job."

An hour later Claire and Brad finished breakfast and Claire grabbed a box of things to bring into the house and sort through. When she entered the kitchen through the back door she saw something that made her blood run cold. Propped up against the kitchen island was the oil painting of the little girl, her eyes dancing menacingly against the canvas.

Claire stood a moment, staring at the painting that she swore was staring back. Every time she saw the paintings that she found in the attic, especially this one, her stomach clenched in a way that she could not understand. They seemed more alive and fresher, the color more vibrant. The blue of the little girl's eyes appeared to pop off the canvas and follow her around the room. Who could forget the night last week when she could have sworn that it actually winked at her? Now, here it was in her kitchen when she distinctly remembered leaving all the canvases in the parlor.

The sound of the front door opening cut through the silence like a drum. Claire whipped around so hard, she felt a muscle pull in her neck and dropped the basket of items she removed from the cottage house.

Heavy footfalls sounded and Brad appeared in the doorway to the kitchen. "Are you okay, Claire?" he asked, rushing forward to help her pick up the items that spilled onto the floor.

"I'm fine," she absently worked her neck muscle with one hand, while cleaning up the debris with the other. "I came in from the cottage and got quite the shock." She gestured towards the painting.

"Oh, I put that there. I'm sorry. I didn't mean to scare you," Brad took the basket from her, placed it on the counter, and helped Claire to her feet. "It was propped up against the fireplace in the parlor and I was working in that area. I didn't know if this was important and didn't want it to get ruined, so I brought it in here. I hope that's okay."

"What about the other ones?"

"What other ones? This was the only one in there."

Claire stared at him a moment and then waved her hand in a manner that she hoped was carefree. "Of course, I forgot. I brought it in there last night to see if I maybe wanted to put it above the mantel in place of the mirror. I guess I was so tired I forgot."

"No worries," Brad smiled. She wasn't fooling him; she was clearly shaken. And why shouldn't she be? This *was* Blackwood Manor. He didn't have the superstitions of the other people in town but there was a reason he wouldn't come here after dark and he often wondered about Claire late at night and hoped she was okay.

He ignored the whispers in town at the grocery store, the post office, and the hardware store.

*"Blackwood Manor, yes. She's out of her mind. Yes, and she hired that insane convict because he's the only one desperate enough to go there."*

The whispers always stopped once he made his presence known, as word had already gotten out that he was working on the old house. His family was old and respected, even if he wasn't, and no one would dare say anything to him. He saw the stares. Careful as they were to look away.

"I got awful dirty out there in the cottage," Claire laughed awkwardly. "I think I'll go upstairs and take a shower."

"Sure. I'll get back to the parlor. Do you want me to dump this?" he asked, gesturing towards the basket.

"Not yet," she shook her head. "I want to go through it and make sure there are no important documents in there. You can just leave it. "

"Okay."

Brad made his way toward the parlor and Claire mounted the stairs.

After grabbing a fresh towel from the linen closet, she shut herself into the upstairs bathroom. The lock on the door was rusted and would not lock. In fact, the door would not latch all the way. She added that to the growing list of things to fix before pulling back the curtain in the claw-foot tub and stepping under the spray.

She hadn't wanted to admit it. Not to Brad. Not to anyone, but she was shaken. She didn't hold much stock in ghost stories. Sure, it was fun speculation as kids. Scaring the hell out of each other was just part of growing up, right? She and Emma had played basically every paranormal game there was growing up and gotten spooked a fair few times. Claire had eventually grown up. Sometimes she worried that Emma had not.

Still, she couldn't deny the feeling of being watched ever since she found the oil paintings; and the little girl, in particular, seemed to pop up in the oddest places, watching meticulously, as though she had a life of her own, and Claire could never remember moving the painting.

As she shampooed her hair, Claire heard the familiar creak of the door hinges.

"Brad, I'm not done here. Try the downstairs bathroom."

She went to rinse her hair and stopped when she realized that the door had not creaked again as though it had been shut. Not to mention there had been no response. The silence was heavy, and the air suddenly felt heavy in a tight, oppressive way.

"Brad?"

There was a high-pitched giggle that seemed to come from just outside the curtain. Claire splashed her face with water and put her hand out to pull the curtain back when something suddenly rushed the curtain. There was a distinct impression of the outline of a face with empty sunken eyes. A disturbing substance that looked horribly like blood appeared to form where the eyes should have been.

Claire jumped back, repulsed, and screamed out as her foot went out from under her. Before she could brace herself, her head hit the tub just below her temples. Her vision became black and spotty and she knew she was on the floor of the tub.

"Claire?" came the sound of a voice that seemed far off and close at the same time, jumbled. Emma's voice.

"Oh, my God! Claire!" The curtain jerked back and the water shut off. Claire instinctively put one arm tightly around her stomach as Emma knelt to help her. Emma placed a bracing arm around her and helped her to sit up. It was Emma. It was just Emma. "Are you okay? What happened?"

"I—I, Claire sputtered. No, she couldn't have seen what she thought she had seen. She was overheated and tired. That was all. She couldn't tell Emma. Not when her friend was finally here. "I fell."

"It's no wonder. No bath mat. Haven't I always told you-" Emma broke off to grab the towel off the rack and help Claire get to her shaky feet.

"I'm okay, really," Claire wrapped herself with the towel and stepped out. She felt better already. "What are you doing here?"

"Well, we've decided to help you. I figure I'm still nervous but Michael has convinced me that everything must have just been rumors after all. If anything was going to happen, it would have by now, and you would have told me."

"Right," Claire gave her friend what she hoped was her best smile.

"Well, come downstairs as soon as you're dressed. We brought breakfast. And I'll take a closer look at the cut on your forehead." Emma swept from the room as fast as she had come in.

Claire looked in the replacement mirror that she had fixed over the porcelain sink. She had a gash on her forehead. She glanced back at the tub and saw a streak of blood running toward the drain slowly. The curtain was completely free of the blood she thought she had seen.

When she stepped out into the hall to turn towards her bedroom to get dressed, Claire saw the painting of the little girl balanced against the wall, smiling mischievously.

## CHAPTER FIVE

*Ten-year-old Claire pulled the borrowed Ouija board out from under the couch and began to set it up. She was sitting with Emma in the cramped living room of Emma's New York apartment. It was Emma's apartment, but Claire had the dominant energy and naturally took over the room. They had become obsessed with the paranormal lately; devouring books about ghosts and demons and watching scary movies in the dark.*

*Emma was convinced that her apartment was haunted. Neither of them knew if it was true or if the girls had simply been scaring themselves with too much "Halloween" lore, as Claire's mother liked to call it.*

*Claire had been the one that thought of using a Ouija board to put their minds at ease; one way or another. She'd talked the teenage girls in the apartment upstairs into letting them borrow theirs in exchange for cleaning their bedroom every weekend for a month. Neither her parents nor Emma's would have allowed them to have the board.*

*Now, she placed the board between her and Emma, balanced on a milk crate from the kitchen as Emma lit candles on either side of them. "Who do you think it is?" she asked excitedly.*

*"No idea," Emma answered. "We're probably just scaring each other. This is dumb." She bit her lip and darted her eyes briefly to the door.*

*"It's not dumb. It's fun," Claire insisted and pulled her wild hair back with a ponytail holder to get it out of her face. "Your parents probably ticked off some spirit and it followed your family home to mess with you. It happens ALL the time," she said knowingly. Emma's family was totally uncool.*

*"Are you sure you know what you're doing?" Emma asked nervously, flicking her eyes from Claire's mischievous face to the board between them.*

*"What's to know? Ask questions and get answers," Claire's eyes gleamed, and she shrugged her shoulders. "Now, place your fingers on the message indicator."*

*Emma followed Claire's lead; neither of them was ever the same.*

Claire was pulled out of the memory by the smell of coffee as she walked into the kitchen to find Emma, Michael, and their kids seated around her kitchen island.

Emma looked up from the plates she was passing out for the donuts. She took in Claire's pale face and wet hair hanging limply in her face barely obscuring the plain wide band aid she'd just applied.

"Are you okay, Claire?" The concern was evident in her voice, and Michael and the kids all turned to look at her.

"I'm fine," Claire took a seat on a bar stool and shook her head as Emma tried to slide her a plate with a fat chocolate donut sitting temptingly on it. "I already ate."

"Are you sure?" Emma still had her own plate suspended in mid-air as her hand reached for a donut, not yet grabbing one. "Did you hit your head too hard? I can take you to the emergency room."

"Em, I don't need to go to the ER. I'm fine. Really," Claire poured a cup of coffee and sipped it calmly and pointedly as though it would magically sway her friend to think all was well.

Emma looked at her, not convinced, but turned back to the box of donuts to help herself. She made her mind up to keep an eye on Claire. She loved Claire, but if there was one thing she was horrible at, it was taking care of herself. She looked as though she had seen a ghost, which was crazy. Claire didn't believe in ghosts. Anymore. She had blocked everything out. Maybe that was for the best, or so it had seemed for so long. Now, following the Brock Business, as she called it, she seemed to be reverting to her ten year old self. Maybe it was coming back. Or maybe it was this place. Emma still didn't like that Claire had taken on Blackwood Manor. But the money was spent and what was done was done. No matter what the reason was, she was acting more like Claire of years past than the woman she had grown into.

"Well, if you're sure you're okay," said Michael from the end of the island, "You've made the papers."

"What?" Claire batted her eyelashes a few times in response. He completely sideswiped her with that bit of information.

Michael picked up a newspaper sitting in front of him and slid it down the island to rest in front of her. It was a copy of the tiny town paper and she was somehow on the front page. The grainy picture had been taken from the road and zoomed in on her in the most unflattering angle right in front of Blackwood Manor, in all her run-down glory.

"It's all about the renovation. Guess your neighbors have been talking. Or maybe the people you've tried to contract to work."

Claire read the article silently and snorted in indignation when she was finished. It was full of people saying the new owner was clearly unhinged or dabbling in the occult, trying to bring that monster house back to full power. It was absolutely ridiculous. Wasn't it?

"Apparently people think I'm taking quite the risk," she said sarcastically.

"Financially you are," Michael was quick to point out. "As for the rest? It's a bunch of bull. Nevertheless, it seems you're going to be hard-pressed to find anyone to help you. We've decided to help you when we aren't busy with work."

"That would be great," Claire let out a small sigh of relief. "I'll admit I was worried about how long it would take to do the majority of the work on my own. I've only found one person to help me. The guy working on the wiring for me. Brad. Thank God, he agreed to help with the overall project."

Michael looked up from the cup of coffee he had just drunk from. "Brad Morse? You know he's an ex-con, don't you?"

"I don't see that it matters as long as he does his job," Claire shrugged and looked back down at her cup. "Plus, he told me why he was locked up and it was a bogus charge anyway. The man is harmless." Emma noticed that she had been absently running her fingertips along the rim of her coffee mug.

"Were you kids playing upstairs a few minutes ago?" Claire asked, hoping her voice wasn't shaking as much as she felt her heart was.

"Nope, we've been down here. About ready to starve to death," Bailey laughed and turned to look at Claire. She immediately stopped laughing at the look on Claire's face. "Aunt Claire, are you okay?"

"Yeah," Claire waved a hand absentmindedly as she took a seat on a stool. "I thought I heard something."

"Ooh," Bailey's eyes went big with excitement and she leaned in closer to Claire. "And so it begins."

"Bailey," Michael said sharply as he let Callie down on the floor. "We've been through this before. There are no such things as ghosts. If something were going to happen here, if all those stories were true, Claire would have said something by now."

He took a donut and one of the pigs in a blanket that Emma handed him and looked back toward his daughter again. "It's normal for old houses to make noises. Claire was in the shower. She could have heard anything. Don't jump to conclusions and let your imagination run away with you."

Bailey rolled her eyes and popped a donut hole in her mouth. "Dad, you're such a bore. This stuff is interesting. Why do you need to take the fun out of everything?"

"You're thirteen years old, young lady," he told her, raising his voice only slightly. "It's time you realize that ghost stories are child's play and start living in the real world."

"Mom believes it," Bailey replied, challenge in her tone, her blue eyes dancing.

Claire looked over at her friend and couldn't hide the smirk from her lips or her raised eyebrow. Bailey was definitely growing up to be a pistol. She reminded her so much of Emma when they were kids. What had happened to that girl?

Emma looked up from her plate, tightened her lips into a fine line, and tried to choose her words carefully. "I do believe in something. I do believe our loved ones watch over us. I believe if you play with things you don't understand you can start something you can't control." Her eyes met Claire's with such an intensity that Claire was forced to tear her gaze away and out the window.

"Demons?"

Emma grimaced but nodded. "I'll admit, I was scared of this house. I believed all the stories I've heard ever since we've lived here. Quite honestly I still find it way too old and creepy. Sorry, Claire," she shot her friend an apologetic look before continuing, "but Claire's been here long enough we'd know in the rumors were true."

Claire looked down at her mug absentmindedly. She sent up a silent prayer that they couldn't hear the booming of her heart. She felt it was going to bust right out of her chest.

"I realize now that I let my imagination run away from me and that can be a very dangerous thing," Emma was cut off by Callie tugging on the hem of her shirt. She looked down to see something tucked tightly into the girl's fist. "What have you got there, honey?"

Emma bent down and took the object from her daughter, looked at it for a moment, and exclaimed, "Oh my God!"

Emma brought the object closer to her face to examine it. It was a rusted piece of metal that looked as though it had been broken off something with a thick, sickening-looking substance on the end. "I think this is blood. What is this thing?"

She handed the object to Claire, who held it up to the light. "I think its part of a fireplace poker. There's one in the parlor that's missing the end."

Claire and Emma's eyes met briefly. Emma's were full of horror and she turned back to the little girl, her voice tender. "Honey, where did you find this?"

Callie pointed towards the walk-in pantry that was still mostly empty, though its door was ajar.

Richie placed his napkin on his plate and turned to Claire. "Aunt Claire? Can I use your bathroom?

"Sure, honey. If you turn next to the staircase and go all the way back, turn right and you'll see a door to the bathroom."

"Actually," Emma interjected, "I went in there before I followed your screams, Claire. I don't like the look of the broken glass in that mirror. I'd rather he use the upstairs bathroom."

Emma turned to her son and pointed to a door open a quarter of an inch. The door was heavy and warped and led to a back staircase. Claire had discovered it when she'd had the large and decayed shelf removed last week. She suspected that it was mainly for servants' use once upon a time. "Just go up that staircase. The bathroom is at the end of the hall."

"Oh, but-" Claire tried to protest. She didn't want Richie to use that bathroom after what just happened but wasn't sure how to say so without scaring her friends.

"Claire, you don't have anything but boxes up there right now. Really, what trouble can he possibly get into?" Emma gestured for her son to go on.

He had no more than stepped through the door when it slammed heavily behind him. Everyone sitting at the island watched dumbly for a fraction of a second before the screams began.

Richie began screaming in a terrifying blood-curdling way that had Emma on her feet and racing to the door, desperately pulling at the doorknob. Michael was beating on the door, throwing his weight against it in an attempt to break it down, but it would not give.

Richie continued to scream. "Let me out!" he cried, and they began to hear sickening scratching sounds. "Don't let her get me!"

Emma snapped around to look at Claire, anger and fear on her face. "There's no lock on this door. Why won't it open?"

"I don't know," Claire answered. "I've never used it before." She couldn't stop herself from trembling.

"Dad! Mom!" Richie screamed through the door, the scratching becoming louder. "Get me out!"

Suddenly, Claire remembered seeing a staircase upstairs that led down, but she hadn't explored it yet. She wanted Brad to check it for stability first. She grabbed a flashlight from the counter, raced to the front of the house, up the stairs, and made her way to the mystery staircase. Clicking the light on, she ran at full speed down the stairs, not checking to make sure they weren't rotting. This was definitely the right place. Richie's screams were growing louder.

Finally, the light illuminated about a foot in front of her. She saw the swish of what looked like a black dress and a silhouette. When she got closer though there was nothing there. Nothing except Richie balled up on the floor, his arms over his head, sobbing uncontrollably.

The door snapped open, hitting the wall behind it. Emma was through the door like a shot, pulling her son into her arms. "Richie! Oh, your poor hands!" His fingertips were bloodied from scratching at the door in an attempt to get out.

"Mom!" he cried, throwing his arms around her. "It was the lady! The lady had horns! She tried to get me!"

Emma held her son and looked up the stairs at Claire with an accusing stare.

## CHAPTER SIX

"She hates me," Claire said into the phone with a defeated sigh.

"She doesn't hate you," her friend Jennifer told her. "But she's scared. Just give her some time. She'll cool down."

"I hope so," Claire said in a tired voice. "The two of you are pretty much the only friends I've got."

"Oh, come on. I'm sure that isn't true."

"Yeah, well. Hey, did you get that email I sent you with the photos of the house?"

"Yes, it's so beautiful. I hope I can come to see it soon."

"I think I can make some room for you," Claire teased.

Jennifer laughed. "Hey, I gotta go. Just got an email from the boss man. I'm behind on my prints."

"You got it," Claire said and hung up the phone.
She grabbed her pink bandanna and pulled it over her messy bun, pulled a soda from the fridge, and headed up to the attic to start her deep clean.

Claire sighed and made her way to an old roll-top desk with a broken lock in the corner. Emma hadn't been back to the house since Richie had been locked in the servant's staircase. This proved Claire's suspicions that Michael and the kids had dragged Emma to the house.

Michael continued to come by to help three weeks later and was now fixing the shingles of the roof. He dismissed his son's hysterics as merely getting scared about being locked in and even occasionally brought lunch for her, knowing she didn't have the time to go out.

Claire glanced at the opposite wall at the oil paintings that she had brought back up with her before she began to clean. She had turned them to face the wall, continually repeating "I don't believe in ghosts," in her head. She *wouldn't* believe in ghosts. Even so, she couldn't deny how peculiar it was that she kept finding the paintings all over the house. After all, she was working on the house from sun up to sun down and was exhausted. Most likely, she was exhausted and kept forgetting where she was leaving them. She *knew* that. It didn't make it less creepy when she would find one of them in a random spot. Like the picture of the harsh-looking woman that was propped up on the bathroom sink this morning.

She couldn't stop thinking about what Richie had said. *"The lady has horns!"* It was normal for a child to become frightened if they got locked in an unfamiliar place without their parents. Richie had never been an easily scared child though. Not to mention he was eight years old, not two. Was it possible that he had actually thought he had seen a woman with horns? Was it possible that it was the woman from the painting?

Claire shook her head and silently rubbed the backs of her eyes with her knuckles. *"Stop it, Claire! You're just going to scare yourself. That's the silliest thing to go through your mind in awhile. You need to just hurry up and finish with this desk and get out of this heat!"* she thought to herself.

She began to fumble in a drawer of the desk and brought out a very old-looking journal. The cover was faded, stained brown leather. She gently turned the pages to look at the text within. The pages were extremely yellow with age. The writing, faded and difficult to read, was in a long, swoopy cursive. She ran her thumb over the date in the upper right-hand corner and brought the page closer to her face, to make sure that she was reading it correctly. April 1864. This entry was written during the Civil War.

There was a loud noise behind her and Claire spun around in time to see a blanket falling from a large ornate mirror covered in grime. It showed the wild ends of her hair sticking out from beneath the bandanna, a spot of dirt streaked on one cheek, and something moving in the darkness of the corner behind her.

It was a woman in her early to mid-thirties. She wore a dirty floor-length white dress, and her face was translucent, like looking at someone's features through a veil. There were indentations where the eyes should have been, an outline of lips but no lips.

Her hands were skeletal with an occasional spot of flesh hanging off the bone. She moved towards Claire, making that awful guttural sound until she stood directly behind her. Claire realized that the sound was eerily similar to breath rattling away in a chest.

Claire couldn't look away.  Her heart raced so hard, she feared it was going to bust right out of her chest. She felt hot breath on the back of her neck and the most God-awful stench went up her nose. The smell of rotting meat, only worse. It was a familiar smell, but she had no idea why.

In the mirror, she saw one bony hand reach up and begin to slowly curl the fingers over her shoulder.

She ran at full speed the long way around the house. She wasn't going to get stuck in that staircase. No way. She didn't stop until she was in the kitchen. She stopped dead when she saw Emma standing at the island, placing a sandwich and a piece of chocolate cake on a plate. Emma was staring at her with a sour, accusing, and at the same time, confused look on her face.

Claire shot a look behind her and saw nothing. She turned back around and dropped to her knees.

"Are you okay? You look like the devil is chasing you," Emma finally said when no explanation came.

"Yeah," Claire said. She took deep breaths to try to still her racing heart. She was tired. The attic was especially hot and not well-lit. She clearly imagined it. "I'm fine. Just heard you moving around and wanted to make sure it wasn't a robber."

"Who would rob this place?" Emma asked bitterly as she turned back to her task. "You're bleeding."

Claire glanced down at her blouse and noticed blood on her shoulder where the creature had been gripping her. Only then did she feel the sting of the pain.

"Em, please don't be mad at me," Claire whined as she plopped herself on a bar stool, ignoring the question. "The house is old. Doors swell. I didn't lock Richie in there, the door was just stuck. I'm sorry he got scared but it wasn't my fault."

"I know that it wasn't your fault, Claire. It doesn't change the fact that you're obsessed."

"Obsessed?"

"Yes!" Emma cried. "Don't you get it? This place is pulling you in. It has some kind of weird hold over you. All you can think about is the house. You don't see the problems. I told you the stories of all the awful things that had happened here. You can't tell me that all those people were full of shit. Then that door swings shut behind my son. I saw it with my own eyes! That is a very clear message that we aren't wanted here."

"Ghosts aren't real, Emma."

"Richie said he saw a woman with horns while he was locked in that staircase. Guess what, Claire? I believe *him*."

Claire's mind briefly went to what she saw in the attic only moments before, but she pushed it right back out and stared at Emma helplessly.

"Just because your brain has been in a dark tunnel since we were kids doesn't mean that everyone else can't see things as they are. You're blind to what's going on here and I'm worried about my husband's safety every time he comes over to help you."

"He doesn't seem too worried."

"He hasn't seen the things that we have."

There was a long, suffocating pause before Claire spoke again, her voice coming out in a hoarse whisper. "I don't know what you mean."

"Maybe not altogether, but you know enough. I'm taking Michael's lunch to him and then I'm leaving and I'm not coming back here. I love you, Claire. I can't stop you from the craziness that is in this house. I don't have to sit back and watch the people I love slowly fall into disaster's lap."

With those words, Emma picked up the plate and headed in the direction of the parlor. Claire immediately jumped up and followed her. "Emma, I don't even know what you're talking about. This is crazy."

They went through the doorway exiting into the entrance hall from the dining room. The massive door stood ajar and a man stood with his hand raised about to knock. Emma stopped dead in her tracks, her eyes going wide.

"Can I help you?" Claire asked, surprised.

The man was young, maybe mid twenties, and dressed in dirty jeans with holes ripped at the knees, a white tee shirt stained with grease, and a faded denim jacket. He had messy sandy brown hair that brushed over his green eyes and a matching five o'clock shadow. He was taller,

Claire estimated he had to be at least six foot three, as he towered over her five-eleven frame. He had broad shoulders and solid muscle. There was a massive pack thrown over his shoulder.

"The door was open, ma'am. I didn't let myself in."

"It's quite alright. We've been leaving it open while we do renovations. What can I do for you?"

"I'm passing through and will probably be here a few months. I'm looking for work and was told in town that you might be needing help."

"Yes, yes, goodness yes. Please, come in," she gestured to him inside.

Emma unfroze, rolled her eyes, muttered "for goodness sake" under her breath, and shot the stranger one last glance before continuing into the parlor.

The man watched her go. "I seem to have come at a bad time."

"Don't worry about it," Claire reassured him and led him back into the kitchen. "She'll come around. You'll soon learn this house has quite the reputation."

"If it didn't, as old as it is, I would be worried," the man set his pack down next to a bar stool and took a seat.

"Thank you!" Claire smiled and poured two cups of coffee, sliding one across the counter to him. "I hope it won't scare you away."

"Don't worry," he blew the steam coming up off the cup and set it back down on the counter. "I was warned of the stories at the same time I was told you were looking for help."

"Ridiculous, isn't it?"

"Not necessarily. I do believe older places have a certain energy. Possibly even ghosts. Honestly, they're probably more scared of us."

"Well, that's something at least," she smiled again. "I'm Claire Donahue."

"Donovan O'Ryan," he grinned back at her. "When do I get started?"

"Right away if you're able."

"Oh, I'm more than able," Donovan took a weary breath and nodded towards his pack. "Does the job include room and board?"

Claire looked up and raised her eyebrows suspiciously.

"No expectations, of course," he said in a rushed sort of tone. "Please don't misunderstand me. It's just that I'm a drifter with no permanent address and from the looks of it, this project is going to take awhile."

"Do you need it to be included?" she asked warily.

"It would help save on hotels," he admitted. "If you're not comfortable with it I'm sure I can find a hotel with a weekly rate in town somewhere. I just figured with how big the place is, how long the project is going to take, and of course the daily trip out here, with it being so far back in the hills, that it might be a possibility."

Claire considered for a moment. She didn't necessarily like this. She wasn't overly trusting of strangers anymore, particularly men. But she had to admit to herself that she was finding herself freaked out lately and she would never fully be comfortable living in seclusion as long as Brock was a free man. Not to mention what she had seen in the attic just a few moments before. Donovan had kind eyes and he had an air that seemed to scream authority. His frame was bulkier and more intimidating than Brock's. She didn't think that many would mess with him. She couldn't help feeling like she'd probably feel safer with him around.

"You can have the room upstairs, second door on the right. You'll have to clean it up yourself, I'm afraid. I haven't had a chance to do much on that floor. When you get settled, come and find me. I'll put you right to work if that's okay with you. I want to make it clear that this is my home and my land and I am in charge. Do not presume to think that you can run things or bully me. If you step over the line your ass will be gone faster than you can say 'boo.'"

"That'll be fine, ma'am. I wouldn't have it any other way," he smiled and made his way toward the front of the house, swinging his pack over his shoulder once again.

"Who is that?" Michael's voice came from behind her.

Claire jumped and swung around and then placed her hand on her chest. "Michael, you scared me. I didn't hear you."

"I'm sorry. Who is that?" he repeated.

"Donovan O'Ryan. I've just hired him to help for the next few months."

"Why's he going upstairs?"

"He's a drifter with no permanent address. It's more efficient to have him here than hiking in from town every day."

Michael raised an eyebrow.

"What, Dad?" she playfully shoved his shoulder and walked past him into the parlor.

"You don't think that's just a little weird?"

"Not really. It wouldn't be worth his time if all his pay was going to hotels and cabs."

"If it was me or Brad I'd agree with you but we don't even know this kid. It doesn't look right, Claire."

"I'm a tough girl, Michael."

"I don't like it," he frowned.

She chuckled. "I'll be fine. Really."

There was an awkward silence and then Michael continued. "Listen, I want to apologize for Emma. She'll come around. She's just been having a real hard time."

"I love that woman. I love her, and I want to strangle her," Claire admitted. "I don't understand her hatred. It's an old house and the doors swell. I'm so sorry he was scared. I am. You have to know that."

"I know."

"But she was already against the house and looking for any reason to be pissed. That's no way to go through life."

"Well, this spiritual stuff…." he paused, trying to choose his words carefully. "It cuts her deep. Between your childhood and things that have happened over the years…"

"Like what?"

"Well, did she ever tell you that her grandmother visited her after she died? Was maybe an hour. Her dad had called to tell her, and she was crying in her room. Her grandma appeared and told her that they had to look behind the stove in her old cabin. Emma was in disbelief and hysterical but her grandma kept appearing and kept insisting until she called her dad and told him to look behind the stove. She found an envelope with $20,000."

"No, she never told me that. But why would she be scared of that? That's a good thing."

"Because of everything that came before it."

Claire downcast her gaze.

"Claire, her unease with Blackwood Manor isn't only centered on you. She has had a fear ever since she moved here. The first time we drove past she told me to go faster and she seemed shaky. I swear she had to have been holding her breath the entire time. She didn't even know the stories yet. You buying the place was like her worst fear being realized. I understand you don't believe in ghosts and to be honest, I don't either. But I do know this. Emma is sensitive to something. She has a connection with the other side. You just have to be patient with her."


*"Emma...do you believe the fates are on your side tonight?" Ten-year-old Claire lit a candle stick and knelt on the floor next to the game set up on a milk crate in the corner of the tiny apartment. She tossed her messy blonde curls over her shoulder and nodded at her best friend.*

*Emma flipped the light switch, engulfing the room in darkness. All she could see was Claire's face behind the flickering candlelight. She walked over and knelt across from her friend. "Only time can tell."*

*Both girls were dressed head to toe in white. They were obsessed with scary movies and books, which their parents hated, but they loved the thrill and the fright of it. Two weeks ago they had seen a movie that had inspired their new adventure obsession. The Ouija board. They couldn't remember the name of the movie now. But it didn't matter. They needed to do this, though.*

*As if by some magnetic force, they put their fingers on the planchette at the same time.*

*"Is there someone here with us?"*

*The planchette moved to the word YES.*

*"Claire, stop messing around," Emma snapped.*

*"I'm not doing it," she whispered. "What do you want?"*

*The planchette slowly spelled out the letters Y-O-U and the candle went out with a sudden burst of wind.*

*"Claire?" Emma whimpered slightly.*

*Then they heard the creaking of a door directly across from them. Their eyes met in the dark, and they slowly turned their heads toward the noise.*

Claire's eyes snapped open. She hadn't had the dream in so long it had honestly startled her. She glanced over at the clock on her bedside table. 3:33 am. She'd been asleep for less than an hour. She felt icy cold and brought the covers up around her tight, trying to wrap up like a cocoon. Still, she couldn't get warm. What was the deal? It was summer. She reached over and turned on her lamp, then went to sit up. She let out a short scream.

Directly across from the foot of the bed was a window that was completely covered in frost. As though they had been hit by a blizzard. In the frost were letters that had been trailed out by fingers. The letters read, "Help Gloria."

There was a knock and her bedroom door creaked open as Donovan stepped in, wearing gray sweatpants low on his hips and no shirt. "What's the matter? I heard you scream."

Her eyes hadn't moved from the window. "Did you do that?"

He walked over to see what she was looking at. "No. Why would I do that?" He examined the letters closer, touching the glass, then pulling his hand away. "The letters were written from the outside."

"What? How is that even possible? We're on the second floor."

"I don't know."

Claire ran her fingers through her hair and closed her eyes. What the hell was going on around here?

## CHAPTER SEVEN

The next day when Brad arrived for work and made his way to the kitchen for breakfast, he suddenly stopped at the sight of Donovan behind the counter, starting a pot of coffee.

"Umm...Hey," he said tentatively.

Donovan looked up. "Hey," he smiled warmly. "You must be Brad."

"Umm...yep," he took a cautious step forward. "Who are you?"

"Oh, I'm sorry," Donovan stuck out a hand. "Donovan. Claire hired me yesterday."

"Oh," relief swept through him and he shook the extended hand. "I'm sorry. I wasn't expecting anyone new." Brad took a seat down at the island. "God, how long have you been doing this? You seem a bit young for this kind of work."

Donovan laughed. "Well, I spent a couple of summers doing construction with my uncle in High School. Also, I was an army brat. We moved a lot. We often stayed in fixer-uppers and flipped whichever house we were in while we waited for my dad's new assignment."

"So you know your stuff then?"

"You could say that." He winked. "Sorry, breakfast is gonna be a bit late. Claire should be down soon. It was kind of an eventful night."

"What happened?"

Donovan quickly told him about the frost and the message in the glass.

≈

Meanwhile upstairs, when Claire woke up, she sat bolt upright in the bed and stared at the window. It was now clear of the frost and its creepy message. The room was no longer freezing as it had been. It was once again the summer day it should be, warm with the sweet smell of honeysuckle.

She let out a sigh of relief but she let her mind wander to everything that happened as she got dressed. The oil paintings, the child giggling, and her experience in the bathroom all greatly concerned her. She was worried about the hallucinations. Maybe the house had toxic mold. She would talk to Brad and Donovan about it. Or she could be suffering from lack of sleep. She'd had many sleepless nights since Brock. Either way, she would need to find a doctor soon and figure it out.

She made her way down to the kitchen where Brad and Donovan were both waiting for her.

"I hope you don't mind," Donovan said, "I made some coffee."

"Oh, that's perfectly fine," she said, taking a seat at the island.

"You look like hell," Brad told her, sliding a mug of coffee across to her.

She chuckled under her breath and took a deep sip. "Thanks."

"No disrespect, of course. I was just talking to the new kid here and it sounds like you had a pretty eventful night."

"Yeah," she reached across the island and grabbed a few Polaroid photos of the window. The message in the frosty glass was perfectly visible along with a white streak that was present in each photo. Donovan had taken the photos with an old Polaroid camera they found in the attic. Thankfully it had film in it and worked perfectly fine. She would have used her equipment but at the late hour, she'd been unable to grasp developing the film.

"You call the cops?" Brad asked.

She nodded. "Sheriff dropped by for five minutes. He said there were no signs of forced entry and the writing had been done from the outside—just like Donovan said. When I suggested vandals he practically laughed in my face. Said no one would come near here and it was just something I was going to have to accept since I bought Blackwood Manor."

"You're kidding," Brad took one of the photos and looked at it. "That frost is something else. It's enough to give a person the creeps. Who's Gloria?"

"Who knows?" she sighed deeply.

Claire saw Brad staring at her and she flushed. Sometimes she felt the man was a mind reader. She knew she looked exhausted and he could probably tell she wasn't sleeping. He probably thought she had no idea what she was getting herself into.

"What's on the agenda today, Boss?"

"Brad, I would like you to paint the inside and outside of the cottage. The one that was the servant's quarters. I've finally gotten it completely cleared out. Donovan, if you could start clearing the pathway up to the house from the road, that would be great. I don't expect it done today but it'll be nice to be able to park by the house."

There was a strong knock on the front door and Claire made her way to the front of the house. "Let's regroup around mid-day and see where we are."

When she opened the door, she found herself face to face with Emma, who had her arms crossed over her chest and a scowl on her face.

"Em," she opened the door and stepped to the side. "Do you want to come in?"

"No. I don't even want to be on the property," she replied curtly.

"Okay." Claire stepped out onto the porch and shut the door behind her. "Why are you here, then?"

"Our friendship goes back too many years to end over a house," Emma began. "Over this inherent evil."

"Emma, don't be ridiculous. There are no such things as ghosts or demons."

"You know damn well that isn't true." Emma's voice was hoarse, shaking so hard it creaked.

"What I know is that I outgrew the silly games we played and you never did. Look, I'll admit what happened with Richie was scary. Doors get stuck. It's not anyone's fault."

Emma narrowed her eyes and her face flushed in that way it always did right before she was ready to blow up. It had been a long time since Claire saw her that way. Emma was not the angry type. "The door slammed shut. We all saw it. Doors may stick but they don't slam on their own."

Claire couldn't stop herself from rolling her eyes before turning her head away.

"Someone was in there with him! He said it was a woman in a long, black dress with no face and horns. His fingers were completely bloody and two of his fingernails had come out from clawing at the door."

"So, he was stuck in the dark. He got scared and imagined it. It's not that far out of the realm of possibility for a child his age."

"Then how do you explain the bruises on his back?" Emma demanded, her voice rising.

"What bruises?"

Emma pulled out her cell phone and stuck it under Claire's nose. There were pictures upon pictures of bruises and scratches on Richie's back. Long, angry scratches in rows of three.

"Maybe he fell into something."

"Oh my God, wake up, Claire! There was nothing to fall into! It was a fucking staircase! Don't be oblivious to what's right in front of your face. Don't let *it* happen again!"

"Let what happen again?" Claire couldn't keep the annoyance out of her voice anymore. Her oldest friend in the world wasn't making sense anymore. Her impatience was growing with each accusation. She loved Emma but she wasn't sure how much more of this she could honestly take.

"You know what happened when we were kids. What happened to you. What almost happened to you. What almost happened to me. We were lucky to get out of that. Don't let your ignorance over this property cloud your ability to see the signs."

"You've been watching too many ghost movies," Claire turned on her heel and opened the door to the house.

"You're obsessed! Don't you see why?"

Claire stepped through the threshold into the house and turned to face her friend one last time. "Don't come back until you calm down and have a clear head." She then snapped the door shut, let out a deep sigh, and walked into the parlor to peek out the window. She watched Emma running towards the overgrown driveway, her hand over her mouth, a gesture she unconsciously made when she was fighting back sobs. Her shoulders were slumped forward in defeat. Despite her elegant height, she looked so small and lost. Her black hair bounced behind her. Poor Emma. She wished she didn't have to be so harsh. She knew Emma truly believed this ghost stuff. But it was the only way she knew of to get through to her. She could not be harassed about her property at every opportunity.

There was nothing wrong with this place other than age and a few squeaky floorboards. She tried to push the nagging thought away, "Where did the bruises come from?" Her eyes followed movement on the far side of the drive once Emma was out of sight. She saw Donovan looking up towards the house. When his eyes met hers he turned away, pulling on gloves to begin his work.

≈

Outside, as he gathered his equipment to clear the path Donovan glanced up towards the house again. He saw the door snap shut in Emma's face, and she turned to step off the porch looking completely defeated. He hadn't been able to avoid overhearing their argument. It sounded as though a child had been badly attacked and injured. He couldn't say he was surprised. This place was burning with evil, especially towards children.

If that was Claire's attitude towards the reality of the place they could have a problem. It would most likely take moving mountains to convince her of the truth. He wondered if he should tell her yet. If she would even believe it.

His eyes met Claire's in the parlor's window, and he realized he had been standing here watching the house for too long. He turned back towards the equipment and pulled on an old pair of work gloves as he found himself lost in thought.

≈

Upstairs, Claire entered the attic and pulled her hair up, tying it off with her pink bandanna. She tried not to let the incident with Emma get to her. They'd be okay. They'd had fights before and they were always there for each other when it mattered. Once Emma calmed down from Richie getting stuck in the stairway, and her Mama Bear claws went back in, then they'd be okay. She couldn't afford to think about it. There was way too much to do.

She went over to a dusty old roll-top desk in the corner and resumed the job she'd been interrupted from the last time she was up here. She tried to roll the top back but found it was locked. Her breath briefly caught in her throat. Hadn't the desk had a broken lock the last time she'd been up here? No, of course, it hadn't. She closed her eyes in frustration. Please God, let the key be in one of the drawers. She needed everything to go smoothly today. She just needed it.

She sat down on the floor and began going through the drawers from top to bottom. There was an old pen and pencil set, an actual feather quill, and a bottle of dried-up ink in the top drawer.

In the bottom drawer, there were a lot of yellowed papers. She almost tossed them in a pile for trash, but ultimately decided to go through them. There may be something of value concerning past ownership of the house.

Old newspapers, an extremely old Bible with names and dates written in it going back to the early 1800s. She briefly scanned the names for births, written tiny on the inside cover, and the deaths on the back cover for the name, *Gloria*, but did not see it. She then went on to see handwritten letters dated during the Civil War. A glance told her that they were letters to Margaret Blackwood from her husband, who was probably off fighting. Claire ran her hand around the inside of the empty drawer but still did not find a key for the roll top.

She got to her feet and placed the stack of letters on the desk and ran her hand behind the desk, trying to feel to see if the key was maybe taped to the back of the desk. She heard the deep guttural growl come from behind her. She slowly straightened her spine and began taking deep breaths to calm herself.

"No," she finally managed to say, though it was nothing more than a whisper. She squeezed her eyes shut, willing the woman away. She then felt the pressure on her shoulder and a surprisingly strong grip in the squeeze of those bony fingers. It was a firm grip, though surprisingly gentle.

The woman leaned in close to her ear. Claire was suddenly freezing from the hand that felt as though it were about to give her frostbite. The breath next to her ear was like a cold wind on a winter night. "Gloria," the voice croaked out among the guttural groans.

Claire finally found her strength and wrenched her shoulder out of the woman's grip and ran towards the staircase leading down to the second floor. She then ran the length of the hallway to the main staircase. She stopped suddenly before descending.

"Claire?" a very small, young voice said from behind her. She slowly turned to see a little girl. The child couldn't have been more than three years old if that. She was much too skinny and wore a grimy brown rag for a dress that was much too large. Her head seemed much too big for her body and her eyes were so huge they looked like they were about to pop right out of her head. Her blonde hair hung in stringy tatters and was congealed with a mass of blood that was clumping it together, and the blood poured down her face.

Claire let out a tiny whimper, but again she couldn't move. The girl stepped towards her. "I like you," she said. "Will you be my mommy?"

The girl threw herself forward and wrapped her arms around Claire's legs. Claire could see the back of her head then. She could see, *Oh God, it's horrible*, the messy lumpy mass under the blood. *Brain matter?*

Claire lost her footing then and tumbled backward down the stairs. Rolling to the bottom. The pain was everywhere and she couldn't get up. She turned her head slightly. Propped on the wall next to the parlor was the painting of the little girl. Her eyes appeared to be dancing on the canvas. That was the last thing she saw before she blacked out.

"Oh, my God. Claire! Claire!" Donovan's voice sounded far off, as though it were coming through a wind tunnel.

Claire fought to open her eyes but they felt so heavy. She was aware of the heaviness of her body as she was scooped up in Donovan's arms and carried into the parlor, then laid on the broken-down sofa.

"Get her a damp washcloth," she could hear him saying to someone. It sounded closer but still far away all at once. It echoed slightly, making her head pound. She attempted to open her eyes again. Her vision was blurry but her eyes stayed open this time.

"There you are. Don't try to sit up," Donovan gently pushed her shoulders back down as she tried to sit.

"Here we are," Brad was there, laying a cool washcloth on her head. "What happened?"

"I found her at the foot of the staircase, unconscious," Donovan answered, then turned back toward her. "Claire? Did you fall? Was it a bad step?"

She shook her head, caught her breath, and finally answered in a whisper, "There were people upstairs. I was running to get help. I must have tripped."

"You said there are people in the house?" he asked her, meeting Brad's eyes over her head.

"A woman in the attic and a little girl in the hallway upstairs. Squatters. Probably harmless. But still," she sat up with shaky arms.

"Hello?" called a voice from the open door in the entryway. It was the neighbor from the nearby plantation, Kate Wilkes. She made her way cautiously to the doorway of the parlor. "The door was open. Is everything alright?"

"Ma'am, would you mind sitting with her for a minute while we check the house?" Donovan asked, ignoring her question. "She's had a bit of a scare."

"Yes, of course," Kate walked in and took a seat next to Claire on the couch, taking her hand.

Donovan and Brad walked out into the entryway, talking among themselves so low that she could not hear what they said. Then they split off and went in opposite directions.

"You look like you've seen a ghost, dear," Kate said. Her bleach-blonde hair was piled up high on her head again and today she wore bright blue eye shadow, heavy eyeliner, and too much blush, making her look like a caricature.

Claire looked at her blankly, not knowing what to say.

"Oh, I'm sorry," Kate chuckled and patted her hand. "Poor choice of words considering where we are."

"Kate," Claire asked carefully. "How long have you lived on your property?"

"Oh, probably about forty-five years now. Although my family has been there for generations. It isn't quite as old as this place but still pretty old. My mother went to New York for college and she met my father and had me there. I inherited the land and came here when my grandmother died."

"Have you ever heard the name Gloria in connection with this place? Maybe one of the Blackwood family or a servant?"

"Gloria?" Kate furrowed her brow in thought. "No, can't say it sounds familiar. Why do you ask, dear?"

Claire hesitated a moment and then thought of the old letters in the attic. "It was in some old papers I found. I was just curious."

Her face must have given her away though because Kate gave her a knowing look.

"Well, I know this place was built in the early 1800s by Gerald Blackwood. It stayed in the family for quite awhile but it was eventually bought from the outside. Did you know that you can go over the property records at the library? They probably won't go back to the beginning, but you could get somewhere."

"That's a good idea," Claire nodded her head and absent-mindedly rubbed her temples. "Did you know the owners who were here before me? I know the place sat empty for thirty-four years, but it fits in the timeline of you being here. Did you know them?"

"I met them," Kate nodded her head in agreement. "We weren't particularly friendly. They were private people."

"When I talked to the husband on the telephone about buying the place, he said they moved because of health issues his wife was having. He made it sound like she's still alive though, so I've been thinking it was strange."

"Oh, yes. They lived here for maybe six months. I remember it was very strange. They were young, early twenties. The woman, Lois I think her name was, had a heart attack and tumbled right down those very stairs. Nearly broke her neck."

Claire lifted her hand to her neck and rubbed it, her eyes never leaving Kate. Her mind was replaying what happened to her at the top of those stairs. Did the same thing happen to Lois?

"The ambulance tore them out of here in the middle of the night and they never came back," Kate was looking off into the distance. "Tom left word that she had a serious heart problem and they were going to this fancy treatment center. No one believed that. Speculation grew even more when they decided not to sell the place. Not until now at least."

Just then, Brad and Donovan came back into the room together.

"There's no one here," Donovan announced, kneeling in front of her.

"That isn't possible." She shook her head in denial. "I was at the foot of the stairs. They couldn't have gotten out without going right over me..." she paused. "What about the hidden stairway?"

"Door shut tight," Brad answered. "Claire, maybe it's time you face the possibility that you just saw something that scared you. It's not that unusual around here."

"There are no such things as ghosts," she answered hotly, her voice rising. "I know what I saw. There were people in this house. They must still be here."

"We went over every square inch of this house," Donovan told her. "There's no one here."

She stared at him; lips pursed tight.

Donovan sighed and ran a hand through his hair. He turned to Kate and Brad. "Would you two give us a moment, please?"

Brad's eyes narrowed with confusion and he glanced down at Claire.

"It's alright," she told him in a way of dismissal. Kate soundlessly rose from the couch and swept from the room behind Brad.

Donovan followed them to the doorway and when he was satisfied that he and Claire were alone he returned to her side.

"I didn't want to get into this. But someone needs to make you see..."

"See what?" she asked sharply.

"I haven't been completely honest with you. I am a drifter. It started at an early age.  My father was in the military so we moved a lot when I was younger. I was a classic military brat. I've been here before." He took a deep breath and looked into her eyes. "Shortly after my family moved to this town when I was fifteen, I broke in here with some friends on a dare for a Halloween party. I'd heard the stories, but I didn't believe in that stuff. Just like you. So, I decided to do it. I thought it would be easy money. Break in, spend the night, get a hundred bucks in the morning."

"Yeah?" she asked. Where was he going with this?

"There were four of us. We broke in through that window." He pointed at the one directly across from the couch. "At first everything was cool. We holed up in here, talking. Telling stupid stories. Then we decided to explore. We split up."

He got to his feet and began to pace the room. "I don't know if it's because we were young or because we were messing with things we didn't fully understand, but the night got bad extremely fast. There was no power. All we had were a couple of flashlights. I was walking along the upstairs hallway and I could hear my friends yelling things. Calling out to the spirits. Calling them names. All that junk. Then suddenly there was a face in mine. Only it... wasn't. It was the shape of one, but it wasn't a face."

Claire sat up a little straighter, watching him intently.

"There were the most God-awful groaning sounds coming from this thing. Then it grabbed my shoulders." He instinctively shrugged his shoulders as though they had a chill. "Then I heard the screaming. I ran to the stairs and I looked down and my buddy, Eddie was at the foot of the stairs and he was in the air. Floating there, arms spread, feet not touching the ground. His head was thrown back. His girlfriend was on the floor in the corner, screaming her head off. This other girl, Stacey, was being dragged across the floor, and her hair was sticking straight out behind her like that's what's being used to drag her."

He came back and knelt in front of Claire once again. "The door swung open and she was dragged onto the porch. Eddie suddenly hit the ground in a heap and we all ran for the door. I came back because this place has been in my dreams every night since then. I keep seeing that face and hearing the voice that came with it. That night, whatever that thing was had said 'Gloria', and then 'Help Gloria' gets written in frost in the window? That's no coincidence. That same figure kept telling me to come back because someone needed help. I think that someone is you."

Claire looked over his shoulder, towards the wall, and did not answer.

"Claire, I didn't use to believe in this stuff any more than you do. Not until it happened to me. But it did happen. And it's happening to you now. Something horrible happened here. We have to figure out what it was or this place is going to come completely alive and rule everything and everyone."

"Houses aren't alive," she finally managed to say.

"This one is," he took her hand. "Blackwood Manor is very much alive."

"Now, look," she rose to her feet and screamed out as a searing pain tore through her knee.

Brad and Kate both ran back into the room. "What's wrong? What is it?"

"My knee," Claire managed to get out.

Kate reached down and felt her knee through her jeans. "It's swelling up. We better get you to the emergency room."

"No. No emergency room. I'm fine," she went to take a step and her legs buckled. Brad caught her before she could hit the ground. "Okay, I guess I do need to go. Damn it. There's so much work to do."

"I'll take you," Kate said, looking up at the men. "That way, they can keep working and we can have some girl time."

"Some girl time," Claire chuckled with sarcasm, then winced.

Brad lifted her and carried her out to Kate's car, placing her gently in the passenger seat. "Take care of our girl."

"Of course, I will," Kate smiled brightly and she reversed.

On the drive to the emergency room, Claire sulked silently with her head propped up against the headrest.

"So, what happened, dear?" Kate finally asked.

Claire hesitated a moment and then she answered, "I fell down the stairs. There were squatters in the house and I was trying to get help. The boys searched but they didn't find anyone. Now, I have to go to the damn emergency room, and I DO NOT have time for this." She thumped her head against the headrest violently and crossed her arms across her chest.

Kate didn't answer her, just kept looking straight ahead.

"They aren't going to believe me anyway," Claire mumbled under her breath.

"Why wouldn't they believe you?"

"Experience," she let out a sigh and turned to look out the window.

"No offense, dear, but you look like doggy doodie run over sideways."

"Yeah, I haven't been getting much sleep," she rubbed her eyes. "So much to do and weird vibes."

"Why don't you go see a doctor about getting on some sleep meds? At least until things settle down."

"I've thought about it but I don't even have time for that."

"I'll give you Dr. Conner's number. I've been going to see him for years. He's great. Really listens to his patient. Plus, his wait times are short and he's not far from you."

Claire nodded as Kate pulled up outside the door to the emergency room.

# CHAPTER EIGHT

Claire was lucky. She only had a mild knee sprain and had to wear a brace for a couple of weeks. She had also gone to see Dr. Conner at Kate's recommendation for her follow-up. He checked the progress on her knee and wrote her a prescription for Ambien. Over the past two weeks, she slept much better and hadn't experienced any weird occurrences. Maybe it had just been a lack of sleep.

Claire didn't believe in hauntings, and she would not be swayed by that. However, she did believe something was going on. She just wasn't sure what. Up until the Ambien she had been having vivid and frequent hallucinations. Plus, she was not the only one to have experienced something "off" there.

She believed Donovan's story. She didn't have any reason not to. But she didn't think it was what he thought it was. She thought he experienced a bad hallucination as well. There had to be something causing it.

Still, she knew that everyone was uneasy. She knew that she desperately needed a crew if she was going to get any work done on the place in a timely manner. Donovan mentioned finding a few guys in town, which was nice, but Claire didn't feel confident that it would be enough for the scale of the project. She needed more manpower. People needed to see her doing something. She grabbed the notepad where she had jotted down several ideas. *Group hallucinations in old houses? Mold?*

She decided to take Kate's advice and go to the local library to go through the property records as far back as she could. She would look up news reports and see if she could find out if anything had happened there or anything that may be a common link between hallucinations and old properties. Above all else, she had to see if she could find out who Gloria was.

She settled at a table with ledgers and books surrounding her. A librarian had been generous enough to help her find the materials she would need. There was a microfilm machine behind her that she could also use if she needed to. She couldn't help but smile at the old-fashioned machine that made her feel more at home here. It represented a humble, simpler time that she had always been fascinated by and she was so happy to have settled in an area that still had old-time touches. She'd never seen something like this in New York.

She began going through documents of deeds, and documents of sale and traced the ownership of the property back to 1909 when the trail seemed to fizzle out. She assumed that the property was probably handed down from generation to generation without having any documents drawn up. She had this theory because in 1909 Robert Blackwood sold the property to Daniel Thompson. That appeared to be when Blackwood Manor left the Blackwood family. A full one hundred years after it was built. Of course, she knew that she could still be way off the mark.

A study of the buy and sell dates told her one very important thing; with the exception of the couple she bought the land from, no one had owned Blackwood Manor longer than two years. The average was closer to six months. It appeared one unfortunate family only paid the first month's mortgage, and then the bank eventually foreclosed. That looked to her like they stayed a month and left. None of these time frames were that long considering the money it took to keep a place like Blackwood Manor afloat. Plus, other plantation properties in the area had the same owners for years. Those properties seemed to be doing just fine. Heaven's Estate was the perfect example of that.

She had hoped to find the name Gloria in a record of sale, but it appeared she was the first woman to buy the place. All the other owners, and there had been many, had been men. There was no way to tell if any of their family members had been named Gloria.

She sat back in her chair, let out a sigh, and cracked her neck as she tried to concentrate. The sales records had been helpful in telling her just how many people had owned the property and how long they had stayed, but it still wasn't telling her what she needed to know. Why did all those people leave so fast? Who was Gloria? Why had the place stood empty for so long and fallen into such bad disrepair? Hell, why had the previous owners not sold the property after they left? They paid the mortgage until the place was paid off even though they hadn't been living there. That was just strange.

Surely it couldn't be just the ghost stories? She wished she had more information about the one hundred years prior to when the sales records started.

She decided to start looking through old newspaper stories on the Microfilm machines and this gave her a little more information. There seemed to have been quite a few disasters that had happened over the years.

In the 1950s a little girl had been thrown from a horse and broken her neck. This had happened at her tenth birthday party. There were plenty of people around who witnessed what happened. They all said that the horse, usually calm, content, and gentle, had suddenly become finicky, almost panicked. Almost like there had been a rattlesnake in front of it. No one had seen anything different that may have caused the horse to react in such a way.

In 1934 a double suicide was found in the house. The man had left a note saying that his wife had been ill. She had been seeing and hearing things ever since she had moved away from her family and slowly lost her mind. She had tried to slit her wrists but had done it wrong and then blew her own head off with his shotgun. When he saw what she had done he decided he couldn't bear to be without her. He didn't have anyone else. So, he had written the note and hung himself.

There were at least three instances she could find of a woman dying during childbirth in the early 1900s. There was a group of teens that got murdered inside one Halloween night in the 80s. She scanned the names, hoping to eventually interview the families. The first name and picture, Donna Harding, felt vaguely familiar to her, but she couldn't quite place it.

The only reference she found to the actual Blackwood family was a newspaper article announcing that socialite, and mother of two, Margaret Blackwood, died at the age of eighty-eight and that her family would be making a donation to her favorite charity in her honor. That had been in 1904. That was the last article that Claire came across. If she was going to find anything earlier than the 1900', it would most likely have to come from the house itself.

She pulled her notepad back towards her and added to her scribblings. *A woman hears voices? 1934. Hallucinations or illness?*

She cleaned up her mess, gathered her things, and drove home.

Claire let her mind wander on the drive. She hadn't been able to get nearly as much information as she wanted to. Still, she had to wonder about the horse that spooked over nothing, killing a child and the woman that lost her mind seeing and hearing things. Had that occurred since moving into Blackwood Manor? Or had it been going on before?

As she pulled up to the property, she breathed a sigh of relief that the pathway was now completely cleared. She could finally drive up to the house instead of parking on the street and hiking her butt all the way up there every time she needed to go somewhere.

As she pulled the car to a stop, she couldn't help the smile that began to spread over her face as she saw the trucks and workers milling around. She didn't know how he had done it, but Donovan found a crew willing to work out here. She knew it may not be for long, but at least it was something.

She got out of the car and approached a group of the men who were standing near the side of the house.

"Hi," she extended her hand as she approached them. "I'm Claire."

"God damn," one of the men said, stepping forward. He was short and pot-bellied. He had a scruffy beard, and bloodshot eyes, and smelled heavily of whiskey. "Aren't you just a tasty little treat?"

"Excuse me?" she asked, dumbfounded, and pulled her hand back. As she stepped closer she could see that all these men were inebriated in some way. The smell was strong. Alcohol, drugs, body odor, and God knew what else. She was nearly choking on it. She managed to keep from coughing but her eyes began to well up.

"It's okay, honey. I don't bite," said Mr. Pot Belly again, stepping closer. "You and I could get to be really good friends."

"I have no interest in being friends," she told him coldly. "I am the owner of this property. I just wanted to introduce myself. Now, if you'll excuse me, I need to find Donovan."

She turned to step away but he grabbed her arm. Her mind momentarily raced to another time and another set of cruel hands as she tried to wrench her arm from his grasp, but his grip was too strong.

"Now, now, don't run off," he told her. "I'm a good friend. You just gotta give me a chance." He leaned in and tried to kiss her while the hand that was not grasping her arm grabbed her breast.

She brought up a knee into his groin, causing him to howl in pain and drop to his knees instantly. His grip loosened and she wrenched her arm away and threw the hardest punch she could manage. Once he crumpled to the ground, she gave him one swift kick in the ribs and said, "Get the hell off of my property once you're able to move again."

She looked up at the others who were staring, incredulous. One actually had his mouth hanging open. "Get back to work!" she ordered, and turned on her heel, marching back up the steps and into the house.

"Donovan!" she screamed as soon as she was over the threshold and slammed the door behind her. "I want to talk to you!"

Donovan came in from the kitchen, looking puzzled. He was wearing faded, dirty jeans that were slung down low on his hips accessorized by a tool belt. He was wearing no shirt and was covered head to toe in sweat.

"What's wrong? Are you okay?" he asked her.

"No, I'm not okay! This crew is a joke and a liability. They're a bunch of junkies and drunks. Or did you not notice?"

"Do you want a crew or not?" he ran a hand through his hair. "Look, Claire. I agree that the circumstances are not the most agreeable. But no one who is sober will work here. Okay? That's just a fact. These guys will get the job done and they'll work cheap."

"Are you insane?" Claire shot out, shaking with fury. "They can't even do the job correctly fucked up like this! They're costing me money!"

Donovan shifted his eyes down to his shoes. "We need cheap labor, Claire. Checks are bouncing."

"What?" she asked, confused. "That isn't possible."

"That's just what I was told this morning about the late supplies." He shrugged his shoulders. "These old boys may have their vices but they're hard workers and they're harmless."

Claire crossed her arms over her chest. "One of your harmless old boys assaulted me outside."

"What?" his gaze shot immediately to the window. "Who was it?"

"Some prick with a pot belly and a dependence on whiskey."

Donovan squeezed his eyes shut and tightened his mouth in an effort to stay calm. "Willie Perkins. I didn't bring him. He showed up with one of the others. I'm sorry that happened to you. I'll take care of it. Are you okay?"

"Oh, I handled myself. Luckily, I've had to learn to handle myself over the years. If it had been some other woman though it could have been really bad. I already fired him. Now, I want you to know that I am holding you personally responsible for the crew's behavior. So, I suggest you have a long talk with them after the day's work about respecting me in my own goddamn house. And for God's sake, put on a damn shirt. I'm not running a Chippendale show here."

Without another word, she climbed the steps to go up to her room.

Once there she sank down to the bed and allowed herself the tremble she had been holding back since the confrontation outside. No weakness. She could never show weakness. Only here, in the confines of her bedroom would she ever allow that vulnerability to shine through.

Once in her life, only once, she had been hoodwinked. She'd met Brock in college and she had been captivated by him immediately. His flaming red hair, twinkling eyes, and chiseled good looks. Those damn devilish dimples when he smiled instantly melted her panties. He could have had any girl in the school, but it was her he was watching and flirting with.

They married within six weeks of dating. On the honeymoon, he convinced her to disown her mother, which hadn't been hard. She had a strained relationship with her mother from childhood. Her father had passed when she was twelve and there was no other family. Her only true friend, Emma, had moved here, to Georgia, to attend community college and help take care of her ailing grandmother. They saw each other less and less until contact eventually stopped.

With that one act of disowning her mother, she had effectively cut herself off from everyone, at Brock's clever suggestion, making herself isolated and alone. At his mercy. The beatings started shortly after the honeymoon. He would apologize in the beginning. Eventually, as the instances got increasingly worse he stopped apologizing. She was forced to start taking self-defense classes on the sly, and even that wasn't good enough. He was always one step ahead of her. She saved little by little. It was a long process but she was finally able to dig her way out from under him. The sad truth was she couldn't talk to anyone about what had really happened. To do that would be to show weakness. Never again.

Once her nerves finally stilled and she stopped shaking she allowed herself to think about what Donovan told her downstairs. Checks were bouncing. Why the hell were checks bouncing?

She immediately pulled out her phone and called her bank. She knew she should have plenty of money in that account. As she listened to her transaction history, her face fell and her heart began beating at a furious rate. She didn't realize how quickly the money would deplete. She would have to start cutting corners.

She could fix the issue, she knew that. But it was going to take some time. That's when an idea struck her for the first time. She couldn't believe it had never occurred to her before. Sure, people around here may be afraid of the stories that accompanied Blackwood Manor, but there were plenty of people that liked to go looking for spirits. She and Emma had been that way as children, after all. This place could easily be converted into a bed-and-breakfast. The perfect spot for ghost hunters. She picked her phone back up and decided to start searching for numbers for local news stations.

## CHAPTER NINE

Claire hit the dismiss button on her cell phone and turned off the sound. She was sitting on her bed in her room, surrounded by bills. The phone had been ringing off the hook for the last two weeks since she decided to call news stations about her impromptu plans of turning Blackwood Manor into a bed-and-breakfast once it was fully renovated.

She was desperate for money. Money to pay her crew, money to pay the mortgage and utilities, and money to pay for supplies to keep the renovation going. Emma and Michael had floated her a loan for the mortgage and utilities. They knew she was good for it, and Michael had always hated Brock. He called him *the bastard with a bald spot,* and had bent over backward to be there for her as soon as she had picked up the phone and called Emma after so long. Still, she was hurting in so many ways.

Despite being desperate, she did not respond to every call from a reporter. She was holding out for the high bidders. She had done one interview with the local news station that had sparked a front-page article about her sanity in the newspaper. She had been surprised to get a call from a national broadcasting station willing to pay her enough to keep her going for another three months. Her interview was at ten in the morning. They would be sending a crew out.

She had also gotten offers from various ghost-hunting crews to investigate. The best offer was from the producers of a reality ghost buster show. They would pay her $10,000 to investigate for a night but everyone else would have to vacate during the investigation so she hadn't made up her mind yet.

It was now eleven at night, and the phone was still ringing with people wanting to understand what was going on inside her head, how she could be so stupid, and she knew she needed sleep. So the phone was turned off.

She began gathering the bills and past-due notices to place on her bedside table. She paused over the latest bill for the painting supplies. Michael had called in a favor for her. He knew the supplier and the man agreed to work out a payment plan for her, but he would not send out a delivery truck. He said it was because that would come out of his own pocket. So, she would be going with Donovan to pick them up. They were in for a three-hour drive both ways.

She slapped down the bills on the table, swallowed an Ambien, pulled her heavy comforter up to her ears, and shut off the light. She willed herself to sleep but that was proving easier said than done. She hadn't been sleeping well again. While the Ambien had initially helped it no longer seemed to do much. She always had trouble sleeping since her divorce, and since moving into Blackwood Manor, insomnia only increased.

She lay there for maybe fifteen minutes when she heard an undeniable squeaking of a floorboard. She slowly turned her head to see a woman standing in the doorway. This was not the woman from the attic. This woman's face could be seen plain as day. Her lips were a tight line, her eyes cold and calculating. Her raven black hair was carefully done up into a bun and she was tall and wearing a floor-length blood red dress. There was flickering candlelight at her back, making her appear to glow with the occasional ominous shadow moving across her face. Claire had seen that face before. Though it had been older and in black and white in a newspaper article. She was staring at Margaret Blackwood.

She wanted to turn away, to close her eyes, but she was frozen in place. This couldn't be possible. Margaret Blackwood was dead. She died in 1904. Yet here she was, looking at her with those dead eyes, the shadows creating a silhouette on her face that only made Claire think of pure evil.

"Is she asleep, Miss Margaret?" came a familiar voice from behind her.

Margaret turned to reveal the shorter young woman standing behind her. The one carrying the flickering candle. The servant girl.

Claire let out a gasp and her eyes grew wider. This was the woman from the attic. She had a face now, and gone were the skeleton hands and decaying flesh, but it was definitely her. She wore the same white uniform.

"Yes," Margaret answered sharply and turned to walk down the hall, the servant girl following behind her.

As they disappeared, Claire found herself able to move again. She wanted to pull the covers over her head and go to sleep. But there was another part of her that wanted to get to the bottom of this.

She silently slipped out of bed, her eyes never leaving the door, and tiptoed across the room. When she got to the doorway, she found equal parts of herself hoping nothing was there and hoping that something was. She took a deep breath and stepped out into the hallway.

Standing about a foot down the hall, the two women conversed in low voices. They were almost entirely in the shadows but the candlelight illuminated them in an ominous, yet beautiful way.

Claire took a couple more silent steps towards them to better hear what was being said. The closer she got, the more she noticed that their images were lightly flickering, as if they were a film in an old movie projector.

"Isaiah is gone," the servant girl was telling Margaret. "Yesterday he was talking about going to find our brothers in Atlanta. He's been missing the family something terrible since our mama passed."

Margaret sighed and ran her hands down over her belly. Claire saw for the first time that she was heavily pregnant. "No more field hands. Now the best foreman in the county is gone. The house is all but destroyed. The dirty Yankees. What are we to do, Josie? How are we to feed the children?"

"I'll just keep working in the fields like I was with Isaiah," the young woman, Josie, stepped closer to the distressed Margaret Blackwood. "Maybe if you write to Mr. Hampton, he'll send Mr. John back."

"That's a beautiful thought, but they aren't going to send any men home simply because all the servants took off and his family is starving. This war shows no mercy," she sighed, and now her eyes in the twinkling candlelight made her look like an old woman. "Percy, Lucy, and I will just have to help you in the fields."

Josie looked shocked. "No, Miss Margaret. They are only children. Lucy is only five. What can they do? You have the baby— "

"There is nothing else to be done," Margaret was firm but kind in her statement. "The children can pick cotton. As for me, I'll do what I have to do. As always."

"But the baby--"

"The baby be damned," her voice was cold. Then her eyes softened, as did her voice. "You won't leave me will you, Josie? What would become of us then?"

"No, Miss Margaret," Josie's voice was low, barely more than a whisper. "Blackwood is my home."

"Good," Margaret turned and walked into the room directly in front of her, Donovan's room, and snapped the door shut behind her. Josie turned and walked in the opposite direction, holding the candle out in front of her. She walked right past Claire but did not so much as glance at her. She disappeared at the end of the hallway, down the servant's staircase.

Claire went back into her room and climbed back into bed, glad to relieve the pressure from the legs she hadn't even realized had been trembling.

≈

Her mind was reeling. Margaret Blackwood. Josie. Isaiah. Percy. Lucy. All new names to her, save Margaret. The flickering images. She couldn't figure out the difference in Josie. How sweet and soft-spoken she seemed there, but how frightening and cruel she had been in the attic, to Richie in the staircase, and to Donovan as a teen. Margaret Blackwood had been very pregnant there but the newspaper story about her death said she was a mother of two. Assuming that Percy and Lucy were her children, it should have said the mother of three.

Claire laughed softly under her breath. Could it possibly be true? It had to be. These events were way too detailed to be hallucinations, the way they fit together like a puzzle. For the first time, she was acknowledging what was happening in her house. She couldn't help but laugh at the irony. It was finally time to admit that ghosts were real.

≈

"Where are my earrings?" Claire cried out in a panicked voice as she frantically pulled the comforter from her bed the next morning.

"Claire, you need to calm down and take a deep breath," Emma said, chuckling. She was standing at

Claire's closet door, going through her clothes. She had come over early to help Claire pick an outfit for the interview. They'd patched things up after Claire told her about the idea for the bed-and-breakfast."

"I'm surprised you're even here," Claire sat on the bed in the rumpled sheets, "considering your hatred for this place."

"Oh, I still think you're completely nuts for buying this place and living here," Emma pulled out a sharp navy blue business suit with a skirt that would hang at the knee. "I think you're even more nuts for wanting to turn the place into a bed-and-breakfast. But going on national television and announcing it, getting the word out all over town...I can't advise against that. The more people that know your crazy plans, the more people there are to convince you to quit while you're still ahead. Plus, you need the money."

Claire held an internal debate for a minute, then finally let out a slow breath. "Em?"

"Yeah?" Emma chuckled and turned towards her friend. She stopped laughing as soon as she saw the serious look on Claire's face. "What's wrong?"

"I don't think this place is evil, but–"

"But what?" Emma sat next to Claire, her face showing nothing but concern.

Claire pulled in a deep breath and then launched into the story, speaking quickly. She told her friend everything that had happened since she'd moved in. The oil paintings moving on their own, the little girl with wicked dancing eyes, the incident in the shower, hearing Emma call her name when she wasn't there, and seeing the figures of Josie in the attic and the girl on the stairs that caused her to fall. She told her about all the owners' short residence history.

Emma's face changed from concern to intrigue, shock, and back to concern throughout the story. She didn't interrupt. She didn't move. She only listened.

Claire then told her what she saw the night before. Once she was done she looked into Emma's face for the first time. "At first I thought I was hallucinating. Lack of sleep, toxic mold, active imagination. But the servant girl, Josie, that I saw last night. She was the same woman that was in the attic. And I already knew Margaret Blackwood was a real person. I knew her face. There's something going on here. I don't think it's evil. I don't feel threatened. I do feel like they're trying to tell me something though."

Emma appeared to be lost in thought. Finally, she spoke for the first time in several minutes. "So, all the names you heard in that vision or whatever it was. None of them was Gloria?"

"No, and that name is popping up everywhere, so I was super confused."

"The child you saw by the staircase, was that the same girl from the oil painting?"

"No. There is a slight similarity but she's definitely not the same girl. The girl from the stairs looked super sick.

Plus, she had green eyes and the girl in the painting has blue eyes."

"Can I see the paintings?"

"Sure. If they haven't moved again, they're in the parlor."

The two women headed down the stairs and into the parlor. Propped up against the glass above the fireplace were all the paintings. Claire pointed to the painting of the woman. "That's Margaret Blackwood. I'm guessing this is her husband, John, and their two children."

"It's the girl that gives you the most trouble?"

"Yes. That one pops up whenever something strange happens. Her eyes look different every time, too. Almost like they're moving."

Emma gently picked up the painting of the girl and sank to her knees on the floor. She turned the painting over and started trying to take the backing off the portrait.

"Careful," Claire said. "It might fall apart."

Emma gently removed the backing. There were some yellowed documents in the back of the portrait. Written on the back was a name and date in swirling cursive handwriting. *Lucy Blackwood. March 1861.*

"Holy crap," Emma whispered under her breath. "These were painted right before the Civil War. I was kind of hoping it would say Gloria though."

"It's what I thought." Claire knelt and picked up the papers that Emma had set to the side. They were written in handwriting that she vaguely recognized. It matched the letters she had pulled from the desk in the attic.

"What does it say?"

Claire read aloud. She had to pause frequently when the writing was so faded to see if she could make out what it said.

*My Dearest John,*

*If you are receiving this letter, it is because I can not bear the tragedy of our being any longer. The war changes us, as you well know. It has changed Blackwood Manor as well. I do not care for the scars it has left on my heart and my body. The dangers did not go away with you. There was plenty to be had right here at home.*

*The servants left, one by one. The land was overtaken by dirty Yankees. They used Blackwood as their headquarters for a time. The thought still makes me sick. Those of us that were left here were forced to bend to their will, and all that implies.*

*There was an accident. Our Lucy is gone. I haven't told you yet. I don't know how to tell you. So, I shall do so here. I regret to say that it was at my own hand. It was not intentional, I promise. Please do not think that of me, my love. Still, it is a cross I cannot bear.*

*I have not entirely made up my mind. The only thing keeping me going is Percy. Our sweet boy. He is so sweet and giving and tells me every day that Lucy was not my fault. That it was an accident. Sometimes he makes me believe that everything has happened for a reason and will get better.*

*I cannot bear the thought of what may happen to him when I am gone, for he would be here alone. All the servants have gone. It is now just the two of us. If I should die, things would not be pleasant for him.*

*If I choose to bear my cross silently, you will never see this letter. I will keep it as a reminder to myself. I will keep it in Lucy's portrait as a reminder of what I have done. I can never forget.*

*All my love,*

*Your Margaret*

Claire lowered the letter and looked at Emma. "What the hell happened here? She killed her daughter but didn't do it intentionally? All the servants are gone? What about Josie? She said she wouldn't leave, that Blackwood was her home."

"Maybe that's what we're supposed to find out," Emma said solemnly, placing her hand over Claire's.

≈

"Yes, the equipment set up here in front of the window for the best lighting. Claire will sit on the couch but we'll need to place it up against the wall," a coordinator was barking orders at the small crew she had with her.

125

"You!" she snapped her fingers at Donovan who passed by the open entrance to the parlor. "Handyman! I'll need you to move these tools." She gestured towards a box of tools.

"Of course!" he pasted on a smile and lifted the box. "Your Majesty," he mumbled under his breath once he was out of the room.

He began to walk toward the kitchen and froze at the sight of a man hanging from the rafters over the stairs.

He wore a Union soldier's uniform, had eyes that were completely black, and wore a menacing grin on his face. "Donovan," he creaked out.

Donovan threw a quick glance over his shoulder into the parlor and saw the people milling around in preparation for the interview. They hadn't seen or heard anything. He looked back around at the soldier who was still hanging there.

"Quit while you're ahead, Donovan," the man rasped.

Donovan squinted his eyes and squared his shoulders before continuing to walk towards the kitchen, though he paused right at the foot of the stairs and said in his quietest voice, "Don't make me bitch slap you, you piece of shit."

He continued his walk into the kitchen and sighed in frustration. It wasn't the soldier's first appearance and it wouldn't be his last.

≈

Later that afternoon Claire threw together a bag for her road trip to the supplier with Donovan. Her interview had gone well despite the annoying coordinator trying to take over her home. No one had told her when the piece would be airing.

There was a knock on her bedroom door and Bailey poked her head in. "Hi, Aunt Claire."

"Bailey," Claire swept out an arm to hug the girl, "I didn't know you were coming."

"It was kind of an impromptu decision," Bailey plopped down on the bed and crossed her legs. "So, I have a serious question for you."

"What's that?"

"Well, you know that I'm interested in all this paranormal stuff and especially in Blackwood Manor. I've always been interested. A place with such a reputation is right here in my hometown."

"Sure," Claire sat down next to Bailey and ran a hand softly through her hair. "What is it, honey?"

"I'd like to do like a ghost hunt or an investigation with some of my friends. Set up cameras and see if we can see anything. Just for fun. Just to say I did it at least once in my life. Would that be okay?"

"Does your mom know about this?"

Bailey hesitated as if she were choosing her next words extremely carefully. "Well, she knows I'm interested. I overheard her telling Dad about the stuff you told her today. About Gloria. I think it would be fun to see what happens after the lights go down."

Claire looked at Bailey, prepared to say no. Then she saw that spark in her big blue eyes. The spark that had been in Emma's eyes so long ago. The spark that took her back to a youth that she remembered as being pretty fantastic before Emma became irrationally afraid. "Okay. You can do it tonight. Donovan and I are going to pick up painting supplies from your dad's friend. The house will be empty."

"Yay! Thank you so much, Aunt Claire. They're going to love me!" Bailey was beaming from ear to ear.

Claire reached into her purse and pulled out a key. She handed it to Bailey. "This is an extra key. The front door sticks a little. You'll have to push pretty hard. Bailey, be out of here by eleven or your mom will have your ass and mine."

"It's a deal," she couldn't stop smiling.

≈

At six o'clock Bailey slipped the key into the lock of the front door. Her hands trembled with anticipation. She pulled her hand down to wipe her sweaty palm on her jeans. She turned the key and pushed the door. Aunt Claire was right. It stuck a little at first, then gave, swinging open on a high-pitched squeak.

"Eek!" her best friend Alex squealed from behind her, making her and her other friend Jessie chuckle.

"Got the bag?" Bailey asked.

"Right here!" Jessie patted the side of the black messenger bag that was swung over her shoulder. The bag was filled to the brim with cameras and various ghost-hunting equipment that they had been secretly ordering for months, pooling their allowances, hoping for an opportunity like this one.

Bailey held her breath as she stepped over the threshold into the dark entryway. Alex and Jessie followed her. All three girls were shaking as Bailey snapped the door shut.

She waited a moment while her eyes adjusted to the dark. It felt unnaturally cold already and she shuddered as the goose-flesh rose on her arms and the back of her neck.

*"Go back now,"* a voice seemed to boom inside her head, echoing in a stern command, making her jump.

"You okay, Bailey?" Alex asked, looking at her curiously.

Bailey looked over at her friends who were looking at her with wide eyes. Their demeanor hadn't changed and she decided right then and there that the voice had been part of her overactive imagination. "I'm fine," she answered and plastered a smile on her face.

She led them into the parlor and sank down to her knees on the floor, reaching for the messenger bag.

"So, we aren't doing just a regular ghost hunt?" Jessie asked. She swept her wispy bangs out of her eyes. She had hair as brown as chocolate with two hot pink streaks on either side of her face and her hair was cut short and choppy, causing flyaways, but she liked it anyway because it was "edgy."

"Looking for shadows and things moving on their own?"

"We can look for that," Bailey answered as she pulled out the equipment. "But now there's a mystery to be solved too. A mystery that is over two hundred years old. How cool is that? Since my Aunt Claire bought the place she's had a lot go down. I found out about a bunch of it today. Not all of it. Enough to make a pretty fun investigation though."

"Those oil paintings sounded ultra creepy," Alex said. She found a lamp and switched it on, illuminating the room with a soft glow. "Where are they anyway?"

"I don't know," Bailey glanced over at the fireplace. "Mom said they were sitting on the fireplace mantle this morning but they aren't there now. Apparently, they move around quite a lot, especially the little girl."

"Lucy Blackwood," Alex stated.

"Bingo."

"So, are we looking to do something specific?" Jessie asked.

"Well, Aunt Claire thinks the spirits are trying to tell her something. The name Gloria keeps coming up but she can't find any record of it. She and my mom found an old letter from Margaret Blackwood to her husband saying that she had accidentally killed their daughter, Lucy. I think that's why her portrait is more active.

"I want to see what we can find. Any type of information, documentation, or pictures. I'd also like to try and make contact and find out what they want. Just remember that this place is super active, you guys. I can promise you will most likely see something or experience something. Don't get scared and don't freak out. They don't want to hurt you. They just want to communicate."

Bailey started handing out cameras. "Now, let's get these set up, and then we can begin."

≈

Claire stretched out her legs and wiggled in her seat. She was in the passenger seat and Donovan was driving. They were an hour and a half into the drive, and she was getting restless. "I'm sorry about this."

Donovan chuckled. "I'm used to not seeing the end of the road. Believe me, it's fine." He looked over at her and could see how rigid she appeared. She was clearly not used to this amount of time on the road in one go. "I'm surprised you're so restless. Moving from New York I wouldn't think a little road trip would bother you so much."

"I flew out with only the clothes on my back. Emma picked me up at the airport."

"No belongings?" he asked, confused. "But you have money?"

She nodded. A moment later, to break the uncomfortable silence, she said, "It's a long story."
Donovan noted her body language and chose not to press the issue, instead changing the subject.

"So, I heard you roaming around last night. I thought you were going to the bathroom but it didn't seem like it. Sounded like you stopped in the hallway for a few minutes and then went back into your room."

"That's because that's exactly what happened." Claire then recounted the events of last night for him.

"Wow. So, you believe now?"

"Yeah. I can't not believe it at this point. I still think people are absolutely insane to think that the place is evil. They're just trying to communicate any way they know how. I don't believe they're trying to scare us."

Donovan cocked his head to one side. "Well, maybe the place isn't evil. But I wouldn't say they aren't trying to scare us. Since I moved in, I've seen a man in a Union uniform with black eyes hanging from the rafters above the stairs. I've also seen the same woman from my childhood except she had horns on her head."

"You didn't say anything," she said, watching him intently.

"Well, you got so angry anytime someone mentioned anything paranormal. I need this job."

"I'm sorry."

"It's okay.

"So, black eyes? Just the irises?"

"The entire eyeball. Do you want to know something even stranger? He was grinning. He was fucking disgusting."

≈

The girls had cameras set up in all the hot spots in the house. Everywhere that Bailey knew for a fact something had happened. The upstairs hallway, the upstairs bathroom, the kitchen, trained on the door to the staircase, and the attic. She paused momentarily when setting up the camera in the kitchen, her mind shooting back to the sounds of Richie's screams when he was trapped in that staircase. He'd had insane marks on him when they'd gotten him home but nothing else violent had happened in the house. He must have done it himself in a panicked state. Right?

Now they were sitting on the floor in the parlor. Bailey laid out a Ouija board between them and a stack of yellow letters that Jessie had found in the attic next to the board. The room was illuminated by candles. They decided to use candlelight instead of electricity to try to draw the older spirits out with familiarity.

They all placed their fingers on the planchette, and Bailey spoke.

"Is there anyone here with us?" the message indicator immediately slid to the word, *Yes*.

The girls gasped but they did not squeal, move, or speak.

Bailey hesitated a moment and then continued. "How many of you are there?"

The girls watched as the indicator moved to letters instead of the numbers, Bailey was mouthing the letters to herself as they spelled out the number, her heart pounding insistently in her chest. The eyes of all three girls grew wider as the message formed.

*"Three hundred and forty-seven,"* Bailey's voice broke as she spoke the completed message out loud. She looked up at the other girls who were shaking. Jessie was biting down hard on her lip.

"Is the spirit of Margaret Blackwood still here?"

*Yes.*

"Is the spirit of a servant girl by the name of Josie here?"

*Yes.*

"Are there any spirits by the name of Gloria here?"

A gust of wind that could not be explained flew through the room, blowing out the candles. Jessie screamed and Alex grabbed Bailey's arm in a vise-like grip.

A loud sound came from upstairs. It sounded as though doors were slamming over and over again. The sound was deafening.

Bailey got to her feet first and rushed out into the entryway with Alex and Jessie on her heels. She fumbled for the light switch. No light filled the room. The darkness was scaring her in a way she couldn't explain. Like it hadn't done since she'd been a small child. Images of the day she had walked into her mother's bedroom and seen her talking to her dead sister. The same biting nausea clenched her gut, the same sweat began to roll down her back, and that same tight feeling took over her chest. *"Don't even go there, Bailey!"* she scolded herself. *"If you don't keep your cool they won't either."*

"The lights are out. Everyone grab the shoulder of the person in front of you!"

Alex planted her hand firmly on Bailey's shoulder and Jessie did the same at the end of the line.

Bailey began to make her way up the stairs, being careful not to go too fast and cause someone to lose their grip. Being careful not to trip and fall on her face.

"Gloria? Gloria is that you?" She reached the top of the stairs and felt along the wall. The doors all the way up and down the hall were slamming shut, one by one, over and over again.

Her eyes focused on a doorway at the very end of the hall. Each time the door opened; she could see furniture sliding across the floor on its own.

"Gloria? Is there something you want to tell us?"

Suddenly, all the doors slammed shut at once. Collectively. Then a figure materialized at the end of the hallway in front of the door. She was wearing a floor-length gown, her hair piled on top of her head. Her flesh was torn away from half her face, hanging in a sickening strip to the side.

Suddenly there was a deafening roar, and she flew down the hallway toward them, horns materializing as she came closer.

≈

"The images they show us may be scary but I still don't believe it's anything sinister. If I did I never would have allowed Bailey to have her little ghost hunt."

Donovan slammed on the brakes and turned to look at her. "What did you just say?"

Claire just looked at him. He looked wild. Wide eyes with what could only be described as fire behind them.

"Claire, what did you just say?" His voice was louder, insistent. "Answer me!"

"Emma's daughter...Bailey. She's fascinated with the paranormal and ghosts. She wanted to have a little ghost hunt with her friends tonight so I slipped her an extra key. It's no big deal. She's aware of what's going on in the house."

"You're telling me that there are teenagers alone in the house right now?"

"Yes!"

Donovan immediately cut the wheel into an illegal U-turn, driving back towards Blackwood Manor with the speedometer steadily rising.

## CHAPTER TEN

"Donovan, what the hell are you doing? Slow down!" Claire cried out in a panic as the car squealed with a turn he took way too fast. "You're going to kill us! And we have to get to the supplier tonight before they close."

"Those kids are more important than the damn paint, Claire," he growled in a tone she had never heard from him before.

"Oh, for God's sake!" she threw her hands down, smacking her leg. "These ghosts are not going to hurt them. Bailey has been in the house before and nothing has happened!"

"She was never there with her friends, and they were never alone," he insisted.

Claire struggled to make her voice steady and authoritative. "Donovan, this is my truck. As your employer and the owner of this vehicle, I am demanding you turn around and go to the supplier."

"I am not leaving kids in that house alone," he answered pointedly. "If you want to fire me so be it. But we're going back."

Claire slammed her back against the seat angrily and crossed her arms over her chest.

≈

Donovan turned into the drive and approached the house. "Damn it," he muttered as he drew closer.

"What?" she squinted her eyes, trying to see what he was focused on in the dark. There were no lights illuminating the property yet, which created a big pool of blackness. Then she saw it. About a foot away from the porch, sunk down in the grass were two teenage girls. One appeared to be rocking the other. She couldn't tell if one of them was Bailey. Not at this distance.

Donovan pulled the car to a stop and they bolted out of it and towards the girls. As they got closer, Claire's heart began to sink. Neither of these girls was Bailey. In fact, she had never seen them before. They were both on their knees. One girl had her arms wrapped around the other, who was rocking back and forth and sobbing uncontrollably, letting out occasional howls that reminded Claire of a wounded animal. The girl holding her was more composed, but her eyes were wide and like glass, tears rolling silently down her cheeks.

Once they were right up on the girls they saw that the one who was crying had a head wound. Blood was pouring down the side of her face. The silent one looked at them. "Are you real?" she choked out.

"We're real, honey," Donovan sank to his knees and pushed back the hair of the girl with the head wound. She only began to let out more strangled sobs and scoot closer to her friend. "It's okay. It's okay. I'm not going to hurt you," Donovan said in a soft voice that Claire had never heard from him before. "I need to see your head. What's your name? Can you tell me what happened?"

"Her name is Jessie," her friend volunteered. "She just...flew into the wall. I know it sounds crazy–"

"Not here it doesn't," he answered her quietly. He was still trying to check Jessie's head wound but had decided not to touch her again. The girl was scared enough. "What's your name?" he asked the silent friend.

"Alex."

"Alex, are you hurt?"

"I twisted my ankle, but I don't think it's broken."

Donovan looked down at her ankle. She had already slipped off her shoe and there was visible swelling. He gently rolled up her pants leg to assess the damage. Bruising was already running through her foot and up her leg like a spider's web.

"Alex?" Claire said, kneeling beside Donovan at last.

Both Donovan and Alex looked up and toward her, as though they had forgotten she was there. "Where is Bailey?"

Alex shifted her eyes down. "That...that thing just came at us. Then Jessie hit the wall and everything was just so...crazy."

"Alex, where is Bailey?" Claire was more insistent now.

Alex looked back up and pointed towards the house with one shaking finger.

Donovan reached into Claire's jacket pocket and pulled out her cell phone then reached out for Alex's hand

and pressed the phone firmly into it. "Alex, I need you to call an ambulance. We're going inside to look for Bailey."

"No!" her demeanor changed, and her voice became shrill. "You don't want to go in there! That thing...it's not right!"

"It's okay," his voice was soft and calm. "It doesn't affect adults the same way it does kids."

Claire looked at him, puzzled. Either he was just trying to soothe the girl or he was making gigantic leaps. They had both experienced plenty. What the hell did he mean it doesn't affect adults the same way?

"No, don't leave us. Please," Alex was sobbing now.

"We have to find Bailey and get her out of there. She could be hurt," he put a hand on Alex's shoulder and gently squeezed. "You can do this. She needs to have her head checked. You need to have your ankle checked. Bailey may need medical attention too. You can do this."

Alex's breathing softened. "I don't even know the address."

"Just tell them Blackwood Manor. They'll know where to go."

Alex nodded her head and Donovan rose to his feet. He stuck out a hand to help Claire to her feet and they began to approach the house. As they walked they could hear the tone of buttons being pushed on the phone.

As soon as they crossed the threshold into the house Donovan muttered, "Jesus Christ, Claire."

"What?" She looked at him. "Are you saying this was my fault?"

"Let's just find Bailey, okay? That's the priority right now."

"Agreed." Claire reached over to the light switch and flicked it. "No lights. They must have blown a fuse."

Donovan walked into the parlor and tried the switch on the wall. No light. Then he tried the table lamp next to the sofa. Still no light. A tiny glow illuminated a small portion of the room and he turned towards it. There was a candle sitting on the floor that had nearly burned out. Claire pulled a packet of matches out of her pocket and lit a second candle, panning it quickly around the room.

They saw the setup on the floor. The candles, the Ouija board. The yellowed letters sitting next to the board.

"Well, now we know how things got out of control so fast," Donovan muttered. He picked up one of the forgotten candles and lit it with a lighter he withdrew from his back pocket.

"Bailey!" Claire screamed at the top of her lungs, panning the candle that Donovan handed her from one side of the room to the other. There was no answer.

Donovan lit another candle and rose to his feet. "I'm going down to the basement to check the breaker box."

They walked back out to the hallway together and Donovan headed for the door to the basement. The door under the stairs.

Claire was drawn to the staircase. She knew she should finish checking the first floor first, but she felt pulled to the staircase, like a magnet. She slowly climbed the stairs and showed the candlelight down the hall. There was a camera on a tripod at one end. The tripod was at a strange angle, as though it had been scooted across the floor with a good deal of force. The camera was cocked sideways, barely sitting upon the tripod, but the red record light was still on. Claire made a mental note to check it later. A little further down the hall, a load of boxes that she had neatly stacked before was knocked askew, their contents scattered over the floor.

"Bailey!" she called again. Still, there was no answer. She turned to shine the light on the opposite side of the hall and gasped.

Josie was standing within arm's reach of her. Her bony, skeletal hands were still spotted with rotten flesh. Still, there was blankness where her face should be. The rotten smell was overwhelming and Claire's eyes began to water.

She didn't know why, but she didn't feel afraid this time. Maybe it was because she knew who it was, even if she didn't know what had happened. What she felt was an aching in her heart, a sorrow she could not explain. But no fear.

"Josie?" she whispered.

Josie did not speak. She simply lifted her arm and pointed towards the staircase to the attic.

Claire glanced towards the staircase and then back to Josie, who was no longer there. She then walked towards the staircase and began to climb. "Bailey!" she called as she ascended the stairs.

≈

Donovan showed his light over the fuse box, looking for any damage. He heard a noise in the shadows behind him and spun around, casting his light into the darkness. On the floor a little blonde girl sat in the corner under a blanket, crying.

"I'm scared," she said.

"I know," he said in a soft voice. "We're going to get you out of here. I promise."

≈

At the top, Claire desperately began to look around the room, the candle her only form of light. "Damn it, Donovan," she muttered to herself. "You know where the damn breaker box is."

Finally, her light rested on a sneaker poking out from behind the old roll-top desk in the very corner of the attic. She made her way to the spot and found Bailey sitting on the floor, her knees curled to her chest. She was looking blankly ahead, her eyes glassy and unfocused, making the whites of her eyes bright. If it wasn't for that brightness, she could easily be swallowed up in the darkness.

Claire knelt in front of her. "Bailey?"

Bailey didn't answer her. There was no flicker in her eyes. No sign of recognition on her face at all.

"Bailey," Claire set the candle down on the floor and grabbed Bailey's shoulders, gently shaking her. "Bailey!"

She began to shake her more insistently but there was no change. On instinct, Claire slapped her as hard as she could across the face. Bailey began to scream. Loud, shrill, and unrelenting.

≈

An hour and a half later there was more light outside of Blackwood Manor than there had been in quite some time at night. There were two ambulances on site. One had Jessie lying on a gurney. A bandage wrapped around her head wound. She was asleep and her mother was sitting beside her, holding her hand firmly.

The other had Bailey sitting on the tailgate, wrapped in a blanket. The paramedics had given her something to calm her down and she was back to just staring ahead blankly. Michael sat beside her with his arm around her.

Alex's ankle had been wrapped and she'd been given the okay to go home. But not before her father had smacked her hard across the face, scolded her for coming to Blackwood Manor, and screamed at Claire for being "a devil-worshiping idiot."

There were also police cruisers and a news van. The police had set up barricades at the driveway, stopping the reporters from wandering onto the property. However, the cameras were still rolling.

Now Claire, Donovan, and Emma were standing on the porch talking to the sheriff.

"So, none of you know what happened?" the sheriff was asking, the irritation clear in his voice.

"No, sir. We weren't here," Claire explained. "Donovan and I were headed to a supplier out of town to pick up supplies for the renovation. Bailey asked me if she could bring some friends over. She's into the paranormal and the stories about the property...I told her it was okay."

"What made you decide to turn back?" the sheriff asked.

"I forgot the empty paint cans," Donovan said. "We had agreed to give the supplier the empties so that he could reuse them in exchange for a discount."

Claire looked at him but did not correct him. She was amazed at how smoothly he could lie but she completely understood why he needed to. The truth couldn't go in a police report. If anything they would probably become suspects when it came to what happened to the girls. She herself hadn't mentioned the cameras she'd found in the house. She'd gathered them and hidden them under her bed.

"Alex McCarthy said that Jessie flew into the wall," the sheriff said pointedly. As if that was going to make them start spilling their guts.

"We weren't here," Claire said. "They probably just scared each other."

"Probably," the sheriff looked doubtful. "Well, if you think of anything else or if Bailey says anything be sure to call."

"We will," Emma said, shaking the sheriff's hand.

Claire waited until the sheriff had cleared the steps and headed back towards the driveway ordering the reporters away and giving his men the okay to take off. "I'm so sorry, Em. You know I never would have put her in danger on purpose."

"I know. After what we discovered this morning you thought they were innocent spirits stuck here. It's okay."

"I never felt threatened," Claire choked out and clenched her fists. "Even tonight. When I saw Josie I was overwhelmed with a feeling of sorrow. But no fear. I don't think she did this. We'll know soon enough."

"What do you mean?" Donovan asked.

"The cameras," Claire answered. She turned towards Emma. "The girls had set up cameras. They were still on. With any luck, they captured what happened. I'm going over the footage tonight."

"I'm doing it with you," Emma said. "Just let me go tell Michael to take Bailey home."

"Where are Richie and Callie?"

"Our neighbor is watching them. She's such a sweet old lady. We told her Bailey had been in an accident and she came right over."

Ten minutes later Claire and Emma walked into the parlor with their arms full of cameras. Donovan had already set up Claire's laptop. The lights were now magically working. Of course. They sat on the sofa. One woman on each side of Donovan, the laptop laying across his legs. Claire handed him a camera and he fumbled as he tried to attach the USB cable. He blushed. "I'm sorry."

"It's okay," Emma took the cable from him and did it herself.

He clicked on the play button and they watched. This was the camera in the attic. They watched as Jessie made adjustments while looking straight into the camera. This girl was not the blubbering mess with blood running down her face that they had seen. She looked excited.

After she was satisfied with the camera angle Jessie began to explore the attic. She stopped at the roll-top desk and picked up a stack of letters that were sitting on it. "Holy crap," she said, flipping from one to the next. "Hey, you guys! You gotta see this!"

She then walked out of the view of the camera and the light was shut off, triggering the night vision capture.

Emma went to hand another camera to Donovan but Claire stopped her. "Wait. The attic was where I found Bailey. Let's wait a bit and see what happened up there."

Donovan began to fast forward frame by frame, looking for anything unusual.

"Wait," Emma exclaimed. "Go back one."

Donovan went back a frame and hit play. Briefly, in the mirror next to the roll top they saw a shadow pass behind the camera. Then there was nothing again. He continued going forward until they saw Bailey come into frame. He went back to the beginning of the frame and hit the play button.

There was a rustling noise and sobbing and Bailey came into the frame, crawling on the floor, seeming to claw for a handhold. She stopped in the middle of the floor, crying. For a moment, it appeared like she was giving up.

Then they heard a child's soft, small voice, but they couldn't see anything on the video. "Hide. She'll hurt you. She hurt me."

Bailey screamed and scrambled to her feet and ran to the spot in the corner where Claire found her. They began going forward again, frame by frame until Claire entered the attic and found her. They watched as Claire said Bailey's name over and over, as she shook her, as she slapped her face.

Then her screaming. Claire inched away, clasping her hands over her ears. There was a loud rushed sound of footsteps and Donovan came running into the frame.

"I don't know what's wrong with her!" Claire had yelled over Bailey's screams, looking at him.

"Get the candle and walk ahead of me!" he ordered. He scooped up Bailey in his arms and carried her close behind Claire. After they were out of frame they shut off the video.

"Did you hear that voice?" Emma asked, shakily.

"I could be wrong but it sounded like the little girl I saw on the stairs. Hard to tell, though. So many children sound the same until puberty," Claire answered.

Emma handed Donovan another camera and let out a long breath as he hooked it up. "I don't know if I'm ready for this. Who hurt her? Who is she? It has to be Lucy Blackwood talking about her mother."

"No," Claire shook her head. "The girl on the stairs was not Lucy."

"You're absolutely sure?"

"Yes. Besides, her head was bashed in. In Margaret's letter, it said she killed Lucy unintentionally. A bashed-in skull doesn't seem unintentional to me."

"Are you ladies ready?" Donovan asked.

They both nodded and looked at the screen. He pressed play and the upstairs hallway came into focus. Bailey was angling the camera to her liking. She smiled and gave the camera a big thumbs-up before bouncing down the stairs.

Donovan began to fast forward frame by frame. Eventually, the lights went out and night vision came on. They patiently went through frame by frame of nothing until all three let out a collective gasp. In the corner of one frame, they saw a door open. Donovan hit play and they watched as the doors all the way up and down the hall began to slam one by one.

"Gloria? Is that you?" sounded Bailey's voice.

They watched as the girls came up the stairs, Bailey in the lead. She was feeling along the wall and the other girls were holding onto each other's shoulders.

Emma let out a scream as all the doors snapped shut at once and an image suddenly appeared at the end of the hall just the way light would at the flip of a switch.

"That's not Josie," Claire said. "That's not who I've been seeing. Donovan?"

"Me either," he answered, though his jaw was clenched tight.

"Gloria, is there something you want to tell us?" Bailey asked.

There was a roar, and the apparition flew down the hall toward the girls. Horns began to materialize on top of her head.

She blew past Bailey, who fell to the side and into the camera tripod. The camera shook and the view tilted. Alex ducked down to the floor, right where she was standing and the figure ran headlong into Jessie who flew through the air and into the back wall, knocking the stack of boxes to the ground.

All three girls were screaming. Jessie was crumpled on the ground with her arms instinctively pulled up over her face. The figure reared back with an arm, swiping at her.

"Stop it!" Alex yelled, rushing forward.

The figure turned and swiped out with its other arm. Without even touching her, the force pushed Alex back a couple of feet causing her to fall on her tailbone. She crawled towards the staircase banister, whimpering. Bailey ran to her side and sank to the ground. The two of them wrapped their arms around each other. The terror radiating off their bodies was electrifying even through the camera. They watched helplessly as the figure lashed out at Jessie again.

Then Josie appeared through the wall and passed by Jessie's head, seemingly gliding. The figure stopped its attack and looked at Josie and flicked its wrist. Josie went forward, in front of Jessie's crumpled body, her face mere inches from the other woman. The figure smacked her and she put her hands on its shoulders pushing it back.

What happened next could only be described as pure chaos. The doors began slamming again, and the lights were flickering on and off, causing an ominous effect on the camera.

The two women were going for each other now, seemingly ignoring the girls. Jessie scrambled for the stairs then ran down them. Alex followed her. Bailey attempted to go next, but the cold figure flicked out her wrist again and Bailey was levitating and being yanked backward, as though an invisible rope bound her.

The figure turned its attention back to Josie, a snarl apparent on its face despite the sickening flesh hanging from its face.

Josie rushed at the figure, and it disappeared over the banister. The hold on Bailey seemed to have lessened. She fell to the floor with a sickening thud.

Josie turned to face her. Her voice was sharp and insistent. "Go. Go, girl!"

Bailey scrambled to the nearest place, the staircase for the attic. Josie walked back to the wall from which she had appeared and disappeared just as quickly.

Donovan stopped the video and the three of them looked from one to the other not knowing what to say. Emma's cell phone rang, breaking the silence.

"Hello?" she answered. The color drained from her face. She covered her mouth with her hand. "Is everyone okay? Okay. Okay, I'm on my way." She hung up the phone and turned to Claire and Donovan. "Our house is on fire."

"What?" Claire exclaimed. All three of them rose to their feet and made a beeline for the front door.

When they pulled onto Emma's street, the fire was still blazing. The flames licked up high. It was a good thing that there was no wind tonight. The houses on either side seemed unaffected. They bolted from the car and right up to the barricades. Emma and Michael threw their arms around each other.

"Where are the kids?" she asked.

"With Mrs. Tucker," he answered. "It started not even five minutes after Bailey and I got home."

All four of them turned to watch the blaze that the firefighters were working so hard to extinguish. It didn't seem to want to go out. The blaze appeared to grow larger, taller, farther and farther up into the sky. No one said anything, but they were all thinking the same thing. There wasn't much house left.

≈

Claire offered to let them move into Blackwood Manor but Emma shied away from the very thought of it.

"I don't know," she said, nervously playing with the ends of her hair. "After tonight and what we saw on the camera..."

"You can stay in the cottage in the back if you prefer," Claire told her. "That area is completely finished and empty. It's been cleaned and painted. The roof is fixed. The crew just finished it."

"I don't know," she looked up at Michael, her eyes searching his face.

"To my knowledge, no one has experienced anything there," Claire continued. "I'm not sure why but I'm positive that area is clean. There have been plenty of people there and not one person has come to me with any strange stories and no one has mysteriously quit after working out there."

Emma glanced down at the ground, lost in thought.

"She's right, Emma," Donovan added. "Not a single person has come to me with anything suspicious. I've been out there myself quite a bit, and I've never seen anything out of the ordinary. Plenty in the main house but nothing in the cottage. It's small but it'll be comfortable enough for a family of five."

"Maybe nobody reported seeing anything because they weren't alone."

"Believe me, that's never stopped anything before," Claire said gently. "And besides, Brad worked out there alone quite a bit."

Emma looked up at her husband again who squeezed her shoulder absently. "We don't really have a lot of options, Em. We can rebuild, but that's not going to happen overnight. We need to have a more stable place than a hotel to save money."

Emma let out a deep breath and finally answered. "Okay. I'll talk to Brad and see what he has to say. But I don't want any of the kids in the main house anymore. Not until we figure out what's going on."

"It's a deal," Claire leaned forward and hugged her friend.

≈

When Claire and Donovan arrived back at Blackwood Manor that night they were greeted by an ominous message. Written across the fireplace mantle in huge letters were the words, "Help Gloria." The message appeared to be written in blood.

Michael and Emma got a motel room that first night. They didn't wake Richie and Callie, just left them with Mrs. Tucker. Bailey was passed out in the opposite bed after taking medicine that the doctor had given her.

Emma didn't think she would be able to sleep at all but she nodded off relatively easily. It was not, however, a peaceful sleep. She tossed and turned as dark images of leaping flames and women with horns invaded her mind. She eventually settled into a dream.

*Eight-year-old Josie hid behind her mama's skirts and kept peeking out at the pretty bride. Mr. John had just married the most beautiful girl Josie had ever seen. The sixteen-year-old woman stood with her pretty raven hair curled just so and laughing and smiling so bright in her flowing white wedding gown that she looked angelic. Mr. John had his arm around her, and they looked so happy and in love.*

*The wedding was set up behind the house, and Josie was helping her mama and the other girls set up the food on long tables for after the ceremony.*

*"For goodness sake girl, be of some use," her Mama shook her off of her skirts, forcing her out in the open. The pretty bride looked toward them, saw Josie watching, smiled, lifted the train of her dress, and walked towards them. She stopped in front of Josie, knelt, and talked to her for the very first time. She was beaming from ear to ear. "Hello, there. What's your name?"*

*"Josie," the child answered timidly.*

*"Well, I'm Margaret," she reached out and gently popped Josie's nose with the end of her finger, "and you and I are going to be great friends."*

Emma opened her eyes and realized immediately that she had just experienced a full-blown memory of Josie's. "What happened to them?" she wondered out loud.

## CHAPTER ELEVEN

Over the course of the next several weeks, things went from chaos to a new normal. Emma, Michael, and the kids moved into the cottage behind Blackwood Manor and had finally settled in. At one point, the building had been one giant room with beds but at some point had been renovated into a small apartment with three bedrooms, a kitchen, and a bathroom. It was the perfect size for their family.

So far, nothing had happened, just as Claire, Donovan, and Brad promised, and Emma's mind was starting to be put at ease. The first several days she had awoken every half hour and obsessively checked on the kids, looking for any signs of foul play or anything out of the ordinary.

They bought furniture at yard sales and the Goodwill in town and several people in the community donated clothing.

Bailey had finally come out of her funk. She was acting almost like a hybrid of her earlier self; she still made her normal jokes, playfully torturing her brother and sister. Her grades were not as phenomenal as they had been, but they weren't necessarily bad either. Emma couldn't help but notice though that she no longer made any attempts to go to the main house. Emma's feelings on this fact were torn. It saved her a fight but, it also worried her. She had been in a similar situation before, with Claire.

At first, Claire had seemed to be herself, only losing interest in the event that had terrified her to her very core. Then gradually her entire personality changed. Emma didn't want to see that happen to Bailey. Bailey had a magnetic presence. She was so full of life. From the time she entered the world, Bailey had worn a smirk that seemed to say, *"Hey, you. Watch what I'm gonna do."* The thought of her becoming anything else terrified Emma on a level that she couldn't really put into words.

On one cool morning, after Bailey and Richie headed off to school and Michael took Callie to a pediatrician appointment, Emma sidled up to the window and opened it to allow the breeze to flow in while she went to work setting up their new home with pictures and other decor.

The renovations were coming along nicely. She was surprised at the progress as she looked towards the main house. There were men on the roof now, all the windows had been replaced, and the new paint job gleamed making the house almost seem to sparkle in the sun. A good deal of the property grounds was still under weeds and tall grass, but just as large of a section had been cleared. She hadn't thought fixing this place would be possible, that Claire was crazy. But she had to admit that she was doing it.

Emma turned away from the window and towards the stacks of picture frames on the small kitchen table and began to hang them. If they were going to live here, she was going to make it feel like home. She had emailed every living member of her family and Michael's, spread thin throughout the country, asking anyone who may have pictures of them to please send copies since all of theirs had been destroyed in the fire. The idea of losing seventeen years of pictures had put her into a depressed state, but family and friends had come through, and the pictures started rolling in. She hadn't expected much. She currently had a couple of distant cousins she had only seen a handful of times since childhood and there had been a good deal of prejudice from the family members left on Michael's side.

No one had been happy when they started dating, and it got even worse when they announced their engagement. They would try to prove she was cheating by planting false evidence. He would be invited to family gatherings without her, and when he arrived there would be an ex of his there. One much better suited for his affections. So many people were saying that they would disown him for marrying a Black girl. He was blamed for his mother's heart attack; the reason being that she was on the older side and her heart just couldn't take the shame. That was nothing compared to when they started having children. People were saying that the kids would be sickly, or worse, demonic. They were told that they were disgusting and that the races weren't meant to mix and that their children would never be accepted. She shook her head at the thought. When Bailey was born Michael was given one last chance to leave them and take his place back as the head of the family. When he'd refused he'd finally been written out of the will.

`Therefore, the fact that there were any pictures left was honestly a shock to her. She was centering one photo, a black and white portrait from their wedding, when she heard the first sounds. The sounds made her stop dead in her tracks. The sounds of battery-operated toys going off with childish glee. She was the only one here. She closed her eyes and took a deep breath, then she followed the sound of the toy into the girls' room and to a plastic guitar with light-up buttons. She popped the batteries out and went back to the living room and the pictures. Within a minute, she heard the guitar again. Her heart began to race. "It's just a toy, Em. Don't flip out on yourself. You know there is a child here. It probably just made its way out here, drawn by your children. It's just a child. Just a toy. No big deal," she told herself, and picked up another picture frame, trying to ignore the noise.

There were several beeps and squeals of toys and then there was a loud bang as if something had fallen off a high shelf. Emma sighed and turned towards the girls' bedroom. She had to make sure nothing was broken before Callie got home. She cautiously opened the door and stepped into the small room.

Callie's toy box was flipped open and there was a pile of toys between their beds. Lights were flashing on some, others played music. Emma's first instinct was to turn and run but she fought it. She stepped forward and looked down at the toys that were strategically placed, forming letters on the floor.   The message was, *"Help Gloria."*

Emma looked up then and saw her in the corner. The woman that Claire and Donovan had seen. The woman who saved the girls in the video. The servant girl, Josie. Of course. Emma looked at her face, or lack thereof, and completely ignored the smell filling the room. This had been the servant's quarters. It made sense for her to be out here. Why had she assumed it had been the child?

"Josie?" she asked with a confidence that she didn't know she had. One she hadn't used in about twenty-nine years.

Josie nodded her head but did not speak. Emma half expected her to turn and go, as she'd always done with Claire. As she had done when the girls were safe in the video. She stayed where she was though.

"Who is Gloria? Is she an ancestor we need to find to help you move on?"

Josie shook her head no.

"Is she someone who needs our help?" Emma took a tentative step towards Josie, who still did not move.

Josie nodded and Emma's breath caught in her throat. Her heart was racing. She didn't dare blink. She didn't want to lose Josie, and her answers, in that split second.

"Are you stuck here? Stuck between worlds?"

Josie shook her head no again.

"Then why are you still here?"

There was a rattling as her voice came. The sound of an unused voice. Vocal cords were straining to get used to the vibrations. It was hoarse and gravelly. "I won't leave her. Not in this place. Not in the dark. Not with them."

"Who? Gloria?" Emma asked again, struggling to understand.

Josie nodded.

Emma tore her eyes away from Josie, looking down at the toys again and realization entered her mind. She looked up and was amazed to find that Josie was still there. "Gloria is a child. She's your child."

Josie shook her head.

"No? She's not your child?"

"I'm all she has," Josie finally said.

"Where is she?"

Josie pointed through the window at the house. Emma turned to see what she was pointing at and when she turned back around, she was gone. She pulled her phone from her pocket and began to take pictures.

≈

Claire had set up a desk in the parlor, directly in front of the window. She was surrounded by yards of fabric and was still trying to make friends with the sewing machine. She had decided that since the place was going to be a bed-and-breakfast she wanted all the curtains to be uniform and to make them herself. It would be cheaper in the long run and she needed the savings.

She felt content listening to the sounds coming from the far side of the house. The kitchen was being fully redone. She couldn't help but smile knowing that one of her dreams, the dream to have a beautiful magazine-worthy chef's kitchen, was coming true.

She turned at the sound of the front door opening when Emma entered. She wore a weary look on her face as she took a seat next to Claire.

"What's up, Em?" she asked, concerned by the forlorn expression on her friend's face.

Emma held up her phone so that Claire could see the pictures on it. Toys spelling out, *"Help Gloria."*

"Josie did it," Emma said simply. "She was in the room."

Claire watched her. She was waiting for her to go on.

"She used every toy in Callie's toy box. I had a conversation with her. Kind of," Emma shook her head in wonder, still amazed by that fact. "I found out she's not trapped here. She can leave when she wants. But she won't leave without someone who is."

"Gloria?" Claire asked.

Emma nodded and then continued. "She's just a child, Claire. Gloria is a child. But she's not Josie's child. She said, 'I'm all she has.' What do you think that means?"

Claire's brow furrowed in confusion. "Gloria's spirit is trapped here? I thought children could automatically pass on because they are pure or whatever."

Emma shrugged her shoulders. "I thought so too. Of course some stick around but I always thought they could go on if they wanted to, but that's what she said."

They were cut off by a knock on the door and Claire rose to her feet, heading into the entryway. When she opened the door, she had to cling to the door jamb to keep her knees from buckling. Standing before her was Margaret Blackwood. At the very least, a carbon copy image. Older than in her vision, younger than in the newspaper article, but the resemblance was uncanny. She had the same high cheekbones, tall and slender build, and ebony hair. The difference was in her eyes. Though they were the same shape, they seemed warmer than Margaret Blackwood's, and her hair was streaked with gray. Otherwise, it was as if someone had taken Margaret Blackwood's portrait and changed the clothing in photoshop to make her look modern.

"Margaret?" she said before she could stop herself.

"How did you know?" the woman asked. The voice was very similar too. With maybe a slightly higher pitch.

Claire must have looked confused because the woman laughed and a soft light touched her eyes that hadn't appeared in Margaret Blackwood's.

"I'm Maggie. Margaret Blackwood was my great-great grandmother."

Claire relaxed her grip on the door frame and stepped to the side. "Would you like to come in?"

"Very much. Thank you." Maggie stepped inside and Claire closed the door behind her.

"You'll have to excuse the mess," Claire shook her hand. "We're in the middle of renovating."

"Yes, I know," Maggie followed Claire into the parlor and nodded at Emma before glancing around the room. "I haven't seen this place since I was a child. I thought it would seem smaller now but it doesn't."

"I thought the property left the Blackwood family in the early 1900s," Claire said as she took her seat.

"Well, technically," Maggie took a seat on the sofa and faced the two women. "The family got into financial trouble. Robert Blackwood had a gambling problem and was forced to sell the property to pay his debts. His wife and new baby had been threatened. He sold it to his good friend, though. The same man that owned the neighboring plantation, Heaven's Estate. They continued to live here until they finally moved away a couple of years later. After that, his friend sold the land, but for the longest time, it was always someone in the community who owned it. So, it wasn't unusual for the family to visit."

Claire and Emma leaned forward, listening intently. These were the goods they had been looking for. Information. And they were getting it directly from a descendant's mouth.

"Who is Robert Blackwood?" Claire asked.

"Robert was Margaret's grandson. Percy's boy. He was only twenty-one when he got into trouble," Maggie took a deep breath and leveled her eyes at the two women. "I'm going, to be frank about why I'm here. I'm sixty-two years old and I don't waste time beating around the bush."

"That's fine," Claire said, cautiously.

"I saw your interview on the television about opening the place up as a bed-and-breakfast once the renovations are complete," she looked into Claire's eyes. It felt as though she were looking directly into her soul. "You must not do this. I know that paranormal sites have worked before in such a setting but it would be disastrous here."

"Why?"

"That's the question, isn't it? Things have happened here. Horrible things. There are things in the history of our family that we don't share with outsiders, that we either ignore completely or whisper about in close company. Now that you're here, I supposed you're an honorary family member," she let out a grim smile. "There are a lot of things that are a mystery even to us. Some things we've put together over time."

"What do you mean?" Emma piped up. "More than just a haunting?"

Maggie nodded. "More than just a haunting. The dark cloud associated with this place goes back farther than you might think. The family kept it quiet until the property was no longer theirs. The darkness goes back to the Civil War. It may even predate it. No one is entirely sure. But it's said that something changed Margaret. Something in this place."

She shifted in her seat and was quiet for a moment. She was trying to figure out the best way to word what she had to say. "Percy told his children that he watched his mother change before his very eyes. She had been very soft, sweet, and lighthearted. She would hug and kiss him and Lucy and get down on the floor to play with them like she was the same age. Then she grew cold, distant, and in many ways, cruel. This is where the family is divided. Some believe that she was so overcome with grief from Lucy's death that she put up a wall and didn't want to let anyone else in. Others believe that there was some outside force leading her, gradually working its way into her brain, making her toxic."

"What do you believe?"

"I don't know what to believe," she answered honestly. "Certain things don't line up. A lot of people died on the property during the war and I believe it's possible that all that energy did open a doorway. But something that's always kept me from forming my own opinion one way or the other is Lucy's death. She supposedly died of scarlet fever, which was a huge problem at the time. But Percy said that she locked herself in her room for a week after refusing to eat, saying it was her fault. That she didn't mean to kill her. Now, scarlet fever was tragic, and would of course, cause depression in any parent but why would she believe that she killed her? The only way that makes sense is if Margaret had a fever herself and had given it to Lucy. Guess what? Margaret was never sick a day. Even stranger than that? She refused to ever hold her grandchildren when they came along. It was as though she was scared of hurting them."

Claire felt a sting in her palm and looked down to notice that she had her fists clasped so tight that her fingernails were biting into her flesh, causing tiny little droplets of blood. She loosened her grip but never took her eyes off Maggie.

"Did Margaret miscarry her third child?"

Maggie shook her head. "Margaret only had two children."

"Were there any family members from that time or anyone at all who lived here named Gloria? That name has been popping up a lot."

"No. Not that I'm aware of. Now listen carefully. Have you found the oil paintings yet?"

Claire couldn't hide the surprise from her face, but she answered nonetheless. "Yes. I found them on my first day of ownership."

"They appear whenever something unexplained happens?"

"They do."

"Whatever you do, do not attempt to destroy them. You can put them away, but if you try to destroy them, things will only get worse for you. One young man tried to burn them, and his daughter was killed. Thrown from a horse and suffered a broken neck. Plus another several months of torture."

"Why do you think that is?"

"Lucy is angry about her death. The others simply follow her. Destroying the portraits….that's like killing her all over again."


Later that evening Claire couldn't stop thinking about everything that Maggie said and Emma's encounter with Josie. What had Josie meant by saying she didn't want to leave Gloria here alone? If Lucy really died of scarlet fever, then why had Margaret blamed herself? Why had she changed so drastically? Her mind was full of questions swimming around in her brain. Her thoughts were interrupted by Donovan calling out to her from the cellar.

She made her way to the door under the stairs and went down the narrow stairway. The cellar was small with a dirt floor and gray, dreary-looking walls. There was junk spread throughout and Donovan had been sorting through it. Old documents in one pile, antiques in another, and a third that appeared to be moth-eaten blankets.

He was sitting on the floor in the center of columns of boxes and discarded junk on either side of him. He was holding a dusty leather-bound book in his hands. "You have to see this," he told her.

She knelt on the ground in front of him. "What is that?"

"It's a ledger," he answered as he opened the book up, careful not to let it fall apart. The pages were yellow and brittle, barely staying in place. The ink on the pages was almost faded to the point of being unreadable. "Of servants who died. The first entry was in 1850. Look at the last one," he carefully turned to the last page with writing on it and handed it over to Claire.

"*Josie. January 8, 1865. Scarlet fever. My dearest friend.*" Written in the margin next to Josie's name was a single word in different, newer handwriting. Popping off the page in a vibrant red was the word "*Murderer.*"

Claire's phone chirped with an incoming text message. She pulled it out and when she saw what was on the screen her face went ashen.

"What's wrong?" Donovan asked.

"My friend Jennifer," she said quietly.

"Is she okay?"

"She was murdered."

*Josie sat down her quill, sighed, and rubbed her tired eyes. She was sitting on the front steps of the manor house with readers in front of her. Her mama had objected, saying that learning to read and write was a waste of time and downright dangerous; that her time and energy would be better spent cleaning the rooms with her and cooking, but Miss Margaret insisted she learn, and what the people said in the main house was law.*

*"How are you doing, Josie?" came a kind voice from behind her and she turned to see Miss Margaret in the frame of the front door. She wore a sky-blue dress that showed off her trim figure and brought out the blue of her eyes. She elegantly walked forward and took a seat on the steps next to Josie.*

*Josie smiled half-heartedly. "I'm alright, Miss Margaret. My learning's not so good."*

*"Well, let's see." Margaret pulled the paper in front of her. "This isn't so bad for a beginner, Josie. It takes time. You just have to have patience."*

*"I don't want to let you down, ma'am."*

*Margaret chuckled. "That's not possible. I assure you. How old are you now, Josie?"*

*"Ten."*

*"And how is it you've never learned to read?"*

*"I ain't had no schooling."*

*"Don't say that. It isn't proper. Say 'I've never been to school.'"*

*"I've never been to school."*

*"Why not?"*

*Josie shrugged and then automatically decided to compose a more elegant response. "Mama says that it's no place for a colored girl; our kind wouldn't be accepted. She says my time is better spent learning to make the beds and cook without burning the eggs."*

*"Well, those things are important also," Margaret chuckled and gave Josie a smile. "There is so much more to*

*life. I have absolutely no disrespect toward your mama. She has done a wonderful job raising you and taking care of all of us. What she said may be true if you were ordinary. You are special, Josie."*

*"How?"*

*"You're smart. You're probably the smartest little girl I know. You could have a real future. You have to learn to read though. It is important."*

*"Why is it important?"*

*Margaret leaned forward and whispered with a conspiratorial grin. "I have a secret. I'm going to have a baby."*

*"Miss Margaret! That's wonderful!" Josie threw her arms around Margaret's neck in a warm hug. "I'm so happy for you."*

*"Thank you but this has to be our secret for now. I want you to be my nursemaid and the baby's nanny. The family may object and say you are too young. I think you are smart enough and responsible enough to handle it."*

*"I am! I am, I promise. I love babies. I want to take care of it."*

*"You shall, my dear," and she gave her a wink.*

## CHAPTER TWELVE

*Claire and Emma stared at the door across from them that had squeaked open. It was the door to her parents' bedroom, and Claire knew that she wasn't supposed to go in there but she couldn't stop herself from slowly rising to her feet and walking towards the door.*

*"Claire, no!" Emma squeaked out in barely more than a whisper. She suddenly had a twisted feeling in her gut but she didn't want to admit that. She didn't want Claire to think she was a chicken. "Come back. You'll get in trouble. Come on, come back. Let's ask some questions about kids at school."*

*"In a minute, Em. I'm in trouble anyway if I don't close the door. They'll think we were in there."*

*"Well, then close the door and come back. Please."*

*"Fine. I'll just close the door." Claire approached the doorway and grabbed the doorknob. Just as she was about to close the door, she heard a rattling sound from inside the bedroom and her skin suddenly felt like ice.*

*She took a tentative step inside, ignoring Emma's harried whispers to her. She swung around when the door slammed shut behind her and her mouth went dry.*

Claire and Emma both awoke at the same time; the memory digging at the front of their brains. Emma hugged her pillow closer to her and rolled over in her bed in the cottage, falling back to sleep.

Sleep didn't come so easily to Claire, however. She stared at the ceiling for several minutes and found herself quite irritated. Why in the world was she thinking about that now? She never thought about her childhood. At least not the details of it. Her memory had been flooded with the details recently, especially the ones of that night. She simply didn't have time for it.

Fear. Such a strong, complicated thing. The way it makes your heart pound, your mouth go dry, and the chills that run up and down your spine. The way it causes goosebumps on the flesh and the hair standing up on the back of your neck. Claire knew the feeling well. She'd felt it frequently during her childhood and almost constantly throughout her marriage. She felt it whenever she'd have these memories of that night. It irritated the hell out of her.

She sat up and made her way down to the kitchen. She was craving a glass of milk. Ordinarily, she wouldn't go down at this time of night but milk had helped her sleep in the past. She grabbed a glass out of the cupboard and a jug of milk from the refrigerator, not bothering to turn on the lights.

She stood sipping her milk for a moment and then stopped, goose flesh rising on her neck. She heard voices. It sounded like Margaret Blackwood's voice and another that seemed familiar but she couldn't quite place. The voices were coming from the servant's stairwell.

Claire cautiously approached the door, her milk still clasped firmly in her hand. She stopped outside to listen and furrowed her brow when she heard a familiar name.

"Kate, I run the show around here," Margaret Blackwood was saying. "This is my property now and always will be. You will do what you are told."

Claire pushed the door open and recoiled at what she saw. Her neighbor, Kate Wilkes, was seated on the steps. Her eyes were blank; the irises and pupils apparently gone. Her skin appeared to still be there, but it was extremely pale. Still, she didn't look quite right. What would she even be doing here anyway?

As bizarre as Kate's appearance was, it was not what affected Claire, who was instead looking at Margaret Blackwood. Margaret looked different than she did in the video. Flesh still hung from bones, but the face was now a blue-gray color with a scaly-looking texture. There were two horns on her head and her eyes were glowing red. Hooves stuck out from underneath her long dress.

"Claire," she said, grinning in a sinister way that made Claire's blood run cold. "Come to join the party? I have big plans for you." She swiped out then, suddenly, Claire felt a searing pain in her shoulder.

She cried out involuntarily and dropped her glass of milk. The glass shattered and the milk spilled everywhere, including splashing over her bare feet, making her feel colder. She reached her hand up to her shoulder and found that her nightgown was sliced open. She pulled her fingers in front of her face to see that they were smeared with blood.

"Claire?" Donovan's voice came booming through the silence. "Claire, where are you? Are you okay?"

"I'm fine!" she called. "I'm in the kitchen."

There were a few steps and the room suddenly filled with soft light. Claire looked back through the doorway to find it empty.

Donovan rushed up to her. "What happened?" he asked, eyeing the broken glass. He looked at Claire's bloody hand that she was still holding in front of her face. "Did you cut yourself?"

"It's not my hand," she said slowly and looked up at him. "I heard voices so I came to investigate. Kate Wilkes, the neighbor from Heaven's Estate, was in there and so was Margaret. But Margaret didn't look like herself. She...Donovan, I swear she looked like a devil. She scratched me."

She pulled the neckline down so he could see her shoulder. The gown had three long gashes in it with matching bloody gashes underneath it.

"Holy shit," he said, looking closely. "We better get some antiseptic on this."

Claire allowed herself to be guided over to a bar stool at the kitchen island and she sat while Donovan went to get first aid supplies from the bathroom.

He quickly returned and went to work cleaning Claire's scratches.

"Are you sure that what you saw was Margaret?" he asked her.

She hissed through her teeth at the sting from the ointment. "I'm not sure of anything. If it wasn't then it was something pretending to be her. Same clothing, the same build, same voice. Except for hooves instead of feet, and her face was bluish-gray and scaly. She had red eyes and horns."

Donovan frowned as he placed a piece of gauze over her wound. "That sounds like a demon."

"I know. But–" she was cut off by the landline ringing. Who could be calling at this hour?

Donovan walked over to the hanging receiver on the wall so that Claire didn't have to get up. "Hello?"

Claire watched his face. His lips were a tight line and his eyebrows furrowed together.

"Hello, is someone there? It's four in the morning," he looked irritated. "Okay, listen. I can't hear you, so you're going to have to call back at a more reasonable hour."

Donovan hung the receiver and headed back to finish taping down Claire's dressing. "Nothing but a bunch of static."

Claire nodded. "Yeah. That happens sometimes. Bad and crossed power lines from being so far back in the hills. It happens on my cell phone too."

"I could hear someone breathing though," he said. "They were probably talking, and I just couldn't hear them."

"Probably."

"What were you saying when the phone rang?"

"Back to the demon subject. I agree with you that it's definitely what it looked and sounded like. But the question is, is it a demon impersonating Margaret? Or is Margaret a demon?"

"I'm not sure how that works," Donovan said as he pulled her nightgown back down over the gauze. "But considering that it was violent tonight I don't think the kids should go anywhere on the property without an escort until we know for sure."

"Agreed," she said, rising from the bar stool.

"Well, I'm going to try to get a little more sleep. The crew will be here at six sharp."

"Okay," she grabbed a hand towel and the trash can and headed over to the mess she had made with her shattered milk glass.

"Do you need me to help you clean that up?"

"No. That's okay. I've got it."

Donovan disappeared from the kitchen, and Claire's mind wandered as she cleaned up her mess. Why did she keep thinking about that night when she and Emma had been children playing with a Ouija board? Why did she see her neighbor in her stairway? Why did Margaret look like a demon?

All these thoughts kept running through her mind like a river when the dam broke. The sting from her scratches just kept them running.

≈

Later that afternoon Claire knocked at the door at Heaven's Estate. She had been meaning to come by for awhile and return Kate's kindness by bringing a pie of her own. Apple.

A woman who looked around Claire's age opened the door. She had long red hair offsetting bright green eyes and a face sprinkled with freckles. "Yes?" she asked warmly.

"Hi, I'm Claire Donahue. I'm the new owner of Blackwood Manor. Kate came by a couple of times and very sweetly welcomed me to the area with a pie. I wanted to return the favor. Is she home?"

The woman stepped to the side allowing Claire to enter. "I'm Megan Harris. Kate is my mother. I'm afraid she isn't here. I'll be sure to let her know that you were here when she's feeling better."

"When she's feeling better?"

"Mom had a heart attack last night. Well, actually early this morning if you want to get technical."

"Oh, I'm so sorry," Claire exclaimed. "She's okay though?"

"She'll be just fine. They're keeping her for observation at the hospital to be safe."

"Yes. Better safe than sorry."

Megan took the pie from Claire as two young boys came running across the entry firing toy guns at each other.

"You boys either slow down or take that outside!" she yelled after them then shook her head, laughing. "Sorry about that. I've got four kids and they make me pull my hair out sometimes. Do you have kids?"

`"No," Claire said. "But my best friend Emma has three, and they're all living at Blackwood right now. One of them is a boy about their age. We should get them all together to play."

"Well, they're free to come over here anytime," Megan said, but her eyes didn't quite meet Claire's when she said it.

≈

Claire felt uneasy during the short drive back to Blackwood Manor. She couldn't shake the feeling that Kate's heart attack was no coincidence. The timing was too close to when she appeared in the stairway.

Claire drummed her fingers on the wheel. Maybe the bed-and-breakfast was a bad idea. Should she bring innocent people, some of whom may have children, into the house? She didn't want to drop the idea but she knew it wouldn't be wise until she knew more. She knew what she had to do.

≈

The next day Claire opened the door and let in Nadine Lewis. Nadine's gray hair was silky and smooth, hanging to her waist. She wore a bandanna around her head and a flowery T-shirt and jeans. She was a medium that Claire had found in the yellow pages right after her visit to Heaven's Estate.

"The way my process works is I will walk the house. I will not speak at this time. Once I'm finished with the walk-through, I will discuss what I picked up on with you. I don't wish you to give me any details until that time. It could affect the vibrations."

"Should I walk with you?" Claire asked.

"The energy is usually better if you don't."

Claire took a seat in the parlor while Nadine began walking the house. She nervously picked at a hole in the upholstery of the chair she was sitting in. If someone had told her a couple of months ago that she'd be hiring a medium to figure out what was going on with her house she would have laughed and called them crazy.

Now, she sat there anxiously and wished that Nadine would hurry and come back to tell her what she knew. She was grateful when Emma came in and sat next to her.

"Penny for your thoughts?" she asked.

"Nadine–, the medium I told you about last night, is walking the house now."

"How does that work exactly?"

"Well, she said she didn't want to be told anything because it could interfere with her investigation and that after she was finished walking the house we'd talk about what she's picked up on. What she's found out."

They sat there in silence for several minutes before Nadine reentered the room and took a seat in a chair opposite Claire and Emma.

"Do you need to check the cottage out back?" Emma asked.

Nadine shook her head. "That's not necessary. I got plenty from the house."

Claire sat forward. "Give it to me straight," she said. "I can take it."

"First off, let me just say that on a property this old, it's only natural for there to be some kind of spiritual activity. Usually, it's harmless and occurs in a burst. As though the spirits are simply reliving something that has already happened to them when they were living. I picked up on a good deal of that. That's not what's alarming to me."

"But you were alarmed by something?" Claire's heart began to sink.

"There are plenty of spirits here. Hundreds, to be frank. I also picked up on a strong and evil presence. What's going on here is very unique and complex. "

Nadine crossed her legs before continuing. "There are so many spirits here and they all have something that they need or want. There were people who died of natural causes, who died of illness. There are spirits of women who died during childbirth. There are spirits of people who committed suicide and even murder. The murder rate here is alarming, I'm afraid. That's going to be what ends up giving you the most trouble."

Claire let out the breath she'd been holding, squeezed Emma's hand, and waited for Nadine to continue.

"There is a group of spirits that stuck out among the others," she said. "They appeared to me several times, seemed very insistent on what they wanted, and unlike the others, seemed very aware of the fact that they are dead.

"There is a woman who calls herself Margaret. She seems to be in charge and she's very cold and unforgiving. There is a servant girl by the name of Josie. She has no face. There are two children. Both girls. There is a man in a Civil War uniform who doesn't seem quite right. There's something wrong with him. I also saw an elderly lady who appeared to be from our time. She was dressed modernly. Her name is Kate."

Claire and Emma exchanged looks. Nadine definitely appeared to be the real deal. "What do you make of them?" Emma asked.

"Well, I believe a phenomenon is happening here. See, when a person does something particularly wrong when they are alive it blackens a part of the soul. There's usually no issue with this as long as they live unless the person is a repeat offender. However, the blackened soul will keep the spirit from being able to pass on and they will be forced to return to the place they made the offense.

"If they are able to face what they did and make things right, which rarely happens unfortunately, they are able to pass on. However, the more common result is the person will continue to run from their problem, the thing they did, and sometimes continue to try to make sure that their secret stays buried. Sometimes they will continue to do unforgivable things in death. When this happens the soul continues to blacken and the person will begin to decay, poisoning whatever is around it.

"In the case of Blackwood Manor, there have been many such offenses. This is a Civil War plantation and a lot of wrong was done here. People that committed horrible acts returned here even if they didn't die here. So the property is busting at the seams, so to speak. Their refusal to face what they've done and the continued blackening of their souls, is making the place radiate with evil."

"They're all like that?" Claire croaked out in a whisper.

"No. Not all. But more than the norm for sure. The people who died innocent deaths, the ones who never did anything so horrible that they blackened their souls are simply existing. There are a few that are stuck. I get a distinct impression that Margaret, Josie, and the children are all interwoven. Margaret's soul is very blackened. It's almost rotted clear through. She may be the worst one here. One of the children is trapped and is extremely frightened of Margaret. Gloria."

Claire and Emma both gasped at the name, but they didn't interrupt.

"Josie is not trapped but she stays to try to help Gloria. She wants Gloria to be freed so that she can get away from Margaret and cross over."

"There's something I'm confused about," Emma said. "You said Margaret's soul is badly blackened and that when that happens it poisons everything around. What did she do to cause that? We found a letter she'd hidden in a portrait saying that she had killed her daughter Lucy, but that it was an accident and she was extremely remorseful. That doesn't seem like it would be enough to blacken her to that extent."

"Well, keep in mind that I only took a brief stroll through the house," Nadine said. "I don't have all the answers or even all the jumbled pieces of the puzzle. I simply have a place to start. From what I gathered from the spirits that presented themselves and the behaviors of those who seemed unaware of me is that Margaret was not responsible for one death. She was responsible for three."

"Three?" Claire asked, shocked.

Nadine nodded her head. "On top of that, I gather that she has attacked the living on more than one occasion. Every time this happens the soul blackens more and more."

"Is that why her appearance alters?"

"Yes. For every bit of the soul that blackens a human part becomes obsolete. As humanity disappears they become more devilish."

"What will happen when her soul is completely blackened?"

"Then the transition will be complete. She will be more or less a demon and have the ability to bring hell to Earth."

"Is there anything that can be done?"

"There are a few things. The chances are not the best, I'm afraid. The first thing is if you can somehow get her to do something kind or to face what she's done and make peace with it. That will stop the blackening, and depending on how effective her transition is, she may be able to pass on."

"How can we get her to face what she's done if we don't even know what it is?" Claire asked in frustration. "We know she's responsible for three deaths but we don't know whose, why, or how."

"My advice is to pay attention to what they try to tell you. When they appear, pay close attention. It seems to me the other spirits are reaching out for help. They may be telling you everything you need to know and you just don't realize it."

"What's the other option? In case we can't figure it out?" Emma asked.

"There is a rare phenomenon. Occasionally there will be living people who possess a light that counteracts the blackening. They have the ability to take control and reverse it. I call these people the golden warriors. For some reason, this gift doesn't seem to work for one-on-one spirits. It shines when it's utilized in a mass cleansing. I do believe Blackwood Manor could benefit from a golden warrior. You would have to find one though. That is not an easy fate. These people very rarely know they have this power. Those that do know usually don't have any idea how to control it.

The power isn't generally known until it generates in a time of crisis."

"What were you able to learn about Gloria? Her name keeps coming up but we're at a loss."

"Not much. She was three years old at the time of her death. She was murdered. She's trapped. Josie sees herself as the child's guardian and is trying to get her help so that they can both move on."

"Murdered?" Emma brought her hand to her mouth and her eyes immediately began to brim with tears. "Who would be vicious enough to kill an innocent three-year-old girl?"

"The world is full of all kinds of monsters, I'm afraid."

"Aren't children supposed to automatically pass on?" Claire asked. "If Gloria is here, and I'm assuming the other girl is Lucy, I'm confused."

"Typically they would. However, if the events of their death are tragic enough or they're attached to someone with a blackened soul it can lead to confusion when they first pass and they can miss the window. Both girls died at the hands of another and both were young. They were most likely initially confused, so they got stuck.

"Why does Josie want to help Gloria but not Lucy?"

"I believe there is much there that we still don't know."

≈

That evening a tired Claire went into the parlor when she heard her name called. One of the men from Donovan's crew, Pete, was standing in front of the fireplace with a tape measure in his hand. His eyes were glassy, and he smelled heavily of weed.

"Yes, Pete. What is it?" Claire asked. She was tired and ready to go to bed. Let Donovan and Brad handle everything for the rest of the evening.

"Ma'am I've been doing the measurements of the fireplaces so that we know how much stone to order, and I'm stumped."

"What do you mean?"

"Well, I've been a contractor for twenty years. The placement of the fireplaces in contrast to the size of the rooms doesn't add up. There's a good five feet of empty space in the wall behind them. It doesn't make any sense. Plus. all the fireplaces are much newer than the rest of the house."

"Newer?" Claire raised her eyebrow in disbelief.

"Still old as hell. Don't get me wrong. But at least fifty to sixty years newer than the foundation of the house. Aesthetically, it doesn't work."

"It was the 1800s Pete. They probably just threw them up to protect them from the cold."

"You can't just throw these fireplaces up," he shook his head.

"Look," she said in a careful, slow tone. "It doesn't matter why they did it. We'll never know. But we're here now and we need to replace the stone to use them safely. Just do your job and don't worry about it."

Pete bowed his head in embarrassment. "Yes, ma'am. I'm sorry I bothered you, ma'am."

Claire turned from Pete without another word and made her way up the stairs to her bedroom. "Jesus, put down the weed and come to work with a clear head," she muttered to herself before slipping between the sheets. She fell asleep as soon as her head hit the pillow.

## *CHAPTER THIRTEEN*

On Wednesday of the next week, everyone began coming down with stomach flu. Donovan was the only one lucky enough to avoid getting sick. It was believed that Richie brought it home from school. The strain was particularly bad, and the renovation temporarily came to a complete standstill. The children were home from school and Claire was miffed. She needed to be in New York Friday for Jennifer's funeral and yet she couldn't stay out of the bathroom and bed. Brad was granted time off until the illness passed so as not to compromise his daughter's immune system.

≈

Out in the servant's quarters, Emma was gently rocking Callie. The poor girl had been vomiting all night and her skin was pale and clammy. She finally fell asleep in Emma's arms, and Emma walked the short distance back to her bedroom.

Bailey was lying in the opposite bed asleep with a plastic-lined trashcan on the floor beside the bed. Emma gently laid Callie across from her big sister in her own bed and pulled the covers up.

As she turned to walk through the door Emma got hit by a sudden wave of extreme dizziness and tripped over a toy she hadn't seen and fell on her tailbone before she could catch herself. She bit her lip to keep from screaming and rolled around so that she could push up with her knees. That's when she saw it.

A floorboard had popped up slightly and moved with her weight. She almost slid it back down into place but a nagging voice in her mind told her to look under it first. She pulled the board up with surprising ease and looked down into the hole.

Among the cobwebs, there was a book. She reached in and pulled it out. It was leather bound with yellowed pages. She flipped open the front cover and saw that it was dated from the 1800s. Given that fact, it was remarkably well preserved. The writing was barely faded at all. She gently thumbed through the pages and saw that the book was almost completely full. Only two pages at the very end were blank.

Emma slipped the floorboard back into place and got to her feet, carrying the book back out into the sitting room. She was intrigued, and she wanted to read some of it before her next urgent trip to the bathroom.

She had no more than opened to the first page before she realized that this was Josie's diary. She struggled at first with the choppy writing and misspelled words of a woman who was clearly not well educated, but eventually began to pick up on the nuances, feeling with each entry like Josie was an old family friend. She read through years of entries detailing Josie's life in Blackwood Manor, and her unique friendship with Margaret.

Then she got to the entries after the start of the Civil War and her smile disappeared. The entries gradually got darker and darker.

Emma's eyes brimmed with tears the more she read. When she reached the last entry, she pushed back her sickness and made her way up to the manor house to talk to Claire about the diary.

"Claire!" she called out as she entered through the sliding glass door at the back of the house, and she heard a toilet upstairs flush.

She made her way up the stairs and met up with Claire just as she was about to walk back into her bedroom. She looked almost green in the face as she climbed back into her bed.

"You aren't going to believe what I found," Emma said, sitting cross-legged on the foot of the bed with Josie's diary carefully perched on her lap.

"What is that?" Claire asked.

"Josie's diary."

"What?"

"Yeah. It documents several years. The way the dynamic changed during the war, the change in Margaret. Claire—Gloria was Margaret's third child."

"What?" Claire shot up in bed with a sudden energy boost.

"There were enemy troops that took up residence for a few weeks. I already knew that. It's pretty common knowledge around here. But the men that were here were extremely demented. They drove away the remaining slaves because of their treatment. Margaret and Josie were raped constantly in that time frame. They put up with it because it kept the kids safe. The diary doesn't explain exactly how. But Margaret got pregnant with Gloria and fell into a depression, turning cold."

"Oh my God," Claire breathed out.

"According to Josie, Margaret didn't even give the baby a name. She wanted nothing to do with her. Josie ended up calling her Gloria. When she was no longer an infant Gloria was locked down in the cellar, barely fed, and beaten if she made any noise."

"How did she die?" Claire asked. "Nadine said she was only three. What happened to Lucy?"

"It doesn't say, on either count," Emma answered. "But Josie did say that she was worried Margaret was going to 'take care of her.' Apparently, Margaret just got colder and colder and was worried about how she would explain her to John. She was convinced her reputation would be in the mud. Nothing Josie did or said talked her down. Josie said that she was beginning to think she was going to have to take Gloria and run. There were no other entries."

"Wow. So, you think she ran off with Gloria?"

"I have no clue at this point. You should read it though. There is a lot of background information." She set the diary down on the bed next to Claire. "I'm going to go check on the kids."

"Okay. Will do. Thanks for telling me, Emma."

≈

When she woke up again two hours later, Claire felt violently sick. She set the book to the side, she had fallen asleep reading it, and ran down the hall towards the bathroom where she vomited for several minutes. By the time she was finished, she felt extremely weak and shaky. She crumpled on the floor and nearly fell asleep. Just as she was about to doze off she was interrupted by the sounds of giggling.

*"Great,"* she thought to herself. *"Now, I have to go downstairs and usher them out back. I don't have the energy for this."*

She slowly made her way towards the stairs as she pushed her sweaty hair out of her eyes. "Richie! Callie! I'm glad you guys are feeling better but you know you aren't supposed to be in here."

She came to the foot of the stairs and turned towards the parlor, where the giggles were coming from, and stopped dead in her tracks.

There was a tent made up of bed sheets set up in the middle of the floor. She slowly approached it and sank to her knees to pull open the front. Inside were two little girls, both of whom smiled at her.

One of them was the little girl she had seen on the stairs, Gloria. The other one had to be Lucy. The girls looked very much alike except Lucy wasn't quite as skinny and malnourished looking.

Gloria's blonde hair was stringy and matted at the back with blood and brain matter. Lucy's hair was slightly shorter and clean. The front and back of the white nightgown she wore was stained with blood.

"Gloria? Lucy?" Claire asked, looking from one to the other.

They nodded, still smiling.

"What are you doing here?" she asked gently.

"Scared of the dark," Gloria said. "It's cold and dark."

"I want to play," Lucy said, shrugging her small shoulders.

Both girls looked at something over Claire's shoulder and began to scream. They tore through the back of the tent at a run, tearing it down as if they were perfectly solid.

Claire snapped around to see what had frightened the girls. Hanging from the rafters on the stairs, staring directly at them was a Union soldier. He had a twisted grin on his face and small nubs on his head where horns were starting to come in.

"Claire!" said an insistent voice in her ear. Claire was rooted to the spot. She couldn't turn her head. She'd know the owner of that voice anywhere though. It was Josie. "Wake up!"

Claire closed her eyes. When she opened them back up she was back in her bed with the covers pulled up to her chin, the diary laying across her chest.

≈

When Bailey woke up she felt a gripping pain deep, deep in the pit of her stomach. Callie was laid across from her, finally sleeping. She got to her feet and began the short walk to the bathroom. At least this time she wouldn't be puking her guts up.

She groaned as she saw that the bathroom door was closed and she could hear her brother vomiting. "Hey, Dweeb," she called through the door. "Are you going to be in there a while?"

"Yeah. It's bad."

Bailey groaned and her stomach clenched again, as if in retaliation. She couldn't hold it. There was no way around it. She would have to go up to the main house.

She walked out the door and started walking to the manor house as fast as her weak legs would allow her. She pulled the sliding glass door and was relieved when it slid open. She wouldn't have to waste precious time walking around to the front of the house. She knew from hearing her parents talk that the downstairs bathroom didn't currently have a toilet. She ran towards the stairs and squeezed her eyes shut when she reached the landing. She didn't want to look at the area where she'd had her last experience in the house.

She didn't open her eyes again until she was a foot from the bathroom door. She ran inside, slammed the door, and barely squatted over the toilet in time. She could feel her stomach muscles slowly relaxing and she let out a long sigh of relief.

When she was done she flushed the toilet and walked over to the porcelain sink to wash her hands. She looked up into the mirror and groaned at the sight of herself.

She had dark circles under her eyes and her skin was pale and clammy. She leaned down to splash water into her face. When she stood back up and looked into the mirror again she froze. There was a woman standing behind her along the wall. She was wearing what looked like a flapper dress from the 1920s and was covered from head to toe in mud. She had curly black hair that hung just below her shoulders in a tangled mass. Her skin was so white that Bailey was sure she could see the bone underneath. The woman was shaking.

Bailey heard what seemed to be running water and looked over at the bathtub. There was blood shooting out of the shower head and quickly filling the tub. She felt her heart beating as the air in the room became heavier and a sour smell filled her nostrils. She turned back towards the mirror and gasped. The woman was now directly behind her. Bailey could now see that her eyes were black.

The woman grabbed Bailey's head and shoved it into the mirror.

Bailey's screams shattered the silence of the house.

## CHAPTER FOURTEEN

When Claire headed off for New York she asked Brad, Donovan, and Michael, who was feeling much better, to clear the rest of the land. There was about twenty-five percent of the property still under weeds and tall grass.

Emma decided to go with Claire. Neither of them liked the idea of her being so close to Brock without a referee. The divorce had been brutal, and while Emma had not known Brock well enough to have a problem with him, she did expect there to be harsh feelings. She would need someone to run interference. They both knew that there was no way Claire would only see Brock at the cemetery. He would see to that.

Bailey had stayed in her room since her experience in the bathroom. She refused to even eat at first but finally relented when she saw how much she was worrying her parents. Donovan had found her when he heard her screams. She'd been on the floor with her knees to her chest, her head buried in her knees, a huge cut on her forehead from the mirror bleeding profusely over her arms and the legs of the pajamas she had been wearing.

Claire had taken Bailey to the emergency room to have her cut stitched up since Emma was having a violent vomiting attack and Michael had been working despite his own illness. The cut took twenty stitches to close and there would be a pretty prominent scar. Bailey was extremely distraught over this. She went to a school where everyone was criticized if so much as a freckle was shown in a person's appearance and she was still at an age where she very much cared what other people thought of her.

Emma had told her that she could have the rest of the week off school since she was sick anyway, but that she would have to go back first thing on Monday. Emma and Claire's offer to help her find a hairstyle that covered the scar was not acknowledged, and she had been pouting in her room ever since.

Claire had been questioned by the doctors about Bailey's state of mind and repeatedly asked if there had been any changes in her behavior and if she had been depressed at all. She hadn't given Bailey this piece of information, but she told Emma immediately that they might have a problem. Bailey had told the doctor that she had slipped getting out of the shower and her face hit the mirror. Claire had thought it was a reasonable excuse at the time, but she could tell from the doctor's line of questioning that they thought she did it to herself.

After seeing Claire and Emma off as they left for the airport, Donovan was now getting a riding lawn mower ready to go and he flashed a thumbs-up sign to Michael and Brad who were working several feet away with weed whackers. They were a long way back from the house, almost clean back to the woods, but Claire owned all this land too.

He stuck earbuds into his ears and got a playlist of '80s rock going on the iPod he borrowed from Claire before hopping on the mower and getting started. He wasn't sure how long he worked but he had to stop suddenly when he saw Michael running at him, waving his arms. His mouth was moving but Donovan couldn't hear him over the music. Brad was running from the opposite direction.

He stopped the mower and paused the song he had been listening to. "What's up, man?" he asked Michael.

"Sorry, I had to stop you. You would have run right into them."

"Into what?"

"Headstones."

"What?"

"There's a fucking cemetery out here, man."

Donovan hopped off the mower and followed Michael and Brad a few feet to see that there was indeed a small cemetery out there. There were several old, worn, and chipped headstones that were completely hidden beneath the weeds and tall grass.

"Do you think Claire knows about this?" Michael asked.

"I don't think so," Donovan bent over a headstone at random and brushed the weeds back. It was so old that it was extremely hard to read. *Elizabeth Blackwood— February 22, 1786- June 19, 1821.* "She would have said something. I do think we should do everything we can to get this cleared before they get back. Maybe we can get some questions answered when we find Gloria's grave."

"Do you think we should bring the other men down to work on it?"

"No," Brad said instantly. "No one else. The men may be inebriated enough to work here, but even they would scatter like rats if they found out there's a cemetery on the property. People around these parts are too scared."

"Okay, let's do it."

≈

Claire took slow, precise breaths, trying to get her anxiety under control. A few moments ago, the pilot had announced that they would be landing soon. As they had gotten closer, nerves that she hadn't even realized she had come to the surface. She was not looking forward to seeing Brock again. She thought that door was closed. Although what she was doing was necessary, and she knew it, she couldn't shake the feeling that she was walking right into a trap.

Brock was smart. He found unique ways of getting whatever he wanted at any given time. He was good at making himself look like a victim. She had annihilated him in court. The baby had been the last straw for her. She'd painstakingly taken the beatings, and stolen money in small increments from grocery money for months. The night he cut her; she'd known she was making the right choice. She'd taken photographs of her injuries when he wasn't home and squirreled them away in her tampon boxes where she knew he would never look.

There had been months of planning and when she finally saw her opportunity she jumped on it. She hadn't told him she was leaving. She had simply gone to a police station with her photographs when she was supposed to be grocery shopping. They'd gone out to arrest him and she immediately called Jennifer asking her to rent a hotel room for her, only saying she'd left Brock, not giving her any details. The photographs, her medical records, and the unexpected testimony from one of Brock's best friends stating he had seen him hit her at a Christmas party had led to her getting sizable alimony, plus she had been able to successfully sue him for damages. He had to serve a small sentence and she had immediately gotten on a plane and flown out to be near Emma.

She heard several months later from mutual friends that Nick, the friend who had testified on her behalf had been found dead in a ditch with his neck snapped. She also heard that Brock lost his job and was unable to find anything near as prestigious with the lawsuit looming over his head.

She knew he must want revenge. Jennifer was Claire's friend. They had worked together for a short time, but Brock had just enough connections to her that Claire felt he would definitely be at the funeral.

Emma reached over and squeezed her hand. Claire gave her an appreciative smile. Her friend didn't know the specifics of what happened but she knew it had been bad. That was on Claire. She never talked about it.

"You okay?" Emma asked.

"I will be." Claire let out a long breath. "I just hope he isn't there. I thought I was done with him."

"Well, I'm here for you. It'll be okay."

Claire gave a half smile. "I hope you're ready for what we're in for."

On that note, the plane began its descent.

≈

Donovan, Michael, and Brad stared in wonderment at the sight before them. Several hours passed and they finally cleared the land around the headstones. They weren't prepared for the mass site that they uncovered. There were more than one hundred graves in total. Some were still in decent condition but most had crumbling stones and faded inscriptions.

There were two areas of stones; one that appeared to have members of the Blackwood family and another that seemed to be servants. The area wasn't as large, the stones were not as expensive and high quality and most of the markers only had first names.

"This is going to be a real pain in the ass," Michael said, shaking his head. "Let's survey it and see if any familiar names pop up."

Michael started at one end of the family graveyard, Donovan began at the other, and Brad started with the small slave plots. They moved inwards to meet each other in the middle, scanning names and looking for signs of anything unusual.

They found the very old headstones of Gerald Blackwood and Elizabeth Blackwood. They found markers of Blackwoods in the early to mid-1800s whose names they didn't recognize. They found Lucy Blackwood, whose headstone was a marble that must have been difficult to come by during the Civil War. *Lucy Blackwood, August 24,1857-January 8, 1865.* "There's something familiar about that," Donovan stated out loud and jotted the date down before continuing the search.

They worked their way through the rest of the Blackwoods, some names they recognized and some they didn't. They found John, Margaret, Percy, and Robert. The only slave's name they recognized was Josie.

"That's it!" Donovan exclaimed.

"What?" Michael asked.

"Remember that ledger I found in the cellar? The one recording servant's deaths?"

"Yeah."

"Well, it had Josie's date of death listed as January 8, 1865. Her headstone here says the same thing."

"So?" Michael was confused.

"When I found Lucy's headstone, her date of death was marked as January 8, 1865. They died the same day."

Brad's eyes went wide. "Holy shit. What do you suppose that means?"

"Who knows?" Donovan wiped the sweat from his brow. "There's an even bigger question here. All these graves and no Gloria. Not even any unmarked that could potentially be her."

"But she died in the house when she was three years old," Michael nodded, sharing Donovan's frustration.

"So where the hell is she?"

≈

Claire paced the floor of their hotel room. She replayed the events of the day in her head and became more and more convinced she walked into a trap. Emma had been staring at her, bewildered, and telling her to calm down. She didn't get it. Claire couldn't calm down.

When their plane had touched down, she had been shocked by Brock's repulsive voice behind her at baggage claim. "Hello Claire," he had said with his lips twisted up into that grin, the one that made her skin crawl, the one that didn't quite reach his eyes.

Emma had brushed it off in the taxi on the way to the hotel as a coincidence. "You said he was friends with her too," she had said.

"He lives here, Emma," Claire had snapped. "He doesn't need to fly in."

Now, Emma was once again trying to calm her down. "Maybe he was picking someone else up. We're flying home in the morning. You're done with Brock. Sit down and relax. Watch some TV."

"No. He didn't give a shit if anyone needed a ride. He wanted to see the look on my face." Claire said as she walked over to the window to peek out through the blinds. "I'm hardly done with him."

"Well, then what is it about?" Emma asked. "Claire, you've been a mess ever since we were about an hour out on the plane."

"It was about finding me. Don't you see? He knew I'd come back for Jennifer. If he could get me here he could track me home."

"What are you saying?" Emma asked, confused. "That he killed Jennifer just so he could find out where you are? Do you realize how insane that sounds? Brock isn't *that* bad. He's a little cocky, I'll admit that."

"Oh, Em," Claire sighed and turned back to the window, resting her head against the glass.

She just didn't believe that she could tell Emma everything. Emma was a very bubbly, trusting person. She had innocence just radiating out of her like heat, and it was that innocence that made her so wonderful. It made Claire love her so much.

Emma had always gotten along with Brock the few times that she had met him. Emma got along with everybody. Even today when Brock had snuck up on them at baggage claim. Emma had exchanged pleasantries with him while Claire stayed stonily silent, looking for her bag, which is why she could never tell her.

She could never tell her that the beatings had started on their honeymoon and could come for the simplest reasons. For not satisfying him in bed, for not making the exact dinner he wanted, even if he never mentioned what he wanted, and for starting a photography business instead of staying home and having a lot of babies. She could never tell Emma about the time he had held a knife to her throat because a male client had called her about his pictures after hours. She couldn't tell her that she hadn't lost her baby in a car accident like she'd said. She lost the baby when he'd kicked her in the stomach repeatedly until she'd started to bleed. She couldn't even remember why. Worst of all, she couldn't tell her best friend that as a result of that encounter she could *never* have children.

To tell her would be to drain Emma of her light. A light that existed in so few people nowadays and, selfishly, Claire needed her light to counteract her own weary experience and irritation with the human race. She needed the balance. She wasn't the same person that she was before Brock anymore, and she was well aware of the fact. She didn't want Emma to realize it too because she didn't want to lose her.

"Why don't you call Donovan and see how far they got with your list?" Emma suggested.

Claire nodded her head and stepped over to a small table where her cell phone was plugged into her charger. She dialed the landline and it rang five times before Donovan answered.

"Hi, Donovan. It's Claire. How did you guys do today?"

She listened as he told her that part of the land still needed to be cleared and that he, Michael, and Brad uncovered a sizable graveyard, just the three of them with hand tools.

"We didn't think it would be a good idea to get the crew involved," he said.

"I agree. Everyone is scared enough as it is," she replied.

Emma gave her an inquisitive look and Claire held up a finger in a gesture that said to wait just a minute.

"You want to know something weird?" Donovan asked. "We found Lucy and Josie. Claire, they died the same day."

"What?"

"That's what we said. Even weirder? There were absolutely no graves for Gloria. We went through them all twice."

"Maybe she's in an unmarked grave."

"There aren't any unmarked graves."

Claire's mouth went dry, and she clutched the phone a little tighter. "Then where the hell is she?"

≈

There was a nagging tug in the back of Michael's brain preventing him from sleeping. Every time he closed his eyes he saw that damned graveyard. When his eyes were open his entire life flashed before him like a flickering reel from a film projector. His stomach was clenched, but not with the flu that had plagued the property. It was with the fear and worry that had nagged at him for months, years, really.

He loved Emma, and he didn't regret a single day that they had been together. Their relationship hadn't come without its share of consequences and hardships. He'd been raised staunchly Catholic with a God-fearing mother and a father who valued image above all else. So, he'd been expecting the fight the first time he'd brought Emma home. He'd waited until he was sure he was serious about her, which hadn't taken long.

From the moment he had set eyes on her at the freshmen college party, he had been crazy about her. He'd been discussing football with his buddy, Josh, and looked up to see her standing across the room talking to a friend. She threw her head back and he heard that bubbly laugh, and it took his breath away. Her caramel skin seemed to glow under the lights of the kitchen and was so clear she looked like a goddess.

Josh caught him looking and chuckled, making a joke about sweet chocolate. Michael had glared at him and thought briefly about punching him even though he hadn't even met her. Josh just clapped him on the shoulder and said, "Hey, man. I don't really care. She's gorgeous. But your mom will have your ass."

He'd been right and Michael had known it but he hadn't cared. He was hooked. They'd dated for three months and he'd taken her to bed only once before he took her home to his family. They were excited. How long had his mother expressed the wish that he meet a nice girl? He'd talked about her for months. How beautiful, amazing, and smart she was. He still didn't warn them. Maybe he should have. Maybe it would have just started the fights sooner, but he would never forget the look on his mother's face when she swung open the front door. The smile melted away from her face when she saw his arm around Emma.

She'd been polite enough during dinner, though not overly friendly. His father hadn't bothered to stay, just stormed out of the house without a word. When Emma had offered to help clear the table, his mother thanked her and smiled a smile he knew well. It was her fake, reserved-for-image smile, and she'd taken the opportunity to drag him out on the front porch and lay into him.

"Michael, what do you think you're doing bringing that girl here?" she had said.

"That girl's name is Emma."

"Fine," she held up a hand as if she were trying to prevent herself from yelling. "You've been talking about Emma as though you're in love with her."

"I am, Mother."

"No, you're not!" She raised her voice and glanced back towards the house and back to him. "You can't be. It's bad enough you'd mess around with a girl like this. But to bring her home–"

"A girl like what?" His voice was icy.

"A colored girl! This is unacceptable, Michael."

His face had flushed with anger, and he remembered the way his heart had started racing. Somehow his mother's use of the word "colored" chilled him more than Josh's joke about sweet chocolate. At least that had been in good humor. There was nothing light-hearted about his mother's words or her tone. "I don't see what the color of her skin matters. She's an amazing person and I really thought you'd like her when you met her, Mama."

"She's a perfectly nice girl. I wouldn't mind talking to her at the supermarket or the library or hiring her as a nanny," she stepped closer, put her lips a mere three inches away from his ear, and spoke in barely a whisper. "The races aren't meant to mix. You're going to end this tonight."

"No, Mama," he'd said gently but firmly. "I'm not. I've never felt this way before."

"You're lustful, and you're going through a phase. I understand that, though I can never understand why. There will be other girls."

"Not for me."

"Michael, this is non-negotiable! How will we ever explain this?"

"You know what, Mama? I don't really care how you explain it," he had said firmly and walked back into the house to see if Emma was ready to go. He hadn't known until later that she heard everything through the open kitchen window.

Things had only gotten worse as their relationship progressed and his mother no longer bothered to feign politeness with Emma. His father would conveniently never be around at get-togethers and even his brothers had gotten their shots in. Charlie even grabbed her breast saying he might as well have a piece of jungle pie as well, since that was the only way Michael could ever be interested in something like her. *Something.*

When they'd gotten pregnant with Bailey, his mother had literally shot up and started screaming about the demon child they created with their evil. A couple of weeks later, he was called over and told if he divorced Emma now and took his place where he belonged in the family, they would provide savings for the child and no one would ever have to know. As if it were that simple. When he refused, he was promptly cut from the will.

In such an environment the evil he had experienced had been in the hearts and minds of the people around him, in their self-righteousness and their prejudice. He didn't believe in the supernatural or the paranormal, only in the dark souls of close-minded people. But Emma believed, and that had always scared the shit out of him.

She had told him very early on what had happened to her and Claire as children and the story was so outlandish, he found it hard to believe. Emma wasn't a liar. He was certain that she believed it. Claire didn't back the story up, so he just always assumed whatever had happened, her brain concocted the supernatural story as a coping mechanism and he hated what it did to her. He didn't want her around it.

Now, there was the damn graveyard and God knew what that was going to do when she got home. The nagging feeling just wouldn't let up. He knew there was a deeper meaning than centuries-old skeletons buried in the dirt, some greater significance. He didn't know what it was, and he didn't know if Emma would be able to take it.

## CHAPTER FIFTEEN

*Claire couldn't breathe as the thing approached her. It was about nine feet tall, with blueish-green scaly skin and black eyes that seemed to glow red around the edges. It had hooves for feet and long claws that were dragging along the wall, peeling the paint down to the drywall. It made a low, guttural sound.*

*She stood rooted to the spot as it towered over her and lifted its claws up to swipe out at her. Her face began to violently burn and swell as her eyes watered. In the next moment, she realized she was on the floor; the thing had knocked her off her feet.*

*The door burst open, and she heard Emma scream but she could barely see anything. Her eyes were tearing badly and her left eye was almost completely swollen shut now. She was seeing everything in a cacophony of shapes and colors. The blur that was Emma charged at the monster and jumped on its back. It began to roar; a deafening sound that shook the walls and drops of red began to pool on the floor, splashing on Claire's hand. The awful smell of blood filled the room and Claire began to panic as the initial shock started to wear off.*

*"Emma! Emma!" Claire screamed, scrambling to her feet. Damn it! She needed to see now more than ever.*

*She heard a choking sound, and she could make out just enough to put together what was happening. The monster had Emma pinned to the floor with its claw hands wrapped around her throat. She kicked her legs and desperately clawed at the monster's hands, trying to peel them off her.*

*Claire didn't know what to do. She looked around the room desperately. She greedily grabbed the silver cross that was hanging above her parents' bed and rushed forward, pressing the cross into the monster's back. It began to howl and thrash, loosening its grip on Emma.*

*It began to disappear, to disintegrate somehow, flickering in and out of focus. It rushed towards Claire with its claws outstretched before disappearing a mere inch from her face.*

*The air felt lighter and she could breathe again. Emma was coughing hard but she got to her feet and threw her arms around Claire. Claire didn't hug her back.*

*"Claire? It's okay. It's over," Emma squeaked out as she pulled back. She gasped when she looked into her friend's face. Her eyes were black.*

*Neither of them noticed that they hadn't closed the session on the Ouija board.*

Claire shot straight up in bed gasping for breath. She was covered in sweat. The dream had been so intense, it felt real. She glanced over and saw that Emma was still sleeping soundly in the other bed. She looked at the small clock on the bedside table and saw that it was just after three in the morning.

She got to her feet and went to the bathroom to grab a paper cup from the counter and fill it from the tap. She needed water.

She had been having the dream for months. At least, she'd been dreaming the beginning for months. It was a memory that kept playing on repeat like an annoying song you can't help but listen to. She remembered them playing with the Ouija board. The memory had changed though. She didn't know why the dream would project the monster in the bedroom. That hadn't happened. All that happened that day was there were a few knocks that turned out to be the girls from upstairs. They had been on the fire escape smoking cigarettes, heard what Claire and Emma were doing through the window, and decided to screw with them. In fact, it wasn't long after that when she stopped believing in ghosts and lost interest in the paranormal.

*"You're sleep-deprived, Claire,"* she told herself. She leaned forward and brushed her hair out of her face to examine the ever-darkening circles. *"Get your ass to the doctor and get that Ambien adjusted."*

"Great," she said out loud. "Talking to yourself. The first sign of insanity."

She walked back out to the room. She thought she would try to get a few more Zs. She was stopped though, frozen by a sinking feeling, a sickening cramp in her gut. The hair on the back of her neck rose and instinct told her she was being watched.

She crept over to the window and peeked through the blinds. Down on the street, leaning against his car and looking straight at her was Brock, a cigarette glowing menacingly at his lips.

≈

When Claire and Emma pulled up the long drive towards Blackwood Manor several hours later, Claire felt relief swarm through her body. She had been plagued with wariness since she had seen Brock looking up at her that morning. She had felt as though she were being watched when they had gone for breakfast, and again at the airport.

On the flight, she had worried, and let her mind wander to all kinds of scary places. She imagined him somehow finding out where she lived, breaking into the manor house, and giving her an ultimatum; either take him back or accept him slitting her throat with his pocketknife.

That was a tactic he used many times in the past. She would be ashamed to admit out loud that she had always relented.

Now, watching the house loom closer and closer as they pulled up, she smiled with the relief and instant warmth that she felt. Logically, she knew it didn't make any sense. If he had found out where she was, if he somehow followed them, nothing would stop him from breaking in and doing just what her thoughts had dictated. Still, she felt safe.

They walked around back, following the sounds of equipment clearing the land.

*"God, it looks so much better,"* Claire thought to herself. She made a mental note to come out with her camera once there was no machinery in the way. The land was stunning. Simply beautiful, it was turning into the type of landscape that she had only seen in old movies.

She began to scan the land nearest the woods and saw the headstones Donovan had told her about on the phone and began to walk towards them, Emma on her heels.

"Welcome back," Donovan said, meeting them at the front of the graveyard. Most of the stones were crumbling, yet they all remained majestic and had a stunning, magnetic presence.

"Where is everyone?" Claire asked, noting the lack of crew around the house.

"Brad had a family emergency, Michael is working, and several of the men are still sick," Donovan answered. "I have five men here today. Two up on the roof, one insulating the attic, and one finishing up the plumbing in the downstairs bathroom. Pete is repairing the rotten steps in the servant's stairwell. We do have an issue I need to discuss with you in a moment."

"Okay, I want to know more about this first though," she gestured toward the graveyard. "It's tucked back here pretty far. Even uncovered, it was very difficult to see from the house. If I hadn't known it was here–"

"I can't believe the Realtor didn't say anything about it." Emma shuddered and crossed her arms in front of her, trying to rub away the goose bumps that suddenly sprouted up over her skin.

"They may not have known about it," Donovan replied. "It's tucked back here far, and it was completely covered. The last stone is from 1902."

"How many are there?" Claire asked, her eyes still wide in disbelief. "You said on the phone it was small."

"It appeared to be when we first found it," Donovan said. "But the more we cleared, the more we found. There are forty-two here. These are the family plots and about twenty yards that way, hidden beneath the shade from the trees in the woods are seventy-four more. We're assuming they are servants.

"The stones aren't nearly as nice and only first names are listed. Josie is back there but her stone was given a lot more care like she really mattered to someone."

"Well, according to Josie's diary, she and Margaret were best friends despite the time, so that's not too surprising." Emma shook her head.

"One hundred and sixteen graves," Claire pondered aloud. "You're sure Gloria isn't in there? Not even in the servant's plots? Since Margaret didn't want to claim her as her child, it wouldn't surprise me if she wouldn't want to bury her with the family. Maybe you just overlooked it."

"No," Donovan shook his head. "Michael and I both went through all the graves twice and neither of us found her."

"Maybe there are a lot of unmarked graves in the woods," Emma offered. "Bailey told me that when she and her friends did their seance with the Ouija board that it said there were three hundred and forty-seven spirits here. That's more than double what's here."

"But remember what Nadine said," Claire looked at her intently, "they don't have to necessarily die somewhere to get stuck there in death. If they do something horrible enough, they will have to return to that spot. A lot of people worked here once upon a time. Plus, those troops made life a living hell for Margaret and Josie. I'm sure they're here even though we've only seen one man. People died here as well after the property left the Blackwood family. Those people will be buried in a proper cemetery. but that doesn't mean they aren't here."

"Nadine?" Donovan asked, surprised. "The medium you had come out was Nadine Lewis? Jesus, Claire. She's so commercialized. Do you remember the psychic hot-line from the '80s? She was cheesy even then."

"How do *you* know about the hotline? Does it still exist?" Emma cut in.

"I believe her," Claire said simply, ignoring her friend. "Her show hasn't aired since the '90s and the hot-line isn't a thing anymore. Plus she knew things she couldn't possibly have known. I didn't tell her anything other than the property is haunted and anyone in the state will know that. She mentioned names and everything."

"I'm not saying she's a fake," Donovan said gently. "It's just that you know she has to pour on the glamor in the hopes of doing a televised investigation. It's business to her. You might get something a lot more straight forward if you talk to Brad's grandmother. She's a seer."

"I thought she was dead."

Donovan shook his head. "She's very old and is in a nursing home in Macon. From listening to Brad talk, she's still sharp as a tack. She used to work as a maid for one of the owners many many moons ago. She had some stories."

"Brad never mentioned it."

"He knew you didn't believe. He was probably afraid of being dismissed. He needs this job."

"Okay. I'll ask him if he'll take me to see her."

An uncomfortable silence grew among the group. Emma was staring at Donovan.

"Earth to Em," Claire chuckled.

"How did you know Brad's grandmother is a seer?"

Donovan shrugged. "He told me."

"No, he didn't. He only talks about his wife and kids."

"Now that you mention it he's never mentioned it to me either," Claire said "I only knew because Kate told me. Good on you, Donovan, getting that out of him."

"Are you sure I don't know you?" Emma asked again.

Donovan didn't answer her. He only stared back with an equal measure of coolness.

Emma checked her watch. "I'm going to go and pick up the kids. I miss my babies." She gave Claire a quick hug and began a slight sprint to the drive.

"So, what's the issue you wanted to talk to me about?"

"Something Pete brought to my attention. It's concerning the fireplaces. Someone added them years after the house was built. They weren't there originally. The measurements don't add up with the size of the rooms. There's too much empty space in between."

"Yeah, he came to me with that cock and bull story too," Claire said, positioning her hands on her hips. "So someone remodeled the house and put in fireplaces. I don't see what the big deal is."

"I did the measurements myself and he's right. This was an amateur job. While it's pretty aesthetically, it really doesn't make logical sense. Since we don't know what's in that empty space, the concern is it may not be structurally sound. Plus, we don't know how old the addition is. If there aren't proper studs, the wall could potentially collapse."

"Okay, so what do we do?"

"Well, let me show you what I think we should do."

Donovan opened the door for her, and they walked silently into the parlor and right up to the fireplace. Donovan knelt to make his presentation.

"You know how you wanted to replace this crumbling brick with stone?"

She nodded her head.

"Well, some of these bricks are already loose. The positioning of the fireplace in the bathroom indicates there may be a slight pocket in the space behind it. My guess is they had to work around a support beam. Estimation from my measurements is there are about five feet of unused space back there. What I propose doing is working some of this loose brick out. Carefully, of course, and slipping inside to check what we're dealing with before we do any work on the fireplaces or the wall. There won't be much room to move around, but I should be able to fit. Once I know it's safe I'd feel a lot better about continuing renovations on this area."

"Is it even safe for you to be in there?"

"If I move slowly. I know what I'm doing. That's why I'm not opening the wall first."

"Which fireplace do you think offers the best entry point?"

"This one. I carefully examined all of them and the brick here is looser. Now, it'll take some time to strategically work it out safely. I'm not just going to yank it out. I think I can get in in about a week or two."

"Alright let's do it," Claire said. "I really didn't want to open any walls or anything but I don't want half my house caving in. Better safe than sorry. Any chance it's a secret room? I know a lot of old houses have them."

"That was my initial thought, but I checked everywhere in the vicinity of each fireplace and could find no trigger to open an entrance. Plus it doesn't fit the profile.

Normally, secret rooms happen with the original structure and get closed off for whatever reason. The structure here was changed with the way this is designed."

"Okay," Claire brushed her hair out of her face. "I guess we should get started."

## CHAPTER SIXTEEN

"Come on, Bailey. We have to talk about this." Emma was sitting next to Bailey on the couch and holding her report card. Her grades had dropped dramatically. She had F's in every subject except English where she had managed to scrape up a D. Bailey had always been a straight-A student. The grades on her last report card had dropped too but hadn't been nearly this bad. She had been through a lot and they all knew it. Emma had chosen to give her a break that time because she was still passing, and it wasn't a habit. She couldn't let it go this time, though.

Bailey just stared straight ahead, her arms crossed in front of her, her lips set in a tight line. Her hair hung string like in her face. She had abandoned the hairstyle that hid her scar when she had been so worried about it not too long ago. She wasn't the same kid anymore.

She was dressing all in black, her clothes sloppy, and she would hardly ever come out of her room. She barely ate and if she spoke, it was usually to say something snarky.

"I promise I won't be mad, sweetheart," Emma's tone was pleading. "But you have to tell me what's going on so I can help you."

Bailey didn't answer. She just stared straight ahead as if she hadn't even heard her mother.

"Are you on drugs?" Emma asked tentatively.

"Mom!" Bailey finally yelled, looking at Emma with livid eyes, disbelief all over her face. "Are you fucking kidding me?"

"Language, young lady," Emma said sharply.

"Well, come on. You really think I would touch that stuff?"

"No, I wouldn't believe it. But something is clearly going on."

"You know what's going on," Bailey snapped, her voice low and shaking. "I was attacked twice. I'm disfigured. And no one has done a goddamn thing about it."

"Language!" Emma warned again, her voice rising.

"Well, Jesus! Richie was hurt too, and you guys just sit around examining the house's history instead of worrying about our fucking safety! Something is after me, Mom. You and Aunt Claire have your noses so far up the ass of these demons to see the real issue!"

"We're trying to get to the bottom of what's been going on. We aren't ignoring anything. And I'm not going to tell you again to watch your fucking language!"

Bailey shot to her feet and began waving her arms as she yelled, "It doesn't matter if you figure out what happened over a hundred fucking years ago! It's not like you can get rid of them! We need to get the hell out of here before someone is hurt worse."

"That's it. You're grounded. Go to your room. Your father will deal with you when he gets home."

"Whatever. You don't give a damn about me. Fucking bitch."

Emma swung out and hit Bailey so hard across the face that her head snapped back, and her own hand began to sting. She hadn't thought about doing it. It just happened. Like a reflex.

Bailey raised her hand to her cheek, where Emma's handprint stood out violently. She had a cold hatred in her blue eyes, making them look almost black. Emma looked back into her eyes unable to hide the surprise of what she had done from her face. "Get to your room," she said quietly.

Bailey shot her one last loathing look then turned sharply around and stomped off to her bedroom without uttering another word.

Emma sat rooted to the spot for several minutes. She shouldn't have hit her. She hadn't meant to hit her. But still, Bailey was out of control. Emma's lips trembled as she saw the look on her daughter's face, and in her eyes. She had seen that look before but not on Bailey.

The last time she had seen that look, it had started months of hell; events that still haunted her nightmares. The last time she had seen that look it had been followed by devastation and death. The last time she had seen that look it had been on Claire's face.

≈

Claire couldn't put her finger on why she was nervous when she pulled into the parking lot of Shady Oak nursing home with Brad. He had talked about his grandmother on the drive and described her as an incredibly sweet lady who was very sharp despite her ninety-two years.

If someone had told her four months ago that she would be going to visit a ninety-two-year-old seer who previously worked in her home to ask her about her experience, she would have laughed until she was hoarse.

Now nothing surprised her. So much had happened in such a short time. She couldn't deny what was happening on her property as much as she wanted to, and she had to get to the bottom of it. She had to. It was eating away at her brain every conscious moment like acid would eat away at a person's bare flesh.

"Are you sure you're ready for this?" Brad asked her when he parked his truck.

"Ready as I'm going to be," she sighed.

She followed him into the nursing home silently and waited as he checked in before leading her down a hallway toward his grandmother's room. They came to a stop outside a door that was cracked open at the sound of voices.

"Mary, you need to find a way to let your daughter know that there aren't any hard feelings." There was a pause and then, "Yes. You can. If you want to badly enough, you can."

Brad knocked softly on the door and opened it, leading Claire inside. The room was empty except for one very old woman perched on the end of her bed facing an easy chair. "Hi, Nana," Brad hugged the woman and kissed her wrinkled cheek. "Who were you talking to?"

"My friend, Mary," she sighed. "She was on horrible terms with her daughter when she passed. She regrets it deeply, and I've been trying to convince her to make amends."

Claire wrung her hands nervously. Was this lady as sharp as Brad and Donovan said she was, or was she just a senile old woman?

"Nana, this is the woman I told you about. The one who owns Blackwood Manor now. Claire Donahue."

"Hello, Claire," the woman said, grasping her hand tightly. "I'm Sadie Collins. I must tell you, dear, you have some set of balls to own and live in Blackwood Manor."

"Oh–" Claire's mouth dropped open in surprise. She had never heard someone Sadie's age speak in such a way.

Brad's chuckle lit up his eyes. He knew how open his grandmother was, and he had been waiting for Claire's reaction. He was not at all disappointed.

"Dear, just because I'm old doesn't mean I don't speak my mind." Sadie smiled warmly. "Please sit down."

Claire took a seat in the easy chair that Sadie was already facing, and Brad sat down next to his grandmother on the bed.

"Now," Sadie said, smiling again. "What can I help you with?"

"Brad said you used to work at Blackwood Manor."

"Yes. A long time ago. Must be nearing sixty years ago now."

"He also said you're a seer?"

Sadie nodded.

"So, since the average person is still so greatly affected at Blackwood Manor, I would assume it must have been amplified for you?"

"You could say that." Sadie's eyes were dancing. "That place radiated with activity. I picked up on every emotion in the book. Sorrow, anger, love, hate, greed, and, yes, evil. It was like a vortex wrapped up in pretty paper with a bow, ready to explode when opened."

Claire visibly shuddered at the description and cast her eyes down.

"Don't get me wrong, dear. I'm not insulting your property. I think it's wonderful what you're doing. A place with that much history should be a landmark. But it can't be properly appreciated unless it's understood."

"I agree," Claire nodded her head. "That's what I'm trying to do. I'll admit, I used to be a skeptic. But too much has happened for me to ignore it. People are scared. I'm trying to understand. I can't shake the feeling that the spirits, one of them at least, is trying to tell me something but can't really."

"It is possible. When I worked there, I constantly saw a woman without a face who would beg me to help someone named Gloria, but she didn't seem to be able to tell me how."

"Did you find out who Gloria was?"

"I'm assuming it was one of the little girls that I saw a lot of, but I never got any verification."

"We did. One of them was Gloria. The other was Lucy Blackwood. Gloria was Margaret Blackwood's secret third child."

"Well, that's juicy," Sadie said, her eyes glowing though there was no hesitation or surprise in her voice.

"I have a feeling that a lot of the activity is about something involving her. Not everything, of course, but a lot of it. This medium that came out told me that she was murdered. Josie, the servant girl with no face that you saw, is desperate to help her to the extent that she won't pass over herself. We found her diary where she said she was planning on running away with Gloria."

"Do you think she did?"

"No, I don't. There weren't any entries in the diary after that, but Josie is buried on the property. We found a graveyard. Gloria, however, doesn't have a grave. If she ran off with her either they would both be buried there or neither would."

"That's a fair assessment," Sadie said. She was leaning forward unconsciously, very glad to be getting juicy information.

"Nadine Lewis came out a few weeks back. She walked through the house and told me about some of the spirits she encountered. She said a bunch of stuff about people getting stuck in a place where they did something terrible or had something terrible happen to them in death, not necessarily where they died. She said that the more wrong a person does, the more it blackens their soul and makes them turn into a demon and there are people who can stop them, but they are hard to find. When she left, a lot made sense to me, but I was also really confused about other things."

Sadie was nodding. "She didn't lie, but she did withhold information. That's how those television personalities do. They dangle just enough to bait and hook you in the hopes of you allowing them to do a televised investigation on your property. Blackwood Manor is well known throughout the state. Of course, she would do that to you."

"So, how do I–"

"I don't know how it works for everyone else," Sadie interrupted calmly. "Not everyone's gift works the same. For me, when I see something I also see colors. This doesn't necessarily just happen with the dead. I see hues typically in six colors. White means a person is innocent and pure and hasn't been tarnished by anything too traumatizing. I see white on living people. It's very rare for me to see it on the dead. After all, most people stick around because they don't have a choice because of something that has happened. I'll get into that in a minute.

"Yellow means a person has gone through some things but not anything too bad. Blue indicates sadness. Something bad has happened to them that keeps them guarded. Purple indicates a person has had something so horrific happen to them that they cannot move past it. Red, now red is very complex. Red generally means someone is extremely wicked. The more bad things they have done, the darker the shade becomes. Black is pure evil."

"What's my color?" Claire asked.

"Oh, I never tell anybody what color I see on them. People tend to obsess over that and stop being who they truly are. That is never a good thing."

"Okay." Claire sat up a little straighter, disappointed, but she didn't want Sadie to stop talking.

"Anyway, what my experience has shown me is that people with a white hue pass on almost instantly unless they choose not to. People with a blue hue have the option to pass on but they tend to get confused and miss their window of opportunity. I'm not really sure why. It may have something to do with reliving their past tragedies at the moment of death.

"Purple hues are interesting to me. These people haven't done anything bad, bad has been done to them, but still, they cannot move on. It seems they either don't know they're dead or that something so terrible happened that they are scared of doing anything, even passing on and they become stuck. However, if they're able to move past what happened to them, they can pass on. These people also have the rare ability to evolve almost as if they are living. They can move about more freely and even age slightly, further causing confusion. This is where living intervention typically comes into play. Say a murder victim is stuck and someone living uncovers the truth and gets justice of some kind, then their soul is free, and they can move on.

"I've also seen this happen when people go missing and their bodies are not found. Once the body is recovered and properly taken care of, the spirit can move on.

"Red. When a person does something especially despicable they get a light red hue. Any shade of red means that they will not pass on. They will be stuck after death and they will be stuck in the place where the terrible act happened. I believe this is what Nadine was talking about when she brought up blackened souls.

"The purpose is to face what they have done so they can be absolved and move on. The problem is most Reds fight it. They don't want to think about what they did, or they don't believe they did anything wrong. The longer they fight it, the meaner they become towards the living and the dead and the more their hue darkens. As it darkens, they will physically begin to change. Once their hue turns black, they essentially become a hell creature. Is that making sense?"

"I think so," Claire spoke slowly. "Once it's black, they're a demon."

"Let's talk demons," Sadie said. "This is where I feel Nadine misled you. Demons are different. They already exist and they create a hell on Earth all on their own. They were never people. However, throughout the Red process, their physical appearance changes and they become *hell-*

*like* because they are essentially becoming soulless. They are not demons, though. They are bad people who won't answer for their crimes with the chance that they are given so they must answer it by eternity in hell."

"So, Margaret Blackwood, for example. People would tell me about a woman with horns, but they didn't mention anything else off. This was before I saw her myself," Claire explained. "My best friend's daughter held a seance in the house one night. She and her friends were viciously attacked. We actually managed to see what happened on videotape. Margaret attacked. She looked like a normal woman except for the horns and claws for fingernails. Their house burned down later that same night."

Sadie furrowed her eyebrows. "Margaret Blackwood was red when I worked there. At the time, she seemed cold and the other spirits did seem to fear her, but her appearance was completely normal. I never saw her physically attack anyone. I don't see the fire as a coincidence, but it wasn't Margaret. These spirits can't roam freely, except for whites who stay behind by choice or purples. Purples cause no harm. They don't form attachments. Demons form attachments. Demons follow. Demons can mimic too. They even mimic the dead occasionally. You said your friend's daughter held a seance before they were attacked. Was a Ouija board used?"

"Yes."

Sadie sighed. "Blackwood Manor doesn't only have angry and confused ghosts. It does have demons too. They were dormant while I was there, but the energy was there, and I heard through the grapevine that demonic activity had happened way back in the days the Blackwood family still owned it. Ouija boards are powerful spiritual tools that should not be used by someone who doesn't know what they are doing. I fear these girls awakened the dormant demons and the girl got an attachment. That is what caused the fire. What I'm confused about is the attack itself. They shouldn't be strong enough to attack that fast. The attack may have been Margaret, and a demon attached itself to the girl. If that's the case, things are going to get way worse than they ever were with the spirits alone. Be on the lookout for personality changes and withdrawal."

"That's already happened. She wasn't only attacked one time. She had another experience in the bathroom, but she wouldn't tell anyone what happened. All we know is there is now a broken mirror and a permanent scar on her face. Her behavior has rapidly changed since then."

"You may want to find a way to bring her to see me. I may be able to tell you more if I see her."

Claire nodded. "I saw Margaret Blackwood another time, and she looked half woman, half something else. Hooves, scaly blue skin, red eyes, and of course, the horns."

"Her transformation is nearly complete," Sadie said, surprised. "When she's no longer recognizable, all hell will break loose before she finally goes down into hell."

Claire shook her head in frustration. "I'm so confused by all this. From everything that I've found,

Margaret seemed like a nice person. She was best friends with Josie. That is especially remarkable given the time period. It simply didn't happen. She donated to charities and was a respected member of the community until her death. I did find a letter that she wrote to her husband that she apparently never gave him saying that she accidentally killed their daughter, Lucy. She stressed, though, that it was an accident, and she was full of remorse. She even considered suicide over it.

"Of course, there's the matter of Gloria being kept a secret. But even then, you can halfway understand her position. Margaret bore a child who was not her husband's at a time when that was not acceptable. Even if she was a child of rape. She probably just didn't know what to do. So, how did she get here? How did she become this thing?"

"I got the impression when I worked there that Margaret's spirit wasn't only affected by something that she had done. Something was done to her as well. I couldn't figure out what it was."

Claire exchanged a look with Brad, unsure of how to phrase the next question. He had spent enough quality time and become good enough friends with her that he felt confident he knew what to ask.

"What do you know about golden warriors, Nana?" he asked, picking up a hairbrush to run softly through his grandmother's hair.

"Golden warriors?" Sadie asked, dumbfounded. "What are you on about, boy?"

Brad couldn't help but chuckle. Here he was in his forties and she still called him "boy" if she thought he was being stupid or reckless.

"It's something else that Nadine Lewis brought up," Claire mentioned. She launched into the story that Nadine had given her. The story of golden warriors; the rare gifted people who could stop a particularly bad haunting, especially if it's violent. Sadie did not interrupt her.

"She said that these people don't usually know they even have this gift until something major happens and that they don't have full control of the power."

Sadie nodded. "It's an extreme rarity. Many seers, mediums, what have you—, they can see things and know things but they can't stop something truly wicked. There are people in the world–, a very small handful–, who can stop a bad attack. The power normally comes through in a moment of extreme desperation and is not fully controlled. Many only have to use the power once. Others will help people with extremely affected properties who are in extreme danger. These people tend to have better control because they do it more often and learn the process."

"But because they're so rare there's nothing we can do to find one? People are getting hurt. We have a cemetery on the property with more than one hundred graves. The seance indicated there were over three hundred spirits and you've admitted that there are demons as well. I want people to be safe on my land."

"There is no official name for this talent. However, there are telltale signs you can look for. If a person has been nearly killed by a spirit in the past they are more likely to have the power. If someone tends to have frequent encounters with spirits, if a person can stop a demon with little to no effort. You may be able to find someone to help with enough research, but it could take years to find someone who legitimately has the power."

Claire sighed and went to stand up. She extended her hand. "Thank you so much for your help, Sadie. I understand things more. I just have no clue what to do about the activity. The more time that passes, the more seems to happen. The place is radiating energy now."

Sadie took her hand and squeezed it. "You needn't worry, dear. I feel you may have someone with the gift on the property already."

Claire's eyes widened in surprise. "What makes you say that?"

Sadie smiled. "The activity is escalating for a reason. You said it yourself. Some spirits seem to be reaching out for help. There may be bad activity and demons at Blackwood Manor, but there are also people that are just plain stuck and need release. I believe they know help is near."

In the hallway, listening from the door, a man pulled out his cell phone and walked away. "Yeah, it's me," he said when the line was picked up. "It's definitely her. Not sure why you're even bothering, though. She's a nutter. Believes her property is swarming with ghosts and demons."

"Never mind that," Brock said coldly. "Where is she?"

<u>PART TWO</u>

## CHAPTER SEVENTEEN

"Are you sure the old lady isn't just nuts?" Emma asked Claire as they beat the dirt out of carpets on a line in the back of the manor house. They were trying to see what could be salvaged. Claire was determined to keep the decor as authentic as possible.

"She seemed extremely lucid to me," Claire answered. "She said things that matched what Nadine had said but better explained. Plus, she brought up certain points before I even had a chance to get to them."

"So you think it's true that someone here is one of the one-in-a-million amplified ghostbusters?" Emma raised an eyebrow and gave a wicked, teasing grin.

"Everything else rang true, so I do believe it's possible." Claire swept a curl out of her face and tucked it behind her ear. "Still, figuring out who it is may be a problem. Thanks to Donovan, we have a fairly large crew now, plus all of us that live on-site, and just about everybody has experienced things. I think all of us fit the criteria in some form or another. We've all seen spooky stuff, and we've all been 'targeted' in some way. None of us has come close to being killed or stopped a demon with little effort though."

Emma looked away quickly and let out a small cough before speaking again. "Well, let's try to break it down. Let's go one person at a time, starting with you.

You've had several encounters even though you were in denial for a while. I'm sure there are things you never even told me."

"Yes. There was hearing you call out to me when you weren't here, something rushing the shower curtain causing me to fall and hit my head, Josie in the attic, Gloria on the stairs, Gloria and Lucy in the tent in the parlor terrified of the soldier hanging in the stairwell, Margaret and Kate in the servant's stairwell, the oil paintings, the messages in the glass in the bedroom and on the parlor wall. I never experienced anything before moving here though, so I think it makes sense because I own the place, and I'm inside more than anyone else. I've never been targeted and I've never stopped a demon."

"What about the thing that attacked Richie on the stairs?" Emma asked. "It let him go pretty quick after you went through the other entrance."

"That wasn't a demon. It was Margaret."

"How sure of that are you? You said you didn't get a good look."

"Very. I saw a dress and horns. Very similar to Margaret in the video. What about you? You have been having encounters with spirits since we were kids, and you are the only one who had a full-blown conversation with Josie."

"Yes, but she's the only spirit I've actually seen here. I mostly just feel sick and get really bad feelings to the point where it's hard to breathe. And you had experiences when we were kids too."

"No, I didn't."

"You really don't remember anything do you?"

"Remember what?"

Emma opened her mouth to answer but stopped when she heard a squeal of joy and turned to see Callie running towards her. "This isn't the time," she said, wrapping her arms around her daughter and pulling her tight.

Claire went to interject but was cut off as Emma started walking back towards the cottage with Callie in her arms. She crossed her arms in front of her chest and let out a growl of irritation.

≈

Later that night Emma swallowed two aspirin and massaged her temples before crawling into bed with her back against the headboard and her knees drawn up to her chest. She wasn't sleeping anymore. She couldn't sleep a minute without seeing what happened when they were kids as clearly as if it had happened yesterday. She didn't know how to tell Claire that she believed she was the golden warrior. She literally fit all the criteria from their nightmare situation but she didn't seem to remember any of it.

She was struggling with trying to figure out the best way to make Claire remember. She had to remember and soon. The energy was suffocating.

≈

While Emma was trying to figure out how best to jar her best friend's memory, Claire was walking from room to room in the house, checking every nook and cranny.

Her nerves were on edge tonight, and she had no idea why. She hadn't had any paranormal experiences today, but she couldn't shake the feeling that something was very wrong. She had chills running up and down her spine, goose flesh on her arms, and the hair on the back of her neck was standing on end. She felt a heaviness in her heart, her stomach was sour, and she had *that* feeling. The feeling that she was being watched.

After circling through the kitchen for the third time and finding nothing out of the ordinary, she leaned against the counter, ran her hands nervously through her hair, and stared out the window.

*"You're cracking up, Claire. Get it together,"* she thought, giving herself a mental shake. She was about to turn away from the window when she stopped, leaning closer to the window, her nose almost close enough to touch the pane. She thought she had seen something in the distance. A shadow at the tree line, a shaking branch. She found herself desperately wanting the floodlights that she had been meaning to put up. She jerked the curtains closed sharply and backed away from the window until her back hit the island. She was shaking despite the fact that the house was warm and she found herself unable to blink as she watched the curtains, almost expecting them to move.

She slowly edged around the island and began to back away towards the door, never taking her eyes off the window. She stopped when something cold touched her leg. A painful feeling like jumping into a lake in the dead of winter shot through her body at lightning speed. She closed her eyes, pulled in several deep breaths until her lungs stopped burning, and turned around, looking down.

Gloria's hand dropped back to her side. She looked up at her and smiled, her lips blue, her eyes much too large. Claire tried to not run at the sight of the brain matter that clung to the top of her head and the blood clumping the hair together. She allowed herself to see the child and only the child.

"Claire," Gloria said, her voice small but somehow authoritative. "Don't go out there. No matter what." Her huge eyes were unblinking and serious. Her small mouth was in a tight line that Claire didn't even know was possible in a child.

"Why not?"

"The bad man. He'll hurt you."

Claire swung back around toward the window, but the curtains remained closed. No visible shadows moved on the other side. She turned back towards Gloria, but she had gone.

She walked briskly upstairs and wrapped urgently on Donovan's door.

"Claire, what's wrong?" he asked her, his eyes puffy with sleep.

"I've had a feeling for a while like I'm being watched," she walked into the room swiftly, shutting the door quietly behind her, and strode towards the window to look down. "Not the normal feeling like with the ghosts but something else. I was downstairs in the kitchen just now and I could have sworn I saw something in the woods. Gloria appeared to me and she said that 'the bad man' was out there."

"Who do you think it is? The spirit of the person that killed her?" he asked, suddenly very awake.

"No. She made it clear I'm in danger. Donovan, I should tell you that my ex-husband was an extremely abusive man. I left at great risk. When Emma and I were in New York I saw him outside our hotel window in the middle of the night. Watching."

Donovan set his mouth in a straight line, threw his shoulders back, and went to move towards the door. She ran in front of him so suddenly that he nearly lost his balance and threw her arms wide in front of the door. "You can't go out there. Not alone."

"Okay," he walked over to his bedside table and seized the landline phone they had set up when he moved in and sat on the bed as he dialed. There was a brief pause before he spoke. "Sheriff, it's Donovan at Blackwood Manor. Claire has reason to believe her ex-husband is in the woods behind the house."

Claire stood in the doorway and nervously bit her nails as she watched the expression on Donovan's face turn angrier. It sounded like the sheriff was yelling on the other end of the phone, though she could not make out what he was saying. Suddenly, there was silence and Donovan slammed the phone down.

"Are they coming?" she asked.

"No. He said he's not sending any more men out here because there's never anything of concern and they have more important things to do." He reached into his bedside table and pulled out a small handgun before heading for the door. "Go to your room and lock the door. I'll go check it out."

"No!" she screamed out suddenly and raced forward, throwing her arms around him, her fingers clutching frantically at his shoulders, her eyes wide with fear. "You can't go out there. He's crazy. You don't know what he's capable of. Please, Donovan! Please!"

"Okay," he patted her head in comfort as she sobbed against his neck. "We'll stay in here and I'll stay up and keep watch. I won't let anything happen to you. I promise."

It took several minutes for him to calm her down and lead her over to the bed where she cried herself to sleep. He sat on the edge of the bed and watched dutifully, his eyes flicking from the windows to the door, his fingers never leaving the gun.

≈

Outside, under the cover of the trees, Brock was intently watching the window, watching her in the arms of another man. The whore. He uncurled his fist and took no notice as the blood poured from his palm onto the dirt below. He slipped the wire back into his pocket. The wire he had been planning on using to strangle her when she stepped outside.

He growled under his breath in frustration. It was supposed to be easy. It should have been. She had bought this big-ass expensive place so far from anything else. With *his* money no less. Hadn't even been bothered to put up lights to see more than a foot from her door. She never had half a brain.

This was a complication he hadn't foreseen. She had grown a backbone after all. Balls. Cajónes. To dare to shack up with someone else. It would be okay though. He needed more time. Then he would take care of them both.

*"Isn't she beautiful?" John said with a voice beaming with pride.*

*Margaret looked up from the baby girl in her arms and smiled at him. Her hair may have been mussed and her face smeared with sweat but to him, she was the most beautiful woman in the world. She turned and carefully passed the baby off to Josie, who was standing dutifully beside the bed.*

*She carried the baby over to the bassinet sitting in the corner and smiled at the three-year-old little boy sitting next to it in knee shorts. He had lots of curly brown hair and pink, plump cheeks.*

"Baby!" he cried and pointed at her.

"Yes, Percy," Josie smiled. "This is your baby sister, Lucy."

"Can I hold her?"

"Not yet, sugar. She's too little." Instead, she lifted him up and leaned him down over the bassinet so he could get a better look at her.

"Pretty," he said and leaned down to touch a tiny fist.

"Yes, she's very pretty."

"John, could you take Percy out back and play with him a bit?" Margaret asked. "I need my rest."

"Of course, dear," he leaned down and kissed her on the forehead. She crossed the room and took Percy from Josie before leaving the room.

Josie made her way to Margaret's side and fluffed her pillows. "That is one perfect baby girl, Miss Margaret."

"Thank you, Josie," Margaret grabbed the girl's hand. "Thank you for your help today. You were wonderful."

Josie smiled. "Seems to me you did all the work."

"Still you've blossomed. You've come miles from the shy child who was scared of her own shadow six years ago. You're becoming a young woman and you are so good with children. It won't be long before you have your own."

"Oh, I don't think I could ever–do that," Josie said and hung her head down, embarrassed.

Margaret laughed. "You forget the pain as soon as it's over and that little bundle in your arms makes all the *pain you went through worth it. You'll make a wonderful mother someday."*

*"I really don't think so. I can't see the boys around here being good husbands."*

*"Well, who says it has to be around here?"*

*"Ma'am?"*

*"You've come a long way with your reading and writing. Your writing could still use a little work, but you read very well." Margaret paused a moment and then smiled. "Eventually, you will be free. All of you. I can feel it in my bones. When that happens, I feel confident that you will be able to do anything you set your mind to. You're already two steps ahead." She gestured towards the bureau across the room. "Look in the top drawer. There is something there for you."*

*Josie walked to the bureau behind her and pulled out an envelope on the very top.*

*"Go ahead and open it."*

*Josie slipped a hefty load of cash from the envelope and sank to the foot of the bed as her knees weakened. "Miss Margaret!" she gasped.*

*"It's your payment for everything you have done for me over the past six years."*

*"Miss Margaret, I can't...you can't. You could be jailed."*

*"Everyone deserves payment for honest work and no one works harder than you, Josie. If you prefer, we can keep it between us."*

*"But Mr. John?"*

*"John knows," Margaret said gently, smiling, "and he agrees with me. No one else needs to know."*

*Josie looked at her, speechless. She was blown away by the knowledge that someone out there cared about her so deeply.*

*"I want you to have the resources and opportunities you deserve when you are finally free. As I said, you deserve it. I told you before you're going to have every opportunity open to you."*

*"Why are you so good to me?"*

*"Because you deserve it."*

## CHAPTER EIGHTEEN

"Alright, so we're spreading out in three-man teams covering a one-hundred-foot radius each," Donovan was addressing the crew the next morning. He had already told Brad and Michael what happened the night before. and they were ready to help him execute the search. This was the deep south and no one messed with their women. No one.

"Shouldn't the police be taking care of this?" one of the men, a quiet young guy named Andrew Tate, asked from the back of the group.

"Of course, they should," Donovan said, barely able to keep the irritation out of his voice. "Unfortunately, due to the *history* of the property and previous false alarms, the sheriff won't send any men out."

"Well, how do we not know that's all it is this time? Seeing things around here isn't all that unusual. We all have," Tate said again, gesturing towards the other men who were murmuring their agreement and nodding their heads.

"Look here, boy," Brad growled out. "You're not being paid to ask questions, you hear? Now the lady said there was someone in the woods and there was."

"Twelve hours ago!" Tate was annoyed now, his nostrils flaring up and putting emphasis on his bloodshot eyes. "They won't still be there. And watch yourself calling me 'boy' when you're expecting us to take orders from this kid!"

"That isn't the point!" Michael shot out. "The point is that we need to find out how close to the house this person was or any sign of who it may have been. There is more than the matter of trespassing to deal with. Claire believes she's in danger. Now, I don't know about all of you but I have a wife and three kids to protect. Doesn't everyone here have a wife, a mother, or a daughter that they would like to see safe at all times?"

Silence fell over the group of workers, but it didn't stop Michael from speaking.

"What if this were happening to one of them? Suppose your daughter called you and told you someone was stalking her, Will?" he asked a short, balding man in the front of the group. Will's daughter had just moved out of the house the week before and he was constantly worrying aloud about her, much to the disdain of the other men. "What if she called you and told you someone was watching her? Creeping around outside her house? What would you do?"

Will mumbled something incomprehensible and stared nervously down at his shoes, which he was pattering absentmindedly in a patch of mud.

"What was that? I couldn't quite hear you."

Will looked up and unclenched his jaw before speaking. "I'd find the son of a bitch and I'd kill him."

Michael nodded in agreement and locked eyes with Donovan.

"Wait, now," a man whose name Donovan couldn't remember called out from the group. "I can't be involved in nothing like that. I'm on probation."

"No one is talking about murder," Donovan assured them. "We just need to know what we're dealing with." He walked among the men, dividing them into groups of three and handing each group a whistle that he had gone out that morning to buy. "If you find anything out of the ordinary, anything at all that doesn't belong, give three sharp blasts on this. Wait approximately two minutes and do it again until the rest of us join you."

Everyone murmured that they understood what they were supposed to do and they fanned out.

≈

Inside the cottage, Claire and Emma were seated around a small two-person table in the kitchen. Claire was holding a steaming cup of coffee between her hands and Emma was watching her warily. She didn't look good at all. Her eyes were wide and red, looking as though they were sunken in and her cheeks were hollow as though she had lost weight overnight. She wouldn't comment on it now, but she also saw a significant amount of gray in her friend's hair that hadn't been there just a few days before.

"Why didn't you ever tell me?" she gently asked.

Donovan had come down that morning and told them what had happened. She had been shocked. She knew they had a bad breakup. She knew that Claire hated him with every fiber of her being but she hadn't known about the abuse. How could she have not known?

Claire let out a long breath and let go of her coffee cup, bringing her head down to rest in her palms, her arms shaking. "There were a lot of reasons. I didn't want pity for one. For another, I was ashamed. Ashamed of what I'd become."

She looked up at Emma and there was nothing but defeat and worry on her face.

"What do you mean?" Emma reached out and grasped her hand.

"I used to be strong," Claire's voice began to crack. "I never understood those girls. Why would someone stay with someone who hurts them? How hard could it be to just walk away?" she shook her head furiously. "Then I turned around and put up with it for ten fucking years."

Emma gently squeezed her hand. "Hey. Hey, look at me." She waited until Claire met her eyes once more. "It wasn't your fault. We always tell ourselves that we would do things differently until we find ourselves going through it. The human psyche is a very complex thing. Why does anyone do the things they do?"

"It started on our honeymoon, Em," she croaked out in no more than a whisper. "Our honeymoon. I should have walked away then. But I told myself he was just drunk, and it wouldn't happen again. But it did. Over and over again. I got extremely creative with my excuses too. Forget the old

*'I ran into a doorknob'* line. For me it was *'I was at a baseball game and my face got too close'* and things of that nature."

"What finally did make you decide to leave?"

Claire leaned back and lifted her shirt clear up to her breasts. There was an angry red scar running from her breastbone clear to her pelvis. "This. He sliced open my old appendectomy scar to see what I was hiding. While I was asleep. I woke up to the knife tearing through my flesh and the blood spilling over my side and onto the bedspread."

Emma was about to open her mouth and tell her the truth. Tell her that wasn't an appendectomy scar, but she was stopped by a distant sound and Claire's sudden silence told her that she had heard it too.

The sound was coming from the girl's bedroom. A low whisper saying, "Just a little closer."

They rose to their feet in unison and slowly made their way toward the door. Just as they reached it, they heard an unmistakable cry. A child's cry. Callie's cry.

Emma slowly opened the door, and they were met with the sight of Bailey sitting on the edge of her bed with Callie perched on her lap. She had one arm firmly around her sister's waist and the other held a knife tightly to her throat. The edge was piercing her skin and blood ran down in rivulets, staining the collar of her shirt. Callie was remarkably still, though tears flowed openly from her eyes. Bailey's head was bent down, whispering something in her ear.

"Bailey!" Emma called out sharply.

Bailey raised her head and grinned. A grin that was not hers. A grin that did not touch her eyes. Those eyes were now a piercing black.

It was then that Emma began to scream.

≈

The men in the woods did not hear the screams coming from the cottage. They were too far out and too few in number.

Donovan, Brad, and Michael had purposely taken the section of woods that held the cemetery, still not wanting the other men to see it, but they were beyond that now.

"Do you think he left anything?" Michael asked.

Donovan shrugged his shoulders and continued looking in every direction for any sign. "Not if he's smart. The thing is though, men like him are never smart. They get too damn cocky and think they can do anything. Leads to mistakes. Big ones."

"Did either of you know?" Brad asked. "About her husband?"

They both shook their heads no.

"I knew it was a messy break-up and divorce despite there being no children," Michael said. "I knew something had gone down but I never imagined that."

"So, you know him?" Donovan asked.

"I never liked that little prick," Michael growled. "Too cocky for his own good. Too smooth. He made my blood boil the first time I ever met him. Something was very wrong with him. You could see it in his eyes. He didn't like me either. I think he knew that I could see right through him."

They were cut off by the sound of a whistle blowing and followed the sound until they reached a small group of crew members. Andrew Tate was standing over something, his knees bent in a squat. Between his legs, Donovan could see a puddle of blood.

"There's a boot print over here," one of the other men called out. He was standing a couple of yards away.

Donovan made his way over and bent down to examine the boot print. These weren't work boots. The prints reminded him of something you might find on some big city businessman. The sunlight gleamed on something almost completely hidden under a pile of leaves. He brushed them aside with his hand and picked up the item, a good long length of wire. A piano wire from the looks of it. He stared at it for a couple of minutes before speaking, his eyes not leaving the wire.

"Brad, did those flood lights ever come in?"

Brad was silent for a moment before answering, his voice cracking. His mouth was completely dry. "Yeah. They're in the maintenance shed."

## *CHAPTER NINETEEN*

"Bailey," Claire stepped forward cautiously with her hands raised.

The thing that was no longer Bailey growled and pushed the knife a little harder into Callie's throat. She whimpered and more blood slid down the blade and her skin.

"Claire!" Emma screamed again as she pulled desperately at her hair, tears flowing down her cheeks. "Claire, do something!"

"What?" Claire asked, feeling defeated.

"Do your thing! Make it leave her alone!"

"I can't!" Claire screamed, her own voice a panicked octave as she stared at that unnatural look on Bailey's face and those black eyes, so glossy that she could see her reflection in them. Going on instinct she reached out and grabbed the first thing she could reach. It was a picture book off the dresser and hurled it as hard as she could at Bailey.

The book hit her squarely in the forehead at the corner, busting the skin open right at the new scar from the bathroom incident. Bailey let out an other-worldly scream, her voice echoing as though she had two sets of vocal cords. The blood flowed down her face as she took Callie and threw her to the ground before rising to her feet and advancing on Claire.

"Come on!" Claire taunted, backing up towards the door. "Come and get me. You big bitch." She backed into the hallway, never taking her eyes off Bailey who was walking towards her slowly.

When they were no longer in her field of vision Emma raced forward and gathered Callie, who was crying hysterically, up into her arms. She held her tight for a moment and then pulled back to examine her neck.

She felt rooted to the spot until she heard the sound of breaking glass coming from the living room. "Okay," she said as she walked towards the window. She opened it and gently lowered Callie to the ground below.

"Mommy! No!" Callie was frantically screaming.

"Run, Baby! Run! Find Daddy!" and she slammed the window closed before running out to the living room to help her friend.

She found Claire pinned to the floor desperately trying to fight Bailey off. Bailey, whose hands were turning purple as they wrapped around Claire's neck. Bailey, who was exhibiting way too much strength.

She raced forward and grabbed her daughter's shoulders.

Bailey whipped around, growled, and shoved Emma effortlessly with one hand, sending her flying against the wall and knocking picture frames to the floor. Emma sunk to the floor. She didn't look at Claire before she passed out. If she had, she would have seen Claire locking eyes with Josie, standing just behind Bailey.

"No more," Josie said simply and grabbed Bailey by the back of the neck, flinging her away from Claire.

Bailey growled and slumped to the floor in the kitchen.

Claire struggled to pull in a breath, her vision cloudy. She slowly rolled to her side and pushed up on her shaky legs watching the figure in the next room.

Bailey let out a groan. A normal groan and began to sit up.

Claire stayed cautiously in place as the girl looked at her. Her eyes were clear.

"Aunt Claire?" she rubbed her hand against her forehead, eyes going wide at the sight of the blood. "What happened?"

Claire turned her head towards Josie, but she was no longer there and jumped as the front door crashed open.

Donovan, Michael, and Brad rushed inside and Claire could see the crew members looking nervously inside.

Donovan took in the sight of the mess. Emma was unconscious, Claire on the floor rubbing her neck that had distinct purple finger marks already popping up, all the chaos and destruction of the room. He made a move for Bailey, who now looked so small and terrified, cowering under the kitchen table.

Michael grabbed his arm. "Wait."

Claire rose to her feet. "It wasn't her. It was her but it wasn't her."

≈

Claire felt bad about leaving Emma, Michael, and the other kids alone with Bailey. She didn't know if whatever had come over Bailey would return. Donovan had insisted that she come and speak to Sadie again and tell her what had happened.

They had driven to the nursing home together, the silence palpable. He hadn't asked for details, and for that she was grateful. She wasn't ready to talk about it yet, but she couldn't stop replaying it in her head.

It had been a dangerous game to play and she knew it. Throwing that book could have ended very differently. In a way that got Callie's throat slit. She didn't know why she had done it. She didn't know why she had backed away and lured Bailey to her with no way of defending herself, and she sure as hell didn't know why it had worked.

She only knew that something deep within her had told her it would be alright. That this had happened before.

As they stepped inside, she began to make her way toward Sadie's room. She noticed that Donovan was no longer beside her and turned around to address him. "Aren't you coming?"

"I'm going to grab a cup of coffee," he said, gesturing towards the table in the lobby. "It's been a hell of a long day."

"Okay," she turned back around and continued to the room. Knocking briskly upon the door before turning the knob.

Sadie was standing at the edge of her bed facing the door. She had her hands folded patiently in front of her. "Claire," she smiled. "I sensed you were coming."

Claire went inside, shutting the door behind her. She took a seat in the same chair she had sat in during the previous visit and waited for Sadie to take a seat on the bed before launching into the story. She told her about what had happened with Bailey and about her own actions.

"I don't know what I was thinking," she said as she let out a nervous laugh.

"You were thinking of the safety of the child, of course," Sadie answered gently. "I was afraid that such a thing would happen. A demon attached itself to the girl and is tampering with possession."

"Is she okay now?" Claire asked. "Should we still worry?"

"I'm afraid so," Sadie sighed. "I've seen this happen before. The demon has shown that it's capable of entering her body but is not strong enough for full possession yet. Whether it would have stayed inside her had Josie not interfered is anyone's best guess. It will try again. I hate to say it, but you should probably keep her restrained until you find the one to help you. It's for her own safety as well as the safety of everyone around her, especially her siblings."

Claire nodded, but she felt more lost than before she had come in.

≈

Donovan sat in a chair in the lobby waiting for Claire, lost in his own thoughts.

He hadn't told her what they had found in the woods. Why the men went to the cottage in the first place. He was going to. He was convinced of that. Everything had seemed so small when they had seen Callie running towards the manor house, blood flowing down her neck, yelling, *"Bailey's cwazy!"*

He needed to tell Claire and he would. Soon. There was so much more that he needed to tell her. That he should have told her long ago.

*She won't believe you,* the annoying voice in his head told him. *She'll think you've gone crazy like that nut of an ex-husband of hers. They'll try to throw you in the loony bin and you know how that will go.*

He shook his head and grumbled out a fierce growl, bringing his fist down on the arm of the chair. He cast a nervous smile in the direction of the old lady sitting two chairs over, but the lady didn't look up from her knitting.

He closed his eyes and laid his head against the wall.

≈

Claire exited Sadie's room ten minutes later and headed back toward the lobby.

A small voice called out, "Claire!" to her and she backtracked a few steps to peek into the room the voice had come from and was astonished to see Kate sitting in a chair with an open book in her hands.

265

"Kate!" Claire smiled big and stepped into the room, walking over to the woman and giving her a hug. "I heard about your heart attack. The last I heard you were in a coma."

"Well, it seemed like they were going to lose me for a while there, but I'm a tough old bird."

Claire let out a chuckle. "I guess you are."

"Listen, Claire," Kate's voice was suddenly serious. "I'm sure by now you know that there is something seriously wrong with Blackwood Manor."

"I know," Claire nodded her head. "I'm on the verge of figuring out why though, and I think I can put a stop to it."

"If anyone can it's you," she agreed. "I want you to listen to me very carefully though. That man at your house–"

"What man?" Claire asked.

"The one that searched the house that day you fell down the stairs. Not Bradley. The other one. Don't trust him."

"Donovan?" Claire asked in confusion. "He's been a godsend. I wouldn't have been able to do half the renovations without him."

Kate shook her head. "You can't trust him. He's not who you think he is."

## CHAPTER TWENTY

Claire filled her glass with water, took her sleep medicine, and quickly downed the glass as she watched herself in the bathroom mirror. She set the glass on the sink and turned out the light before making her way down the hall toward her bedroom.

She paused momentarily outside of Donovan's door, ears poised for the slightest sound. Anything that may be off. Just as she had every night over the course of the past week since Kate told her that she couldn't trust him. Just as every night for the past week, she heard nothing but the steady sound of him breathing in a deep sleep.

She continued to her room and slipped under the covers. She lay back on her pillow and stared at the ceiling as she let her mind wander, waiting for deep sleep to come over her.

She just didn't know what to believe. She didn't necessarily believe that Kate was lying, but she had been through a major shock with her heart attack, her coma, and her subsequent rehabilitation. She hadn't been able to give her any specifics on why Donovan couldn't be trusted.

She had been in the area for a very long time. It was possible that Kate recognized Donovan at the house that day and took a while to place him. He admitted he had lived in town briefly as a teen. Maybe Kate knew something about Donovan that he had not yet disclosed. Or maybe she was just confused.

Hard as Claire tried, she could not think of a single incident where he had exhibited any strange or suspicious behavior. He had never lied to her that she knew of. He had done wonders for the property, somehow getting the men to work hard and efficiently when no one else had been able to get things off the ground. He had never made any advances on her to get her guard up. He had never tried to convince her to go in a direction with the property other than what she wanted. He never tried to get anything out of her except room and board, which he was more than earning.

Still, suspicion of men was almost second nature to her. It was Brock's doing, she knew, but now she couldn't help but find herself looking for anything out of the ordinary. Whispered phone calls, numbers being off on her receipts to indicate he was stealing from her, and any sudden movements or guilty looks when she'd enter a room. But there was nothing.

*What had Kate meant?* She asked herself one last time before she was overcome with sleep.

≈

Out in the cottage, Emma lay in Michael's arms long after she had fallen asleep crying. She felt so defenseless. So helpless. Like the world's most horrible mother. What had happened with Bailey had been so terrifying. When Claire had returned from talking to Sadie and told them what Sadie had said about something attaching itself to Bailey and that she doubted it was over; something in this place desperately wanted her; her heart had dropped like lead in the soles of her shoes.

Michael tried to reason that whatever had happened was done now and she would be okay, that she was clearly upset and sorry about what happened. Still, Emma could only think back to when she and Claire were kids. How bad things had gotten before they got better. What had to happen in order for things to get better? She didn't want to subject Bailey to it. She had insisted that she be taken away from Blackwood where nothing could get her. They had packed her up and taken her to the psychiatric hospital in Macon with her begging them every step of the way not to.

Emma had come home and cried. She knew her daughter was not crazy. She knew that she didn't have a personality disorder. She knew that it was *not* Bailey who attacked them. She knew what this was. She had seen it before. Something in this place was pure evil. It was a black hole, and she could feel it swallowing them a little at a time, day by day.

The only reason she was still here is that she knew that there were innocent spirits here as well, and those spirits needed to be freed. As vulnerable as her own children were, she could not stop thinking about poor Gloria and wondering what happened to her. So young and innocent and treated so cruelly by her own mother. She was stuck here, destined to spend eternity battling this evil, and she had to have been terrified. She had to find some way to help the child. Then, she would somehow convince Claire that she was fighting a losing battle. She would get them all out of here. She had to.


*Emma sat against the living room wall with her knees pulled to her chest, unconsciously rocking. She had her arms wrapped around her knees and her eyes could not be torn away from Claire. Something was seriously wrong with her. Ever since that...thing...had shown itself in the bedroom Claire had been acting strangely. She'd been acting strange ever since that thing showed itself in the bedroom.*

*She kept walking the length of the apartment, scratching at the walls. A low, disembodied growl seemed to constantly run out of her without her ever opening her mouth. She kept looking over at Emma and giving her a grin. This grin sent goose bumps and chills up and down Emma's spine. She didn't know why. She did know that grin was not right. It wasn't Claire. Her eyes were very wrong. They were black and glossy.*

*The most frightening thing of all? Claire's cat, Whiskers, had just walked through the room and Claire had jumped on him like a lion pouncing on its prey. She had torn his throat out with her teeth. The blood was still trickling down her face. Claire loved that cat. She would never hurt him.*

*Emma waited until Claire's back was turned to grab the phone off the coffee table. She quickly dialed her mother's number, the only one she could think of at this very moment. Claire seemed to startle, and Emma quickly placed the receiver behind her on the floor, careful not to hang up.*

≈

Brock sat up in a tree with a pair of binoculars, patiently watching. He was a safe distance from the house, but he had a good vantage point to watch. He disappeared during the day. It was too risky. But nights were completely open to him. Nights were a golden opportunity.

It was taking longer than he would have preferred, but he had to make sure to do it right. He spent the nights over the past week scouting the property. He knew when the crew came and went. Emma and her family were in the little house out back. Not right up on the main house but close enough that it posed a possible risk for him.

He had been going straight up to the house, checking doors and windows when all the lights would go out, and he was sure everyone was asleep. The floodlights had gone up two nights before, putting a stop to that.

Brock flared his nostrils in anger and set his binoculars back on the bridge of his nose. That man. Claire's man whore. He was beginning to be a real problem. He was getting between Brock and his objective. He would simply have to be eliminated.

"Brock. Hey! Brock!"

He was shaken from his concentration by the sound of the voice. *God, I've been found out! And I don't have the wire anymore!* He slowly turned his head towards the sound of the voice, and he jumped, nearly falling out of the tree from the shock of the sight before him.

In the tree directly opposite him, there was a man wearing a Union soldier's uniform. He was hanging from a high branch, landing where his eyes were exactly even with where Brock was sitting. His neck was bent at an awkward angle and his eyes were bulging out of his head, but he spoke just the same.

"They're laughing at you, Brock. Claire. That bastard Donovan. He laughs at you while he fucks her, Brock. They're laughing at you right now. Are you going to let them get away with it?"

"No," Brock said firmly. "They will both pay. I have to play it right. No one can know I was here."

"They already know, and they laugh at you. The lights were a slap in your face. To tell you they are invincible, and you will never touch them. That you aren't good enough to touch them. Just look!" he pointed one long finger toward the window he had been watching.

Claire was standing in it, naked. She looked right at him and smiled that bitchy smile of hers, the one that just really pissed him off. She waved. One deliberate finger at a time. Then the man–Donovan? Was that his name?– came up behind her. He was also naked. He put his arms around her and slid his hands up to her breasts. He licked her forehead while looking pointedly at Brock.

"Oh yes," Brock said aloud as he watched the curtains being jerked closed. "They will pay."

He decided he would go into town and buy a gun first thing in the morning.

## CHAPTER TWENTY-ONE

Claire was photographing the kitchen the next morning with a huge smile on her face. It was finally completed, and she was enamored with it beyond belief. The walls were painted a soft gray that made all the modern matching black appliances pop. The tile on the floor had been replaced with a gray linoleum only slightly darker than the paint.

The curtains above the kitchen sink were new and a soft blue brought a splash of color to the room that brightened the place up. The large shelf that had at one point been hiding the entrance to the servant's stairwell was still there but it was pushed along the wall next to the kitchen counter and had been repainted to match the rest of the room, leaving the doorway exposed. She'd had the door removed from the hinges, leaving the oak doorway open. No one else getting trapped in there. No way. No how.

"Claire!" Emma called out to her and she answered back never taking her eyes from the viewfinder.

"In the kitchen, Em!"

She heard the footsteps behind her and began to babble excitedly. "It turned out so much better than I thought it would. If I can sell this to a magazine, it's going to open so many doors." She turned to smile at her friend and her face fell. Emma was extremely disheveled. Her hair hadn't been brushed and hung in clumps around her face.

Her eyes were now ringed with dark circles. Her clothes were mismatched and it was obvious she was still wearing the same shirt she had worn to bed.

"Sit down, Claire," she gestured towards a bar stool next to the island.

Claire was so overcome with concern that she immediately plopped down without question.

"Is there coffee?" Emma circled the counter and answered her own question as she stepped towards the full coffee pot. She pulled down two mugs and poured them both. She slid one towards Claire and patiently got out sugar and creamer.

Claire waited patiently; her coffee untouched in front of her.

Emma finished making her cup and went to take a seat beside Claire at the island. She massaged her temples and looked at her friend with a look that was almost defeated. A look that scared Claire to her very core for reasons that she could not explain.

"Emma, what's wrong? Is Bailey okay?"

"Bailey's fine," she answered simply. She hesitated a moment. As if she were having an internal battle with herself over whether or not to continue.

"I know there's a lot you don't remember, Claire. I need to know how much you do. About that day."

"What day do you mean?" Claire asked, confused.

"The day when we were ten. When we played with the Ouija board."

"Oh," Claire sat back in surprise. "I remember we'd been watching scary movies. Like we always did back then. We'd decided to see if we could reach out to the unknown, so we borrowed the board from my neighbors. Nothing happened except they tried to scare us. You know, it's interesting that you're asking me about that. I've been dreaming about that night for months."

"You have?"

Claire nodded. "It's different, though. Things and details change every time. Small things lead up to big things that never happened. Then there are huge blocks of blankness."

Emma bit her lip and took another big swig of her coffee. "Did you never think it was strange how different things were after that day? That I still believed in the supernatural, but that I was now scared of it? That you suddenly found no interest in those things yourself? That Whiskers disappeared? How much your relationship with your parents disintegrated?"

Claire laughed and squeezed her friend's hand. "Em, people grow up and they change. That's all. I became sensible and realized that stuff was nothing more than fun children's games. Until I came here at least. Whiskers ran off. It's sad, but it happens. My parents didn't like that I became my own person as I grew up and we began to drift apart. Do I wish it could have been different? Absolutely. But what's done is done."

"Claire, a lot of secrets have been kept from you. You're probably going to hate me when I'm done talking. If you do, I won't blame you, but please know that we only kept these things from you to protect you because we love you. It never should have come out. With this place, though, it's become necessary to make you see what has to be done."

"Emma, you're scaring me."

"I'm not trying to, but I am glad," she said flatly and looked deep into Claire's eyes. "That day started the way you remember, but that's where the similarities end. In the dream you've been having, has there been knocking on the walls? The door to your parent's bedroom opening?"

Claire had a chill in her spine and her mouth was suddenly as dry as sandpaper. "How did you know that?"

"Because I've been dreaming about it too. Because we both lived it. Only I remembered and you didn't," she squeezed Claire's hand, which was now like ice. "I somehow knew something was wrong. My gut told me. I begged you to not go into the room but you said you'd get in trouble if you didn't close the door. So you went in, and the door slammed shut behind you. I could hear you screaming."

Emma's bottom lip began to tremble, and tears flowed from her eyes. "I was so scared. I wanted to run away, but I loved you like a sister, and I couldn't leave you there, so I ran in. There was this...*thing*...in there attacking you. It was horrible looking. I tried to help you, but I might as well have been a doll. I did the only thing I could think of. I grabbed the cross that was hanging over your parents' bed and pressed it to the creature. It howled in pain and then it just–disintegrated. I tried to hug you and talk to you to make sure you were okay, but you didn't talk or move. Not for a long time. When you did, you were different. I thought you were in shock at first, but then I noticed your eyes were black. That's when it started getting scary."

She stopped talking, looking deeply into Claire's face. She was waiting for a reaction but Claire's face was pale and unresponsive. Her eyes were furrowed in confusion. Her damn mouth was still dry.

So they had the same dream. So what? It didn't mean anything. If that were true, though, why was she overcome with a feeling of dread? "Just a dream," she whispered. "It's only a dream."

Emma shook her head. "I wish to God that were true, Claire. It's not. You started clawing at the walls and grinning this twisted, unnatural grin. Claire, you jumped on Whiskers and tore his throat out with your teeth! That's when I knew it wasn't you. I managed to dial my mom, but I couldn't speak without you noticing. She listened for several minutes before she heard you talking in a disembodied voice and she rushed like hell to get there."

"That's a damn lie!" Claire yelled suddenly, rising from her bar stool so quickly that she knocked it over. "I would have never hurt Whiskers. I'm an animal lover and always have been! How dare you!"

"That's what I'm trying to tell you, Claire," Emma pleaded with her eyes and her voice but remained seated. "I know it wasn't you. It was your body, but it wasn't you!"

Claire shook her head frantically and began to pace the room, pulling unconsciously at her hair.

"Every time you left the room, I followed you. I just knew somehow that I had to watch you. That I had to keep myself at your back. I made a mistake in the kitchen. I pulled out a knife. To protect myself. Just in case. That's what drew your attention to me. When my mom came in, you had me pinned to the ground and we were frantically fighting with the knife between us. She tried to pull you off me, but you threw her back and she hit her head on the coffee table. I took that split second when you were turned away, and I slashed out with the knife. I didn't want to hurt you. I just wanted you off me. You were cut from your breastbone to your pelvis. You fell to the ground and when you looked at me, your eyes were clear. Whatever had been there was gone and you were crying in pain.

"I called an ambulance and they took you both to the hospital. Mom had a brain hemorrhage. She died the next day."

"No!" Claire yelled out defiantly, and her eyes were brimmed with red as she cried. "I had an appendectomy, and your mom was in a car accident."

"That's not an appendectomy scar. Richie had his appendix removed two years ago, remember? I can show you the scar if you don't believe me. I can also show you my mom's death certificate."

"If all that's true then why were we not in trouble?"

"We were. Not in the way you mean," Emma answered slowly. "We lied. We said that you had shown me the knife and we were playing with it. I was holding it. Mom came in and saw us and ran to stop us. We said she tripped on the rug and fell into me. It knocked me forward, and I cut you. I had to answer a few questions at the hospital. You didn't. You were getting a blood transfusion, and you were very disoriented. It seemed like it was over, though. It wasn't. When they let you go home, you started acting different again and it got to where you were like that even at school.

"Your personality was completely different. You were moody, confrontational, and kept to yourself unless you had an insane desire to insult somebody. You became active in vandalism, your grades dropped crazy fast. You were a completely different person. One night, you asked me to come over for a sleepover. This was about a month after everything had started. I didn't really want to because you honestly scared me. You were my best friend, though, and I didn't want you to feel alienated because of me. So I went.

"You had ripped the heads off all your dolls and wanted to see just how much pressure it would take to break a bone. With me as your dummy. I kept fighting you on it and you got angry. I went out to tell your parents that I wanted to go home, but I overheard your mom on the phone talking about a priest who was coming over that night. She said you were possessed by the devil. Now, I didn't necessarily believe that. Your parents were crazy religious after all. I did think that the thing from that day was making you do things somehow."

Claire crossed her arms angrily in front of her. "I don't know what you're trying to pull, Emma. I think you need to leave."

Emma stood up and strolled over to where Claire defiantly stood. "I know it's a lot to take in. I understand that you don't believe it right now. Calm down and look back on things. Look up your records. You'll see I'm right. Let me know when you're ready to hear the rest. I'll be visiting Bailey if you need me."

She disappeared through the doorway into the dining room and a moment later, Claire heard the snap of the front door closing. Claire sank down to the floor with her back against the wall and began to weep.

≈

Donovan turned around from the parlor fireplace at the sound of the front door closing and watched through the window as Emma hurried down the porch steps, her hands over her mouth as she ran for the driveway.

He turned off the electric drill he had been using and could hear the distant sound of Claire crying from the kitchen. He almost went to her to ask her what was wrong, but he held back at the last moment and reminded himself that it was none of his business. He had a job to do, and he had to do it relatively fast. Claire was going to find out sooner or later and it could go any number of ways when she did. He couldn't allow himself to get close.

He turned back to the fireplace and began to work at the brick some more. He loosened a good chunk of it, but there was no way he or anyone else would be getting in there just yet. There was a small hole cleared and he placed his eye on it. He nearly looked away, but then was certain that he saw something move. Surely that wasn't possible. He stuck his entire arm through the hole up to almost the elbow and tried to feel around with his outstretched palm. There was so much air. So much empty space. He thought he felt his fingertips brush up against something. Something that was not a wall. He tried to reach in farther to get a grip on whatever it was, but his arm would go no farther. The hole was simply too small.

He retracted his arm and grabbed one of the fireplace pokers, carefully sticking the handle in slowly. He was pushing it in the same direction his hand had been, moving it gently this way and that, until he felt contact. He heard a soft thunk and rattle as if something had fallen.

He pulled the poker out and examined the handle. Dust. Dust and something white that he could not quite identify.

"Don't you stop, boy."

Donovan whipped around and found himself face-to-face with Josie. Her face was not even half an inch from his own and he thought he could see the dark shades of eye sockets beneath a veil of nothing. Her voice was not angry. It was not harsh. It was exciting, vindicating him. As though he had made a very good decision and was about to get a treat.

"I can't move the brick fast enough safely. If I pull it out now, the whole foundation could come crashing in." His voice was steady, unwavering. He spoke with confidence and not a single shred of uncertainty.

"Let it come down," she spoke. "There are things that are more important."

He turned back towards the fireplace once more, flipped the poker around, and began to swing at the brick, starting at the weakened hole, with all his might.

≈

Claire woke up on the floor of the kitchen. She was balled up on the floor with a stiff back and her tears were dried on her face. Her attention was drawn to movement in the corner and again she was caught by the flickering focus of Margaret walking the length of the kitchen and holding a candle. It was like watching a film reel, like the time she had a ring sideshow to Margaret and Josie's conversation in the upstairs hallway.

Margaret made her way to the entrance into the hall and Claire scrambled to her feet to rush after her. The house was almost in darkness, but Claire still saw through the flicker of candlelight. As they passed the door to the parlor, she peeked in and was surprised to see one giant room. The sliding pocket doors on the opposite wall were there, leading to what she assumed was an office, but otherwise, it was open. No fireplace. She knew the bathroom didn't exist yet.

Claire tore her eyes away from the parlor and followed Margaret up the stairs. On the landing, she saw a boy with his back to the wall. He was sobbing softly. It must have been Percy. The boy and Margaret locked eyes for a moment but neither of them said anything.

Margaret turned and made her way down the hallway before entering one of the bedrooms. It was the room that Donovan now used. She approached a small door in the wall and opened it up. *What was that?* Claire thought to herself. *Was it a wall safe?*

Margaret leaned slightly inside, her arms extended, and dropped something down inside. There was a moment before Claire could hear the thud of the item making contact with something far below.

Claire let out a sigh of surprise. It was a dumbwaiter shaft. She had never seen any dumbwaiters on the property.

There was a fade out and Claire looked around to see the room with modern conveniences. She was now standing in Donovan's bedroom facing the wall, which was covered by a giant tapestry. She gave it a good hard yank, and it came tumbling down.

There, in the wall, was the rusted door that was the entrance to the dumbwaiter. She opened the door, muscling it hard but not as hard as she had thought she would need to, and stuck her head in to look down. The door had barely opened before she heard a small, distant voice crying, "Help!"

"Hello?" she called down. "Who's there?"

"Claire?" the voice of a young girl answered.

"Callie? How'd you get in there?"

"Stuck! Cold. Help, Claire!" She grabbed the lamp from Donovan's bedside table and held it inside to illuminate the shaft. The ropes appeared to be in place, but she didn't trust them enough to try and bring the dumbwaiter up. She found the location odd. They were not over the kitchen. Where did this lead?

She reached in and grabbed one of the ropes to test it. She felt that it would hold her weight so she placed the lamp back on the table and cautiously began to climb into the shaft. She grasped the rope firmly with one hand, then one leg, then the other hand, then the other leg, and began to shimmy her way down the rope.

She kept throwing her eyes from the darkness below up to the entrance she had come through, which was now a tiny matchbox square of light. There was a groan of metal and the door closed over that box of light, throwing her into darkness.

*"Miss Margaret?" Josie asked.*

*Margaret looked up from her needlepoint and smiled at Josie. Her smile was different though. She had changed so much in such a short time. Her smile no longer* quite reached her eyes and there was a weariness in the laugh lines of her face. She forever appeared apprehensive, tired, and like the world was going to drop out from under her.

"The children are asleep," Josie sat across next to Margaret on the sofa and offered her a cup of tea.

"Thank you," Margaret accepted it and rubbed the bridge of her nose before taking a sip.

"Did Lucy have an accident tonight?"

"Not so far. Though the night is young."

"Isn't that the truth," she sighed. "I worry about her. Still wetting the bed at three years old."

"She's only recently started doing it again," Josie said gently. "Her daddy just left for the war."

"Every night this week," Margaret shook her head. "We all miss John. Her most of all. That's never what she tells me though. She's always talking about monsters and things that are not there."

Josie nodded in agreement. "When I was putting her down she asked me to make sure that the little girl isn't in her closet. I did so to humor her. Maybe she will actually get some sleep tonight."

"Little girl?" Margaret asked. "That's new."

"She says things speak to her at night. I told her it was just her daddy watching over while she sleeps, and she doesn't have to be frightened."

*Margaret smiled. "What would I ever do without you, Josie? You're such a natural with the children and they no longer have patience for me."*

*Josie placed a comforting hand on her arm. "That's not true."*

*Margaret looked into Josie's eyes deeply, tears brimming in her own and then she leaned forward and pressed her lips to Josie's. Softly at first, then firmer. The touch was fire and liquid as her tongue slipped between her lips to meet Josie's.*

*A warmth flooded Josie that she didn't know and didn't understand. The warmth of those lips pressed urgently to her, and she found herself returning the pressure, her tongue gently massaging Margaret's. The fire spread down her body to the tips of her fingers and exploded with an impossible ache between her legs.*

*The feeling excited and paralyzed her. She liked how it felt but it scared her all at once, freezing her in place.*

*Margaret pulled away suddenly with a gasp. She raised one hand to her chest and her cheeks were flushed. "I'm so sorry. I shouldn't have. I'm going to bed now."*

*With that, she was on her feet and fleeing the room, leaving Josie sitting on the sofa wondering what exactly just happened.*

## CHAPTER TWENTY-TWO

Emma sat in the rec room of the psychiatric hospital and absently played with her visitor's badge. She was waiting for Bailey to be brought in. She was fidgeting in nervousness, not sure how this was going to go. It was the first time going to see Bailey since they brought her here, the first time she had been allowed visitors.

The door to the rec room opened and Emma rose to her feet as Bailey walked into the room and over to her. She was unkempt and her eyes were dark and hollowed, but she didn't have that hard edge to her anymore that had been there since the seance. She looked like her baby girl again.

They exchanged an awkward hug and sat down opposite each other on matching couches, each waiting for the other to speak.

"Bailey," Emma began. "I know that you're probably mad about being in here. I doubt you even remember what happened. We didn't think we had any other choice given the circumstances."

Bailey nodded in agreement, surprising her mother. "I get it, Mom. I remember more than you think I do. I wish I didn't. How's Callie?"

Emma had dreaded this question, but she had already told herself that she would answer honestly if it came up. She squeezed Bailey's hand. "She's confused and scared. She doesn't understand why you tried to hurt her."

Bailey looked away in shame and let go of her mother's hand and Emma noticed a shining tear rolling down her cheek. "She's young, honey. She knows it was your face, your hands. She's too young to comprehend that it wasn't you inside. She'll forget in time."

Bailey nodded her head. "I know. I just hate that she's scared of me."

"What happened, Bailey? What do you remember?"

"After the seance, I never felt alone. I always felt like I was being watched. My stomach felt sour. I started having bad thoughts about hurting you or Richie or Callie, but it wasn't like it was my inner voice, it was like something else taking over my thoughts."

"I have to ask, sweetie. Your behavior changed after the bathroom–"

Bailey violently nodded her head and cleared her throat, cutting her mother off. "We'd been passing that flu bug or whatever it was around. Richie was in our bathroom, so I had to go to the house even though I didn't want to. Everything inside was telling me, 'don't go!' but everything was fine until I washed my hands.

"I looked in the mirror and there was a woman standing behind me along the wall. She was wearing period clothes, this green flapper dress like they wore in the '20s and looked like she had wet stringy hair. I heard a noise and looked over to see the bathtub filling with blood. When I looked back in the mirror, she was right behind me. She grabbed my head and slammed it into the mirror."

"Oh, God," Emma whispered. She was unconsciously grasping at her neck with one hand.

"Her fingers were so cold," Bailey went on. Her voice shook, and she went quiet for a moment as the tears rolled down her face. "I sank to the floor, but it wasn't over. She got right down in my face, and I watched her change. Her skin began to rot and tear away from the bone. This horrible smell filled the room and a feeling of dread and hate. She started hitting me. The next thing I knew, Donovan was shaking me, and I could see that he'd kicked the door in. I must have been screaming.

"It still wasn't over. That feeling that she gave me in the bathroom was always there. Constantly. I felt angry, alone, and lost. I felt like everyone around me needed to pay. Then that day it was like I was watching a movie through my own eyes. I saw everything happening, but I had no control over my body."

"Was this woman one of the ones you saw during the seance?"

"No. Her clothes were different."

"You said the '20s?" Emma echoed and unconsciously chewed her lips. "I don't remember anything sticking out about the '20s in the house's history."

Bailey shook her head. "It was weird. Her dress was from the '20s. Emerald green. But she had a punk hair do. I felt like she was faking."

Emma reached out to squeeze her daughter's hand and recoiled as she felt a bolt of electricity shoot through her hand, up her arm, and into her neck at lightning speed. She rubbed her neck and stared down at Bailey's hands. She was flexing her fingers and little threads of electric blue bolts were shooting out of her fingers and flickering out.

"Bailey, what's wrong with your hands?"

Bailey looked down at the little sparks coming from her fingertips and looked back up at her mother. "You can see that?"

"Does that happen a lot?"

"For a couple of months," Bailey answered with barely more than a whisper. "I thought I was crazy."

Emma's eyes went wide with realization. "Oh, my God."

≈

Michael hung up the phone with his wife and made his way back up to the house. He didn't know why it was so important to her that she know exactly when Donovan and his friends spent the night in the house as kids, but she wanted him to find out.

He could hear the loud bangs before his feet ever hit the front steps. The yells of exertion. He ran up the stairs and threw the door open, bounding into the parlor. He saw Donovan swinging a sledgehammer carelessly into the brick of the fireplace. He was using a good deal of force, but ironically, didn't appear to have so much as broken a sweat. Directly behind him were two ominous figures. A black lady in a floor-length white dress and a small blonde girl with brain matter hanging out of the back of her head. Although Michael hadn't personally seen anything up until now, he instantly knew that it was the infamous Josie and Gloria.

"Donovan!" He found his voice and called out sharply.

Donovan turned and grinned, as did Josie and Gloria. He did not flinch or jump at the sight of the two ghosts standing behind him. "Michael!" he answered joyously.

"What the hell are you doing, man?" he asked, ignoring the faces of the spirits, trying to read something in Donovan's face. "You told Claire that had to be taken down super carefully or risk the ceiling caving in! There you are beating the hell out of it haphazardly."

"Oh, it's okay," Donovan answered. "It's secure." His eyes seemed glassy and wild. Not at all like the cool, calm, and collected man that Michael had gotten to know. "But you know something really cool, Michael? Something's in there."

"What?" Michael shook his head in bewilderment. Donovan was starting to scare him, and he didn't like the way the two spirits were still watching him silently and unblinking. "It's a fireplace."

"In the gap behind it," Donovan insisted. "There's a big enough hole now that I can see in. I saw something move. I really did."

Donovan moved forward suddenly, passing through the two spirits who disintegrated as he did so, and he still didn't react. He threw an arm around Michael's shoulders and walked him toward the fireplace. "Take a look!"

Michael shook Donovan's arm from his shoulders and stepped back. He didn't like this. "I don't think you should mess with this anymore until you talk to Claire. I think the heat is getting to you. This is dangerous, and it's her house. Don't do anything else to the fireplace until you talk to her. Please."

"Mike, you gotta take a look!"

Reluctantly, Michael bent down and put one eye to the hole that Donovan had made, but he didn't see anything but never-ending darkness. "I don't see anything," Michael straightened up and turned again to face Donovan. "Promise me."

Donovan crossed his arms over his chest and narrowed his eyes. "Fine. I won't do anything else unless I talk to Claire. Now, was there something you wanted to ask me?"

Michael blinked for a moment, suddenly drawing a blank on the information that Emma had asked him to get. Then he remembered and opened his mouth to answer when they were interrupted by a banging metallic sound.

≈

"Don't panic," Claire told herself when the light from above disappeared. She gripped the rope as firmly as she could and began to consciously stagger her breathing. Once upon a time, she had been extremely claustrophobic. Closets, tunnels, and even being trapped in a car in traffic for too long would be enough to cause her to stop breathing. Life with Brock had forced her to work through that. She'd needed to hide in some pretty inventive, and small hiding places before. Her fear had gotten stronger, but there were still small links to it in her brain.

This was such an instance. She was in the walls of her house, suspended in midair, held up only by a centuries-old rope. Someone closed the door on her, and she didn't know how deep this tunnel was or where it went.

She held tight, giving her eyes a moment to adjust to the dark. There wasn't much improvement. There were no cracks for light to shine through. She began to shimmy down the rope very slowly and carefully.

She breathed a sigh of relief when her feet scraped across the surface. The top of the dumbwaiter. It had to be. She put her feet down firmly and let go of the rope, preparing for something to give away and cause her to fall, but it didn't happen. The air was thick, and she found it extremely difficult to draw air into her lungs. There was a smell of old, and stale rot down here. She felt for the edge of the dumbwaiter and jumped down from it, feeling her feet hit earth.

She dug in her pocket and felt her heart sink to see that she only had three percent battery left on her phone. She flashed the screen around the area before her. It was small and cramped and she still couldn't see more than a foot in front of her face.

She saw that the actual dumbwaiter was sitting at an awkward angle, as if it had fallen and was rusted almost clean through. She was also horrified to see how badly frayed the rope was. She was amazed it had supported her weight at all.

"Callie!" she called out and was met with only silence.

She began to walk along a path in front of her, walking slightly stooped and praying that she would come to the end before her phone died. After walking about three feet, she came to a fork with two paths and she picked the right one at random, following it as slowly as she dared. The hair on the back of her neck was standing on end, she could barely breathe, and she felt like she was being watched, which was ridiculous. There wasn't room down here or enough light for anyone to be watching her. Still, she felt uneasy. She stopped and instinctively put her back to a wall when her phone chirped several times, text messages coming in.

She read them, the first several from Emma. They grew increasingly panicked.

Message one: *Claire, I'm sorry I upset you at the house today. I never planned to tell you all that because I knew it would torture you. Something is going on in that house, though. I believe you are the golden warrior. The only one that can put a stop to all these awful things. I tried to tell you that before, but you didn't seem to get it. I didn't know how else to tell you without telling you the truth. Please don't hate me.*

Message two: *Claire, I know you don't want to talk to me right now. I need to know, though. Didn't Donovan say that he and his friends visited Blackwood Manor on Halloween night? I know it seems like a silly question, but I promise you I have a reason for asking.*

Message three: *Damn it! Don't ignore me! You don't know how important this is! Was it Halloween? Was it? I know you know!*

Message four: *I know who the golden warrior is! I was wrong! I need your answer about Halloween! We can't come back until we know!*

Then there was a message that made Claire's blood run cold. A chill ran down her spine as she read it. This message was not from Emma. It was from a private number. It read, "I hope you suffocate down there."

She had barely finished reading when her phone died, spilling her into darkness once more.

## CHAPTER TWENTY-THREE

Emma pulled up in front of the nursing home and pried her fingers from the wheel, wiping her sweaty hands against her jeans. She gripped the wheel so tightly that her knuckles were now protesting in pain from being ripped from their home on the wheel.

"Mom?" Bailey asked from the passenger seat. She was still wearing her hospital gown. "Why are we at a nursing home?"

"Claire isn't answering me but this woman can help. She knows all about Blackwood Manor. She'll know what to do."

Emma reached into the backseat and pulled out a Wal-Mart bag where she had stopped twenty minutes before and bought Bailey some clothes. She had never thought she would be breaking her own daughter out of a psychiatric hospital. "Put these on. You can't go in there wearing that. They'll know."

Bailey obediently took the bag and pulled items out one by one and put them on. Emma kept a close watch on the mirrors and windows, expecting to see flashing lights bounding down on them at any moment. God, why had she told them about the attack? Pesky court orders.

"So, why do I need to talk to this old lady?" Bailey asked, pulling the t-shirt over her head.

"Because," Emma turned towards her daughter and gave a half-hearted smile. "You are going to put a stop to all this and she is going to tell you how."

When Emma saw Brad's familiar truck pull into a parking spot a few spaces down, she let out a sigh of relief.

The two of them climbed out of the car and made their way toward the truck. Bailey kept wringing her hands, and Emma squeezed her shoulder. Brad got out of his truck. His facial hair was longer and more scraggly than when she'd seen him last, and he had dark bags under his eyes. "Oh, good God, Emma," he said as soon as he saw Bailey. "This isn't good."

"We have to see your grandmother. It's important."

Brad gave her a look, about to protest, but the urgency on her face stopped him. "Okay, but we better make it quick." He turned and led them toward the entrance.

"Don't fidget. Don't let on that something is wrong. We can't afford any delays," Emma hissed at Bailey.

They stepped inside and Bailey's eyes swept the lobby in disbelief at the sight of the employees and various residents.

"Talk about white-washed," she muttered under her breath.

Emma sharply gripped her arm at the elbow. "Watch yourself, young lady. Don't forget you're half-white too."

"Yeah, but not enough," Bailey hissed. "How the hell are we supposed to get in now?"

"That's why Brad's here. Just follow my lead." Emma straightened her spine confidently and followed Brad to the reception desk. They were greeted by a perky redhead that reminded Emma briefly of a pop tart popping up out of a toaster.

"Hello," she chirped. "How can I help you?"

"Yes, we're here to see Sadie Collins."

"How do you know Sadie?"

"She's my grandmother," Brad answered, reaching for the sign-in sheet.

The receptionist nodded to Emma and Bailey. "And what about them?"

Emma paused, only for a moment. Then decided to take a big risk which she knew had the possibility of giving her away. "She's my grandmother too."

The receptionist gave a sweet smile that did not meet her eyes, a smile that said she was not buying the story the least bit, but she directed them towards Sadie's room anyway.

Emma followed Brad down the hallway towards Sadie's room, tugging gently on Bailey's arm to urge her forward. Once they came to the room, she stopped and told Bailey to wait outside the room. She knocked sharply on the door and waited to be greeted before slipping inside and quietly closing the door behind her.

She walked deeper into the room and saw a little lady propped up on the bed reading a book about witchcraft.

"Hi, Nana," Brad greeted, kneeling to kiss her cheek.

"Yes, dear." Sadie smiled, her blue eyes twinkling. "How is Caroline?"

He paused, his breath hitching ever so slightly. "It's touch and go."

Emma suddenly realized that she hadn't seen Brad since the day everything happened with Bailey, and she hadn't even noticed his disheveled appearance. His daughter had taken a turn for the worse. She immediately felt guilty for bringing him here for something she could have taken care of on her own.

"This is Emma Price. She's Claire's friend. She lives with her family at Blackwood Manor."

"Yes, yes. Claire has spoken quite fondly of you." Sadie placed a bookmark in her book and set it on the bedside table. She gestured towards the chair across from the bed and Emma took a seat. "What can I do for you, dear?"

"Well, I think that you're the only one that can help us," Emma began. She explained Bailey's seance with her friends, the subsequent fire, and the change in Bailey. She told her about the attack from the thing that was in Bailey's body, Callie's attempted murder, and placing Bailey in the psychiatric hospital.

Sadie listened patiently, not seeming to be too surprised by any part of the story– and waited a moment after Emma had stopped speaking to respond. She clearly wanted to make sure that Emma was finished.

"Well, dear. I told Claire that I believed the fire at your home to be caused by a demon that was summoned that night. You see, when your daughter and her friends had their séance, they unknowingly opened a doorway, and from the sound of it, they didn't close the doorway. That demon would have attached itself to your daughter."

Emma nodded and took a deep breath before jumping to her main point. The real reason that she had broken Bailey out of the hospital and brought her here. "Yes, I had figured that out. Claire and I went through something similar in our childhood."

Sadie nodded. "I sensed it in her."

Emma's eyes momentarily went wide in shock. *Let's go back to that later,* she thought to herself, but she would not be distracted from the purpose of her visit. Everything had been building to this moment. Everything came down to this. "Well, Bailey is normal now that she's not on the property anymore, and I've recently discovered something about her. Claire told me that she spoke to you about golden warriors, the people who can put a stop to the activity. That you gave her criteria for finding that person. I initially thought it *was* Claire because of our childhood. But now I see crackles of electricity from Bailey's fingertips that weren't there before. As much as I hate to admit it, she does fit the criteria."

"What do you mean crackles of electricity?" Sadie asked, her brow furrowed.

Emma rose to her feet and shuffled towards the door, sweeping Bailey in. She walked her over to Sadie with her hands on the girl's shoulders.

Bailey had a doe-in-the-headlights expression on her face. She subconsciously leaned against her mother and never took her eyes off Sadie's face.

"Bailey, this is Ms. Collins," Emma said, trying to urge her forward.

Bailey resisted the nudge and didn't step forward, though she did speak. "Hello, Ms. Collins."

"Hello, dear," Sadie smiled warmly at her. "It's okay to be frightened. I know you've been through quite a lot recently. Though I can assure you I am very real."

"Bailey, show Ms. Collins your hands," Emma spoke into her daughter's ear. "Go on."

Bailey reluctantly pulled out her hands, which she had firmly clasped behind her back, and held them up for Sadie's inspection.

Tiny little bolts of static electricity were sparking from the girl's fingertips in a brilliant shade of blue. Her hands were noticeably shaking.

Sadie reached out and gently clasped both of Bailey's hands firmly between both of hers. "I understand how confusing this must be for you."

"What does this mean?" Emma cut in, breaking the connection between the old woman's and the young girl's eyes. "Is she the golden warrior?"

Sadie pulled her hands back and reluctantly nodded her head.

Emma let out a low moan and sank back into the rocker. The color drained from Bailey's face, and she raised her hands up to massage her neck.

"This isn't necessarily a bad thing," Sadie said. "It's an extraordinary gift, you must remember that. It does come with certain dangers, as does anything that is truly extraordinary. You must be cautious, there is no denying that."

"That thing already latched itself to her once." Emma shook her head. "I can't take her back in that house."

"That's what it wants, Emma," Sadie said gently but firmly. "It sensed the power in her right from the start and that's why it targeted her. It wanted her out of the way. Things will only continue to get worse without her intervention. You'll give it a nice, healthy surprise if you take her back. It won't be expecting that."

Bailey fidgeted slightly and did not speak.

"Well," Emma hesitated. "How—how do we take her there, and keep her safe, and fight the evil?"

"Very carefully," Sadie said as she leaned forward and took one of each woman's hands in each of hers. "Now, here is what you need to do."

≈

"She's probably starting to panic now," Brock thought to himself and smirked from the darkness of the closet. Getting into the house had been so easy. Easier than expected. The front door had been wide open, and there was a work truck parked right outside the door with unattended tools.

He had strapped on a tool belt and walked right through the front door. The handyman, that guy Donovan, had been pounding away at the fireplace and hadn't heard him. He had almost put the hammer right into his skull. It would have been so easy.

But his busy work would keep him out of the way while Brock dealt with Claire. Then it would be his turn. He had gone right up to her in the kitchen and was ready to take care of her, but she got up out of that cowered position on the floor and walked aimlessly after something like she was in a trance. She hadn't even seen him.

He'd followed her and seen her climb into the dumbwaiter shaft, and he'd barely been able to suppress his glee. He knew of her claustrophobia. Knew that it had improved but was still there in the back of her mind. He'd shut the door, fired off a text to her phone, and slipped into the closet in case she came back out.

The urge to go in after her and take care of her in the darkness between the walls where no one would ever think to look for her was great. This was better, though. Let her sweat it down there until she started to panic and hallucinate, or better yet, broke her own neck. Then he would go in after her and sneak up on her.

He'd been sitting here, patiently waiting, glancing at his watch and letting his mind jump to all the times in their past, gauging how long it would take for her to start to panic. He figured that time was right about now. The thought had him hard as a rock and his heart pounding in anticipation. He made a move towards the doorknob and turned it, ready to step out towards the dumbwaiter shaft. He was stopped by an arm grabbing his wrist and a feeling like ice ran through his body and he felt sure that his temperature had dropped. Damn, it must have been about twenty degrees.

The Civil War soldier stood next to him. "Not now," he said and pulled Brock back firmly.

"Why?" Brock asked breathlessly.

Just then he heard pounding footsteps. It sounded like several people were running through the halls.

"You need to get out of here, boy," the soldier said matter-of-factly.

Brock was annoyed. He wanted to take care of Claire. "This bitch has ruined my life. I'm going to ruin hers."

"Not yet," the soldier repeated and had no reaction to the scowl that Brock gave him. "They are closer to the whore right now than you are. Do you want to get caught?"

Brock sunk back further into the closet, crossed his arms in front of him, and let out a grunt of dissatisfaction.

"Go back out to our spot in the woods," the soldier said, slowly beginning to fade. "I'll let you know when the coast is clear."

≈

Claire's breathing was panicked. She was breathing very fast and struggling to hold air in her lungs. It was pitch black and she could feel eyes on her. He was down here. She knew he was down here. He was coming to get her. For leaving him. For taking him to court. But she couldn't see him. How the hell was she supposed to fight him when she couldn't see him?

Just then, a figure began to materialize in front of her. She let out a scream, thinking that Brock was closing in on her, but it was Gloria. She was emitting a brilliant white light around her, like a halo that hadn't been there before, lighting up the tunnel.

She reached out and took Claire's hand. Her touch was surprisingly warm and reassuring. Gloria tried to pull her down the tunnel, but she kept her foot firmly planted in the earth.

"Come on," Gloria said, her voice small but firm. Much firmer than a child's tone. "He'll get you."

"Who will get me?"

"The bad man," Gloria said simply and began to walk. Claire followed her. She didn't know why she trusted this small child to get her out of this situation, but she did. She followed her to the end of the tunnel where she faced a metal door. Another dumbwaiter door. She slid it open, having to use every bit of her strength.

There was something on the other side. Her way out was blocked. She felt the panic returning, beginning to envelop her.

As if she sensed it, Gloria spoke again, "There's a shelf in front. Bang hard. They'll let you out."

"Isn't there another way?" she asked.

Gloria shook her head. "All the others are closed."

Claire began to throw her weight against the shelf and bang on the metal, occasionally shouting out.

She heard a voice yell out, "Over here!" and heard the scraping of metal as the shelf was pulled away. The brilliant light disappeared. Claire turned her head to look and saw that Gloria was gone just as light filled the opening from the dumbwaiter. A hand reached through to help her out, and she seized it.

She stepped out into the basement and looked up into the eyes of Donovan, Michael, and a few workmen.

"Jesus, Claire," Michael breathed out. "What the hell were you doing in there?"

She didn't answer but gave them both her most serious face. "Brock's in the house," she gestured over her shoulder. "Callie is in there somewhere. I heard her but couldn't find her."

Michael shook his head as he stuck out a hand to help Claire up. "Callie isn't home."

*"I'm sorry about last night," Margaret blushed and crossed her arms in front of her nervously as Josie placed plates of food in front of the children.*

*"It's okay, Miss Margaret," Josie answered softly but she didn't make eye contact. She had had dreams the*

*previous night that she would never be able to discuss with anyone. Shameful, sinful dreams of soft skin against hers. She instantly felt the ache between her thighs at the thought.*

*"No, it's not," Margaret glanced at the children, but they weren't paying any attention. They were too busy babbling amongst themselves. "I don't know what came over me. I have been so lonely. I do love you, but…"*

*"It's okay, Miss Margaret," Josie finally raised her eyes to meet Margaret's. "I understand."*

## CHAPTER TWENTY-FOUR

Michael tapped his fingers on the counter of the librarian's desk, slightly impatient, waiting to be assigned a computer. Wi-Fi had been hooked up on the property just last week but something deep in his gut was telling him that what he needed to do shouldn't be done at home.

They rallied the entire crew and searched the entire house from top to bottom, including the dumbwaiter shaft that Claire had found herself locked in and had not found Brock. He believed her. She had shown him the message she'd received, and in the shuffle and confusion of the men being assigned to different areas of the house, he had caught a glimpse of several other frantic messages; messages asking about Donovan and Halloween night. He had felt the fist of uneasiness twist in his gut. Something wasn't right and everything in him was screaming to figure out why. He had kept waiting after the all clear had been given, and they were all certain that Brock was no longer in the house for Donovan to talk to Claire about the fireplace. He never mentioned it. That fist of uneasiness in his gut had grown into a dark web wrapping around his insides and filling them with dark and sickening warmth.

He had texted Emma and told her to get a hotel room for her and Bailey for the night. He didn't want her coming back to the house if Brock was still on the property, and he didn't like the vibes he was getting off Donovan. He liked the kid but he was hiding something and that just didn't sit well with Michael. The way he had been pounding away into that fireplace, almost obsessive in his actions, without even breaking a sweat, the way he hadn't even flinched at the two spirits standing behind him, the way he'd promised to talk to Claire about the fireplace before messing with it again–only to not say a word to her– Michael had the sneaking suspicion that Donovan would be back at the fireplace again tonight, and Claire would be none the wiser. He didn't like it.

So he'd arranged for Richie to go to a friend's house after school and dropped Callie off at the hotel with Emma. He hadn't stopped to speak to them, and he was ashamed to admit to himself that he couldn't look Bailey in the eye and felt guilty leaving Callie there, ignoring her terrified shrieks.

He plopped down at the assigned computer after what felt like an eternity and pulled up the web browser. He sat staring at the screen—not sure what to be looking for. Claire had already looked up the history of the property. There was nothing about Halloween as far as he could remember.

The thought came to him suddenly to try the back door. Try to find the information he needed another way. Instead of looking up Blackwood Manor and getting the same tired information he already knew about from Claire, he decided to narrow his search.

In the search bar, he typed in the name *Donovan O'Ryan.* He clicked on a few links, discarding them from his mind once finding pictures and realizing that they weren't the Donovan he was looking for. He hadn't thought it to be an overly common name, but apparently, it was. He went from link to link, Facebook page to Facebook page, and none of them was the man he was looking for. He let out the grunt of frustration and jumped at the *ssh* that was hissed at him from the librarian's desk. He gave her a half grin, mouthed *"Sorry,"* and turned back toward the screen.

*Think!* He told himself. *You've known him for months now. What have you been told that you can use to find him?*

He ran several scenarios through his head, disregarding them almost as soon as he thought of them. Driver's license? No, he's a drifter. He showed up hitchhiking. An only child? Sure, and so were millions of other people.

*"I was an army brat. My dad was in the military, and we moved a lot,"* Donovan's voice echoed in his head like an amplified speaker. *"We moved here when I was fifteen. I spent the night in Blackwood Manor to try to make friends and get some easy money. I knew I'd be respected because everyone was so terrified of this place."*

Michael remembered asking him how long they'd stayed, and Donovan had hesitated and said, *"Not long. But that experience never left me. It haunted me."*

*"Okay,"* Michael thought to himself. *"Now we're getting somewhere."* He let his mind wander slightly. His family moved a lot because his father was in the military, and they hadn't lived here for long. It was when he was fifteen. How old was Donovan now? Michael wasn't sure. He couldn't remember him ever saying. He forced his face into his mind and concentrated on it deeply. He had such a baby face. He looked eighteen, but he had to be older than that. Twenty-five? That didn't seem right but he didn't look much older.

He began trying new searches with different variations of *Donovan O'Ryan/military/Georgia-1987-1992.* No hits.

He was frustrated and hovered the mouse over the x button when he saw it. The words that he had almost overlooked flicked up at him now as if reaching out. It wasn't the blue link that stood out to him, but the tiny words underneath that gave insight into what was behind it. He saw the words **LIEUTENANT ROBERT O'RYAN SON MISSING.**

He almost disregarded it and didn't click but that voice came back to him, *"My dad was in the military."*

He clicked the link and began to read, holding his breath. It was a news article dated November 3, 1981.

*"Damn it!"* he thought. *"It can't be him. He's much too young."*

Still, something inside wouldn't let him exit the article. He began to read it.

Lieutenant Robert O'Ryan and his wife Angela are urging anyone with knowledge of the whereabouts of their fifteen-year-old son, Donovan, to contact the sheriff's department immediately. It is believed the boy is in serious danger.

Donovan has been missing since Halloween night. A group of teenagers attempted to spend the night and have a Halloween party in an abandoned plantation home, Blackwood Manor, and tragedy ensued.

One teen in the group stormed into the sheriff's office, bloody, speaking of an attack at the mansion. When emergency services arrived the bodies of four teenagers were found murdered. Donovan was not found. Police say that further examination of the mansion showed evidence of someone living inside. The theory is that the teens disturbed the vagrant who had been living on site. There has been no word from Donovan, and his parents say that is unlike him.

Anyone with information as to Donovan's location should contact the sheriff's office immediately.

There was a grainy black-and-white picture included and he zoomed in and felt the bottom of his stomach drop as he looked into the face of Donovan

O'Ryan. Looking exactly as he did now. He pressed the print button for the article and looked back over his shoulder at the librarian. She was watching the row of computers too closely. He didn't dare pull out his phone.

Instead, he opened Facebook and sent a message to Emma asking why she was asking Claire about Donovan and Halloween. He received a message back almost right away.

*Bailey finally told me about that night in the bathroom. She said the figure of a girl wearing a 1920s flapper dress attacked her, but she felt like she was a fake. That she had a kind of punk hair do. I remembered those were big in the '80s, and I thought I remembered Donovan saying the night that he and his friends stayed in Blackwood Manor was Halloween. He did, didn't he? I thought maybe he knew her.*

Michael opened a new search. This time, he searched Blackwood Manor, Halloween 1981. He found more articles about the tragedy, and he found a scanned memoriam that looked like it was from a yearbook of the teens that had lost their lives that night. He decided to print it and show the photo to Bailey. If one of them was the girl that attacked her, then they had their answer.

Emma lowered the printout that Michael had shown her and leaned against the bathroom counter in the motel room. She raised her hand to her chest, trying to still the rapid beating beneath, and her eyes stared him down with disbelief. She was visibly shaking.

"It's not possible. It just can't be possible," she finally let out in barely more than a breathy whisper.

"That's what I thought," Michael answered her. "But he was beating into that fireplace like the devil was chasing him and he was almost manic. He's been missing since Halloween that year. It all fits. Did Claire ever say that the Realtor mentioned murders on the property?"

"She mentioned a lot of deaths." Emma shrugged her shoulders. "That didn't seem so strange considering how old it is." Her eye went wide again, and she gripped his arm. "Do you think he killed them?"

Michael considered this but ultimately shook his head. "No. If he had he wouldn't come back to the scene of the crime and use his real name."

"Then what the hell happened?"

"I don't know. How has he not *aged*?"

Michael cracked the bathroom door and called for Bailey, stepping to the side once she approached to allow her room to squeeze inside.

He held the second printout in his hands, looking his daughter straight in the face. "Don't ask questions. Just answer me. Do you recognize anyone? From anywhere?" He held it out to her.

Bailey examined the photos and let out a small whimper. "Her," she simply pointed to a picture of one of the girls.

"Where do you recognize her from, sweetie?" Emma asked.

"From the bathroom," Bailey began to sob.

"Okay." Michael took his daughter in his arms, soothing her until her cries died down. "It's okay. You go on out and sit with your sister now."

Once Bailey had left the bathroom he looked down at the photo she had pointed out. "Stacey West," he said, flicking his eyes up to Emma. "She's one of Donovan's group that was killed that night."

Emma was shaking, and she leaned back against the counter. He picked up the printout again, scanning the names and faces. "Honey–"

"Not now. We'll talk about it later."

≈

Donovan checked the last window in the house to find it locked. They had checked the entire house once Claire had been found, and he had checked himself again about an hour before. Still, no Brock to be found anywhere. All the windows were locked. Still, he couldn't shake the uneasiness that had been building all day.

He turned from the window and looked into Claire's room through the open door. She was sitting in a rocking chair looking out her window at the expanse of open space that was lit up by the floodlights.

"He's still out there, you know," said a feminine voice behind him. He turned to see Stacey behind him. Her image was pale and almost translucent, but if he hadn't been looking for it, the effect would have been lost in the soft lighting of the hallway. Her emerald green flapper dress twinkled slightly under the lights.

She walked up next to him and peered into the room at Claire as well.

"Stacey," he said dryly.

"Donovan," she answered back with a dry chuckle.

He leaned his shoulder against the door frame. "Why'd you attack that girl?"

"I didn't mean to hurt her," she sighed. "It's not safe for her here. You know that as well as me. Someone had to get her out of here. I only meant to scare her."

She lazily sauntered forward a step and leaned her back against the door frame. She lifted her chin to look him in the eyes. "It's time to hustle, Donn-O. Shit's about to hit the fan."

"What do you want from me?" he snapped out in a growl. He heard Claire shift in her chair, and he leaned back out of view slightly and lowered his voice. "I'm doing everything that's been asked of me."

"That son of a bitch means to kill her. You can't take your time anymore. There's been enough death here."

"He means harm to us all," came another voice, and Josie stepped forth from the shadows, gliding up to them. "He's angry that nothing is going his way. He'll burn the house down if it comes to it."

Donovan shook his head in frustration. "He knows too much. How the hell did he get in here?"

"Oh, Donovan, use your brain! Isn't it obvious? Someone is helping him." Stacey's voice was low but bewildered. As though she couldn't believe anybody could be so dense.

"Him," Josie answered. "Under her instructions."

"Why would Margaret want to hurt Claire?"

"This is her house. It will always be her house. Now, the fireplace–"

"I promised Michael I wouldn't touch it until I talk to Claire."

"Then talk to her, "Stacey growled out.

"She's not going to believe it. Who would?"

"Most of what's happened around here shouldn't be believed. But everyone has seen it with their own eyes. She may surprise you. Besides, you don't have to tell her everything. Just tell her you think there is a body in the fireplace."

Donovan rapped on the door before he lost his nerve and stepped forward into the room as Claire turned from the window.

"Donovan." she laughed nervously.

He gave a quick glance over his shoulders and no longer saw Josie and Stacey.

"Hey," he grabbed a chair from the wall and placed it down facing her before taking a seat. "I need to talk to you. It's not going to be easy, but I need you to hear me out, okay?"

"Did you find Brock? Or something that belongs to him?" she asked nervously.

"No, no. Nothing like that." He glanced down at the ground and then looked up. "You know the fireplace in the parlor? How the dimensions don't match and it's so much newer than the rest of the house?"

"Yeah."

"Well, I was working down there today. Before everything happened, working on the brick as I have been. I saw something inside, so I tried to open it up more. It was dangerous and I shouldn't have tried to take it down that fast. It was a momentary lapse in judgment. The fact of the matter is, though, there was something in there."

Claire leaned forward, unblinking. "What do you think it is?"

"Well, as I said, I didn't get in. The more I think about it, the more I'm thinking it's probably a body. Maybe even Gloria."

"Gloria? What makes you think it's a body?"

"Well, there isn't much space in there. There are no doors so it's not storage. There are no blueprints for the house so I can't even determine when it was added. It's the only logical explanation as far as I can see."

Claire was about to reply when the floodlights went dark suddenly. She and Donovan both rose to their feet and peered out the window, looking for any hint of movement in the darkness. It was simply impossible to see.

## CHAPTER TWENTY-FIVE

Brock waited in his tree in the woods for hours, meticulously watching the house and grinding his teeth until his gums bled. He was still pissed that he hadn't been able to kill Claire in the dumbwaiter shaft like he had planned or smash in Donovan's skull.

This big property didn't lend nearly as many opportunities as it should. There were too many people, and he was growing tired of it.

When he finally got the signal from his new friend and the floodlights went dark, Brock shimmied down out of the tree and felt the waistband of his jeans to make sure that his new gun was secure.

≈

*Enough is enough*, Michael thought to himself as he marched through the cemetery with the shovel thrown over his shoulder. He waited until his family was fast asleep in the motel and driven back to Blackwood Manor.

Emma didn't know what he was planning. She would have panicked, and he damn well knew it. But he was tired of this. He was tired of people he loved and cared about getting hurt. Tired of the mindless attacks that this place was known for. It was a beautiful property, and for that, he was glad it was getting restored. The attacks though, the danger, needed to be eliminated. The only way to do that was to find out what the hell happened so many years before and what the hell that had to do with that Halloween night.

He hated that he had to do this in secret. It was despicable. He knew that. He knew if he told anyone, they would throw a fit and stop him. That's why he parked on the road and walked his way up, stalking through the woods so he would not be seen in the flash of the floodlights.

Thankful that the cemetery could not be seen from the house, he scanned the tombstones until he found the one he wanted.

He looked down at it for a moment, his face lined with sadness and defeat. Continually flashing through his mind were the facts that he did know, Margaret had accidentally killed her daughter, Lucy Blackwood and Josie died the same day, Margaret was forever changed, Donovan's group had been murdered in the house that Halloween night and Donovan himself had gone missing. So was Margaret's secret child. It was all connected. Every instinct in his body told him that.

*But how?* His brain screamed, echoing inside his skull. He looked down at the grave of Lucy Blackwood and let out a long breath, which ended up being an anguished moan, like the air slowly being let out of a balloon.

"God help me," he muttered out loud and brought the shovel down into the earth. He shoveled as quickly as his muscles would allow, listening to the thud of the shovelfuls of dirt as they hit the ground, strategically out of place so as not to hit any other graves. The sound of the dirt echoed in his ears, and Michael forced himself to keep going as the tears flowed down his face.

His muscles were on fire, and he was covered in sweat, pushing through while trying to not think about the barbaric nature of what he was doing until he heard the thud of the shovel hitting something solid.

He hopped down into the grave and gently pushed the dirt away from the old coffin. It was tiny, too tiny, and the wood was split and warped, really showing its age. He pulled at the lid of the coffin, expecting it to be heavy, to possibly even need to pry it open, but it lifted right up off the hinges, much lighter than he thought it should be. He set it aside, careful to be gentle, and looked down into the coffin at the skeleton of the girl.

He ignored the bugs and the worms, forced himself to look past them climbing over and through her body, and allowed himself to take her in. Her skeleton was small, much too small. The clothes covering her were decomposed and rotting, but he could see enough to know that they had been nothing more than rags to begin with. Her skull seemed oversized compared to the rest of her body. Her eyes sockets were huge, and even now, empty except for the fat worm sliding out of the left one, which appeared to be staring at him.

Something wasn't right. The feeling washed over him in a chill that he couldn't quite explain. He very desperately wanted to lift himself right out of the grave and make a beeline for the house. but an invisible force appeared to be holding him firmly to the ground.

He reached out gently, not even knowing why he was doing it. He didn't notice the floodlights going dark. He didn't notice because there was now a glow surrounding this tiny skeleton that he was oblivious to, giving him just enough visibility to find what he needed to find.

He grasped the shoulders of the skeleton as gently as he could. The crackle of the bones as he lifted her and they broke away, sent a shudder through him, freezing him in place, unsure of what to do next.

*One hand behind her neck, easy now,* some unknown voice echoed in his head and he slowly moved one hand to the back of her neck to try to prevent more damage and slowly turned her. The skull broke free and right into his hand.

He let out a whimper, but he did not recoil. Instead, he felt something not right beneath his fingers. He turned the skull over in his hands, the dirty tangle of what was left of the blonde hair skirting across his knuckles and looked into the massive gaping hole in the back. A chunk of the skull was missing and what was left was caved in unnaturally. He glanced down into the coffin for the remainder of the skull, figuring it had broken apart in all these years, but it was not there.

The hand not supporting the skull gently skimmed the remaining hair, and that's when he saw it, the old stain of congealed blood. Someone had bashed this girl's skull in. How do you do that accidentally?

He turned the skull back over in his hand and let out a gasp as he jumped, nearly dropping the skull. Except it was no longer a skull.

In his hand, Michael held the head of a young girl. A girl with eyes that seemed ready to pop out of their sockets and blood running down her face, plastering her blonde hair to her face.

"L-L-Lucy?" he stammered.

She shook her head no. He physically felt the head turning in his palm.

His eyes went wide. "Gloria?"

Her eyes blinked and there was a trace of a smile puckering at her lips.

"Where is Lucy?" Michael asked.

"She'll never let her leave," Gloria said in a tiny voice. Her eyes flickered over his shoulder, and she whispered, "Watch out for the bad man."

Michael turned his head as he heard the crunch of boots in leaves.

Then an audible gunshot broke the silence of the night.

≈

"Michael!" Donovan yelled as Michael crawled out of the grave. Claire was trailing alongside him, clutching at his arm. He lowered the gun and reached down a hand to help pull him out. "I nearly shot you, man! What the hell are you doing?"

All three of them looked down into the grave at the open coffin and the tiny broken skeleton.

Claire swung her head towards Michael, her eyes wide with shock. "You dug her up?"

"It's sick, I know," he said in way of a half-hearted apology. "But I had a good reason. There are so many things not adding up around here and we needed to know. Margaret's letter said she killed Lucy by accident, but Maggie said she died of scarlet fever! Did no one think that was strange?"

"Dude," Donovan's eyes still hadn't left the grave. "That's fucked up."

"Oh, I can name several things that are fucked up," Michael spat out, fury bubbling up inside him. "Like teenage boys going missing in the house when all their friends are murdered only to show up thirty years later somehow as baby faced as the day he went missing."

They locked eyes, and Donovan's mouth was a thin line.

"What are you talking about?" Claire asked, her eyebrows furrowed in a crease of confusion. She turned towards Donovan. "Donovan, what's he talking about? You're our age. You must be…" she trailed off because now she could see it.

Donovan's face transformed before her eyes as though a veil had been lifted. His lines smoothed, the five o'clock shadow was gone, his eyes became brighter, his hair filled in slightly thicker, and his body leaned. He no longer had the muscle she was used to seeing. He was a teenager.

Donovan pointed a finger at Michael. "What you need to understand about that–"

"What?" Claire interrupted, jumping slightly. "You went missing from the house? Your friends were murdered?"

Donovan looked down at the ground, defeated. "Yes."

"What the hell?" she exclaimed. "Did you kill them?"

"No!" he looked deep into her eyes. "I didn't. I–"

"Why don't you tell us what really happened that night?" Michael asked.

"I was the new kid in town. Just like I already told you. I'd only made one friend. People thought I was weird. They thought I'd get them in trouble coming from a military family. That my dad would be too strict. Ty was my only friend. We'd been here about six weeks. Ty started telling me about Blackwood Manor. The history. How haunted it was supposed to be. He said that his girlfriend really wanted to do an overnight Halloween party here. To show how badass we all were. Most kids were too terrified of the place to even think about it."

"How'd they get you to go?" Claire asked.

"It wasn't hard," he admitted. "I wanted friends. I didn't believe in hauntings anyway. I figured if I came out here, I'd get some credit for having the balls to do it. Plus, Ty said his girlfriend had a single friend she wanted to set me up with. Friends and a potential girlfriend? Hell yeah, I did it."

"So, what went wrong?"

"It was cool at first. We experienced stuff right away. Whispers. Doors slamming. Shadows on the walls. We only had tiny pen lights, so it was creepier. Then Stacey, the girl they were trying to set me up with, went to find a bathroom. A couple of minutes passed, and we heard her screaming. When we found her, she was dead. She was crumpled on the bathroom floor with her throat slit. Blood everywhere."

"Jesus," Michael whispered. He tried to back away but felt some dirt give at his heel and realized he was on the edge of the grave.

"We decided to split up to look for whoever did it. Stupid," he shook his head. "So stupid. Fifteen-year-old kids without weapons. I searched a couple of rooms and didn't find anything. I went into another room and get stopped by Josie. She scared the shit out of me. She told me I needed to go. That I wasn't safe. Then I heard another scream and turned to see Ty falling over the railing to the staircase and I see this dirty dude with long hair looking down at him. Then he turns to look at me and he grinned. It was the vilest grin you could possibly think of.

"I didn't think. I just bolted for the stairs and barely missed his fingers as I flew down them. The door opened and a little girl came in. Eight. Maybe nine years old. She was calling out for Donna, Ty's girlfriend. I scooped her up and ran for the woods. First, she fought me. Hitting my shoulders with her little fists. Then she was screaming at me to run faster because he was right behind us."

Michael's attention was grabbed by something in the distance. "You guys expecting company?"

They followed his gaze to see a soft glow in one of the windows. The light was from a cell phone, as though someone was trying to see without giving away their position by turning on a light.

"Someone is in the house," Claire whispered.

"Someone not of the ghostly variety for once," Donovan chimed in.

"It's that son of a bitch, Brock," Michael growled.

The three of them hunkered together in a protective throng and made their way toward the house.

*"We're going to hell," Margaret whispered. She had her back pressed against the headboard and the sheet pulled up tight over her naked breasts. Josie did the same on the opposite side. She was still enamored by the glow. The smiles and kisses that had been building for months had reached her. She had felt all along that she wasn't the only one who felt it.*

*Then finally those kisses turned into more. Her naked skin brushed against Margaret's, her mouth on her breast, Margaret's head between her thighs, finding that sweet, blissful spot. Every need, every want she felt for years had exploded through her body as she found herself lost in it.*

*"Why would we go to hell?" she asked, barely able to hold back her blissful grin.*

*"That was wicked. Positively wicked," Margaret whispered. "On so many levels."*

*They heard the sounds of horses neighing in the distance, and their eyes met. Josie rose from the bed, ignoring her nakedness, and strode to the window to peek out. "Soldiers. Yankees." She turned back to Margaret, terror in her eyes. "There are so many of them."*

*"We're being punished," Margaret croaked out.*

*Then they heard the sound of the front door banging against the wall downstairs.*

## CHAPTER TWENTY-SIX

When they entered the house the air felt different. It was heavier. Suffocating. Claire sucked her breath in, trying to hold it as long as possible to allow herself to have more oxygen. She felt like there was a weight on her shoulders. All the hair on the back of her neck raised on end and her arms erupted with a mass of goose bumps.

They stopped at the parlor door and Michael slowly backed into it, grabbing a fireplace poker from the stand next to the hearth. He slowly approached them and stopped as Donovan held a finger to his lips and pointed at his feet before bending to remove his shoes.

Claire and Michael did the same thing, and they re-banded together before slowly making their way through the dining room door and back towards the kitchen. The cell phone light they had seen had been coming from the kitchen.

Donovan put a hand to her side and pushed her firmly but gently behind him and Michael. She didn't object. She was the only one without a weapon, and she was fairly certain she knew who the owner of that light was. She didn't notice that Donovan's hand was ice cold and that her own blood seemed to be thick with ice water. She didn't notice that her heart was pounding in her throat. She only knew that she was shaking and that this walk seemed to be taking forever.

When they reached the kitchen, it was empty. Donovan did not lower his gun but strode over to the breaker box that was hanging next to the window.

"Lines were cut," he muttered, fingering the severed wires in his hand.

"Check this out," Michael said. He was gesturing toward the door to the servant's stairwell that seemed to have a light coming from within.

Donovan strode towards it and Claire suddenly got hit by a sickening twist in her gut. Her heart beat extremely fast and her breath seemed to stop. She froze in place as the men walked through the door.

"NOOO!!!!" she screamed just as the massive shelf that had once blocked it shot across the room, back into its original place. It moved with such speed and spontaneity that several boxes and cans flew off the shelves, hitting the walls. She heard them yelling from the other side of the door and saw the back of the shelf move in rhythm with their beating. They were locked in, and she was out here without a weapon. She saw a Union soldier step out from the shadows and he grinned at her manically. She knew in an instant that this man was Gloria's father. She also knew he was working with someone else. Someone very much alive. The owner of the cell phone light.

She dove for the butcher block to find the knives gone. She frantically began opening drawers but they were not there.

The door to the pantry opened and Brock emerged from the darkness, the menacing, wild stare of his face exaggerated by the tiny sliver of moonlight that lit it up. He walked towards her, and she grasped the countertop.

"Come on, Claire," he finally said. "I thought you were smarter than this."

He swung out, and she didn't see the pistol in his hand until a split second before he slammed it into her skull.

≈

Emma sat up in the hotel bed, gasping for breath. She had the old dream again. Played over those months when she and Claire had been children. Then that dream had merged into flashes of the images of Bailey when she had been possessed mixed with flashes of something else. Images of Margaret and Josie naked in bed together when the soldiers arrived. Pictures of Claire in the dark in Blackwood Manor, desperately searching the drawers. Images of that door. The door to the staircase that she loathed so much. A shelf slid across the floor with alarming speed.

"Mom?"

Emma jerked her head to the other bed. Bailey was sitting up straight as a board, her hair plastered to her face. Her nightgown fused against her skin with sweat. "They're in trouble."

Emma wanted to blow it off. To pull the covers over her head the way she had as a girl. But she saw the knowledge in her daughter's eyes. She had seen what Emma had seen. Maybe more. She was the golden warrior after all.

"It's time," Bailey said, more insistently this time. "We have to go back."

≈

Claire felt time stand still as she began to fall from the force of the blow. Brock hit her again after she lost her footing, and she felt her nose explode. A fountain of blood flowed, and the crunch of bone was agonizing. She hit the floor with a force that sent shocked pain through her ribs and stomach, knocking the breath out of her.

She struggled for breath. She couldn't seem to get enough air into her lungs and breathing in through her nose just brought the coppery taste of blood and movement from lodged bones. She reached forward and tried to crawl around the island. She heard the echo of the men pounding on the makeshift staircase door, but it was as though she were hearing the sound through earmuffs.

She felt her ankle wrenched back, and she was suddenly flipped onto her back. Brock loomed over her and suddenly she was back to a time when he'd attacked the moment she walked through the door, immobilizing her before she could react. He'd stood over her with a knife. What had she done then? How had she gotten out?

She struggled to remember, but she couldn't think of anything but the sheer terror standing over her. A monster in man's clothing. A monster without a conscience. A monster who was unaccustomed to the word no, and as a result, would not let go of the one person who had walked away.

He smiled at her then. A slow, devilish sneer that began from a hard thin line of pursed lips and slowly ripped through this face, going ear to ear, his lips peeling back over his teeth that were bared, reminding her of something from a vampire movie. There was no light in his eyes. He was deranged. More so than she had ever seen him.

"Get up," a sharp voice said from behind her. She bent her head back and she saw Josie standing behind a throng of other spirits that were preventing her from stepping forward.

"Get up!" Josie screamed, more insistent this time, "Now!"

≈

"Son of a bitch!" Donovan slammed his fist into the back of the shelf.

Michael turned to run up the staircase, damaged or not, to try to reach the next floor, but Donovan grabbed his arm.

"There's no time!"

"We have to try!" Michael growled, shrugging Donovan's hand off his arm.

"He's going to kill her!" Donovan screamed.

Michael nearly snapped back but something in Donovan's eyes stopped him.

Donovan turned and put one hand on either side of the door frame and stood with his feet shoulder-width apart.

Michael's breath was taken away at the sight before him. Donovan was emitting white light. Subtle at first, but then the light spread until he was completely engulfed in it. Just as Michael was going to look away from the brightness, the shelf exploded into thousands of tiny pieces, flying in every direction.

≈

Claire swung her arms wildly as Brock lowered himself, pinning her to the floor and putting his hands around her throat. She couldn't breathe. Her lungs were burning, her eyes were watering, and her vision was blurry. She stared up into his face, grinning down at her devilishly as he choked the life out of her.

Her hands made contact but with no strength, slapping uselessly at his arms and sliding down.

*"I'm going to die here,"* she thought to herself. *"I'm going to die on my kitchen floor. I'm going to die on my kitchen floor and then be stuck here with all these sad and angry people."*

Then she heard an explosion and she saw that Brock heard it too. He turned to look towards the staircase and his grip loosened slightly.

She attempted to reach out again to hit him, but her arm fell to the ground.

Brock was thrown off her with so much force that she felt air rush over her, and he slammed into the wall. Donovan walked into her field of vision surrounded by a blinding white light.

Brock was then thrown against the opposite wall. He yelled out in fright.

She barely registered that she was coughing and had wrapped her own hands around her throat when she felt firm hands on her shoulders, pulling her to her feet. She was pulled into Michael's chest where she buried her head, refusing to look toward the screams of her ex-husband.

"Please! No more!" he yelled out in a choked sob.

"Alright," Donovan's voice boomed out.

Then there was the sound of a gunshot.

Claire let out a strangled scream into Michael's shoulder but he pulled her back and spoke to her softly. "It's okay."

She turned to see Donovan standing over a lifeless Brock who was lying in a pool of blood.

The light around Donovan was reducing and beginning to turn a soft shade of red before it completely disappeared.

"Donovan!" a voice yelled out.

All three turned to see an army of spirits gathered in the kitchen in various stages of period clothing. The one who had spoken was a man in the front of the group. A tall Black man in a torn shirt and suspenders.

"Miss Margaret will be displeased," he spoke. His voice was strong and deep. "We do not interfere."

"That's the biggest line of shit I think I've heard in this house," Donovan snapped out coldly.

"Donovan?" Claire asked carefully. Her voice was hoarse and cracked, barely more than a whisper.

He turned toward her, and she gasped. He now had cuts on the side of his mouth, pointing downward, giving him a permanent frown.

Suddenly, she remembered everything Sadie had told her about auras. The white light. The altered appearance following the attack on Brock.

"You're a ghost?" she choked out.

He didn't answer but there was pain in his eyes.

"You've been a ghost this whole time?"

"I tried to tell you–" he answered, his voice weak.

She stormed off, running past him into the dining room. He turned to follow her.

The tall ghost spoke again. "This isn't over, Donovan."

Donovan looked at him reproachfully and then walked from the room.

*Two months later, Josie walked into the master bedroom where Margaret was lying in bed, pale and sweaty, clutching a basin where she had repeatedly been sick. They had been tormented by the soldiers, and both of them were raped. They didn't fight after the soldiers threatened to do it* to the children. So night after night, they had both lain down in bed for the men, praying that it would be over soon.

Josie couldn't help but be thankful that she had had a wonderful experience with Margaret before. That she could have lovely memories from it, and not only the memories of pain.

Margaret had been sick for a week now and the men had only vacated two days before. She hadn't spoken to her lover. Had only looked after the children and tried to give them back some sense of normalcy. This was the first time she had been in the bedroom since her interlude with Margaret, and she wished it were under better circumstances.

"Miss Margaret?" she asked timidly. "Shall I go for the doctor?"

"It won't do any good," Margaret snapped out and set the basin aside. "I am with child."

"You're certain?"

She nodded. "How am I to explain this? To bear a child that is not my husband's. It is my greatest shame."

"You were attacked. Surely you can not be blamed."

"Who will believe that after–" she broke off and hung her head in shame. "God punishes us for our sins, Josie. It'll come back around."

# CHAPTER TWENTY-SEVEN

"Found some candles!" Michael yelled as he pulled candles and matches from the workbench in the basement. He lit one and made his way back up the stairs. He saw Donovan leaning against the door frame to the parlor, looking in.

He approached and saw Claire sitting on the sofa with her knees drawn up against her chest. He looked at Donovan and couldn't help but feel bad for him. He had mistrusted him when he'd learned he went missing from the house but now he saw the pain.

The pain of watching his friends drop like flies, being stuck in the house with all the spirits, and making a sacrifice to save Claire even though it was basically condemning him to damnation.

"How much trouble are you in?" he asked him.

Donovan lifted his eyes toward him. There was a flicker of something that Michael could not quite identify but Donovan answered him.

"Probably a lot. We aren't supposed to interfere with the living, but I've seen so much in my time here to know it happens. Margaret is ultimately the one in charge. So, no matter what she does we're supposed to bend to her will.

"Did you know that Gloria was in Lucy's grave?"

"No," Donovan shook his head. "I'm not even sure any of us knew that. Josie has a small group of us tasked with getting Claire to help Gloria. I assumed it was by finding her body, but if she was in Lucy's grave, I don't see the point."

"Well, she'll come around," Michael nodded toward Claire.

"Yeah, but in time? Doubtful," Donovan shook his head and sighed. "It's about to get nasty. The spirits here are divided. Some are downright mean and nasty and want to clear out anyone in their path and others want to help the living in hopes of having the chord severed."

"The chord?"

"The chord keeping us here. We're supposed to be able to get out if we find the right living person to help or if we do enough to help the living. As far as I know, none of them has succeeded."

"Is that why you've been helping Claire?" Michael asked gently.

"Twofold," Donovan admitted. "It was a big conspiracy. Josie always took pity on me. She had always said I shouldn't be here, that the rules were broken by keeping me here in the first place, and that if I did something exemplary, I would be released. She convinced me to go to Claire, help her, gain her trust, and get her to help Gloria. Margaret never would have allowed it. Beyond the obvious reasons, she sensed something in Claire that scared her. That alone gives many of us hope that Claire is the one. We told her that by doing this I could make it easier to subdue Claire at an opportune time."

"And you think that plan is about to backfire?"

"Judging by what happened back there, the spirits divided and–"

"And the dead body in the kitchen?" Michael finished for him.

Donovan inclined his head.

"By killing him, you didn't make him invincible, did you?"

"He'll have power, but he won't know what to do with it yet. He'll be confused for a while. Might not even realize he's dead. And once he does, he'll have no clue how to control his powers. Once he figures it out though–"

"Then why did you do it?"

"She's the one," Donovan answered, his eyes ironically tired. "I know she is. I couldn't let him kill her. Her power would have been useless if she was dead. Plus," Donovan sighed and looked deeply into Michael's eyes, "seeing her so helpless–Claire of all people, that this man had that kind of power over her and used it in this way, it enraged me."

"Why are you so sure that Claire is the one?"

"Margaret is scared of her. She usually views the living as toys, not sources of fear. It means something."

"So, she's the golden warrior?"

"No," Donovan said. "That's a whole other level. Claire can absolve the innocent. Those of us stuck here without anything marring our purity. The golden warrior can cleanse the place and destroy all traces of evil. Claire can make a mark on her own, but with the golden warrior—even we don't know what to expect."

"Do you know who that is?"

"Yes."

"Who?"

Donovan looked him in the eye and did not bother to blink. "You're not going to like it."

≈

Emma swung her car into the driveway and her heart was racing. Her breath caught at the overwhelming blackness. No floodlights. No lights in the house. The house was almost entirely impossible to see, even from the driveway. She felt it in her heart and soul, in her mind. Something was wrong. Something was *very* wrong.

She pressed down harder on the accelerator, willing the car to go faster, but the long drive seemed to be never-ending, freezing them in time.

"Mom, watch out!" Bailey screamed suddenly.

Emma slammed on the brakes before she saw what her daughter was seeing. A woman on the road appeared, almost as if from thin air. She was wearing a full skirt that draped to the ground, her hair was done up into a tight bun. She had horns protruding from her head, her eyes were red. The claws hanging down from her hands were like shiny razors, illuminated only by the headlights of the car. The skin, she could see even in the dark, was a series of blue scales.

"Margaret," Emma breathed out in realization just before the car spun out of her control. She groped helplessly at the wheel but could not gain back control of the spin.

She saw the tree only seconds before slamming into it.

≈

Claire's head jerked towards the window at the sound of the crash. She got up from her place on the parlor sofa and approached the windows. She saw the glow of the headlights of a car that was not moving about halfway up the long drive but was surprised to find she felt nothing.

Her eyes flickered to her slight reflection in the window glass and cocked her head in amusement at the sight of her destroyed nose. It was nothing more than a flap of skin under the blanket of blood that covered the rest of her face.

*"Funny. It doesn't even hurt anymore,"* she thought to herself as she raised a finger to poke at her nose, registering no pain and finding the blood dried.

She barely heard the screams of the men and the loud banging of the front door as it hit the wall of the entryway as they rushed out towards the distant car.

"Claire," a voice said behind her.

She briefly raised her head, seeing the figures of Donovan and Michael far off from the house. So who was the man behind her? The man with the vaguely familiar voice?

She slowly began to turn around.

≈

"Bailey!" Emma was screaming hysterically when Michael and Donovan reached her.

The sight of her was frightening. The windshield exploded inward on impact, and she had a large piece of glass sticking out of her forehead, with blood rushing down her face like a warm and sticky river.

She had undone her seat belt, but her leg was pinned beneath her. The car had flipped, trapping her.
The passenger seat was empty.

"Bailey!" she screamed again, her voice growing hoarse. She ignored the figures of the men outside the car. She screamed again and again as one of the men climbed up on top of the car and wrenched the passenger door open.

"Emma! Emma!" Michael screamed sharply, cutting off her screams. He reached inside. "Take my hand!"

"I can't! My leg is pinned!"

Michael turned towards Donovan. "Get the tractor."

Michael turned back towards his wife as Donovan disappeared off into the distance. He slid down inside the car as gently as he could to try to evaluate how bad a shape her leg was in.

"Forget about me!" she cried out. "Go get Bailey!"

"Bailey was with you?" he asked, shocked, and dread coursed through his veins in building terror.

"Yes! Margaret–" her voice broke off, and she began to weep.

"Did Margaret take her?"

"Bailey threw Margaret away from her somehow and then ran into the woods. Margaret headed after her."

Michael's heart sank. Bailey was here. Of all nights. This wasn't going to be good. He reached into his pocket and pulled out his phone and was immediately annoyed to see that he only had one bar. "You've got to be fucking kidding me," he muttered and dialed the first crew member he could find, Brad.

"Hey, Brad," he said hurriedly when Brad answered the phone. "It's Michael. Listen. I don't have good service so I'm depending on you. I need you to gather the crew and get them here. Bad shit's gone down."

There was the crackle of static on the line and Brad's voice cutting in and out.

"What -*crackle*- say-*crackle*-to-*crackle*- there?"

"I don't give two shits what you tell them!" Michael uncharacteristically bellowed. "Just get them here, Brad!"

The line went silent.

"Brad! BRAD!" Michael screeched and then threw his phone into the night in frustration.

He turned to the sound of the roar coming down the driveway towards them. Donovan was coming. He breathed a sigh of relief and looked back toward Emma.

"I'm okay," she nodded. "Go. Go find her. He'll get me out."

Michael leaned down and kissed her. "I love you."

"I love you too. Now go."

≈

"*One,*" Bailey thought to herself quietly as she clutched the tree branch. "*Two.*" she exhaled slowly and narrowed her eyes into the darkness. She couldn't see anything. "*Three.*" Images from the crash were trying to force their way back into her mind, but she clamped her eyelids tightly shut and continued her exercise. "*Four.*" Her eyes were still tightly shut but she felt the creep of tiny hairs rising on her arms and on the back of her neck. She could feel the goose bumps peppering her skin. "*Five,*" She felt a sense of calm, cautious calm—but calm nonetheless wash over her, and allowed herself to open her eyes.

She still couldn't see anything, but her breathing slowed, and now she was able to think. She had lost the woman. The woman from the seance. She now knew the woman was Margaret Blackwood. But she had no idea why she was after her.

She shimmied her way down the tree she had climbed in the dark and tried to find her bearings. She had run aimlessly into the woods after her mother screamed at her to run. She had refused at first, wanting to help her mother out of the pinned car. She smelled gasoline and was scared that it would blow up with her mother still inside. But then Margaret had started to advance on her; looking positively evil and she just ran into the woods without thinking. She had run for a long time, getting more and more lost by the minute. When she heard the crunch of leaves nearby she darted up the closest tree—something she didn't even know she could do.

Now, she looked in every direction, looking for any sign of light, trying to remember which direction she had come from. *Why did I have to go and run into the woods?* She internally chastised herself. *"I've never even* been *in the woods. Why didn't I run towards the house? There were other people at the house!"*

"Stop it," she muttered to herself out loud. She chose a direction and began to walk, wishing there was at least moonlight to guide her,. but there was only darkness and stillness for miles around her.

She walked about ten minutes before she felt lightheaded, and she crumpled to her knees and scooted up so that her back was to a tree and tried her counting and breathing exercises again. This time, it wasn't working. She was fairly certain that her vision was blurred, but it was hard to tell when the only thing she could see were trees.

"Bailey," said a soft voice right behind her.

She jumped, let out a squeak, and spun around. A little girl, maybe eight years old, with a blood-stained nightgown stood there peeking at her from the opposite side of the tree. She didn't look menacing, but she didn't look particularly inviting either. She walked around until she was right in front of Bailey and knelt. "You need to rest."

"I can't," Bailey shook her head. "She's gonna find me."

"She's gone. She got exactly what she wanted. To separate you. You're getting too far out."

"Good," Bailey muttered. "I don't want to go back to that place. Let me come out on the other side."

"No," the girl said sharply. "You are too important. You all are. You need to save your energy. You're going to need it."

"No," Bailey said stubbornly. "What for?"

"You have people depending on you."

"Who? A bunch of dead people who mean nothing to me?"

"Them, yes," the girl nodded. "Not just them. The people you care about too. The living and the dead."

The girl looked up at something just past Bailey's shoulder and nodded her head, only slightly.

Bailey felt something make contact with the back of her head and pain spread throughout her body. She slumped to the ground as her eyes began to feel heavy. Just before she slipped into unconsciousness she heard Lucy Blackwood mutter, "I'm so sorry."

## CHAPTER TWENTY-EIGHT

2:35 am. Emma looked up from her wristwatch and exhaled. They were approaching the witching hour and she didn't like it.

She was sitting on the parlor sofa with her leg thrown across Michael's lap as he dressed her wound.

Donovan had dug her out of the car and helped her back to the house, and Michael had searched the woods for almost two hours. He hadn't found Bailey, and she wasn't responding to his calls either.

The entire crew had shown up around two and Michael had sent them out to search in three-man teams, very similar to the search for Brock.

Donovan walked back into the room and sat down in the chair directly in front of Emma. He had been searching the house for Claire once they all got back to the house and realized that she was nowhere to be found. Bailey and Claire were both missing. This was bad. This was very bad.

"So, how did you know?" he asked her, jumping straight to the point.

"Excuse me?" she asked.

"You were asking everyone if I was here as a teenager on Halloween. How did you know I'm dead?"

"What?" He had her attention now. Her eyes were wide as saucers and her mouth went completely dry.

"You didn't know?" he asked, surprised.

"Umm–no," she had a chill, but she was still fascinated.

"Well, I guess the cat's out of the bag anyway," he shrugged his shoulders.

"He had to exhibit ghostly powers on Brock tonight," Michael attempted to explain gently. "He was telling me his story when we heard the car crash."

Donovan repeated what he had told both Claire and Michael throughout the night before continuing. "I heard that little girl tell me he was getting closer just before I felt my legs go out from under me. We hit the ground and then he was over us with a knife, looking wild and crazy. I told the girl to run. All I saw was this small girl with big brown eyes and light caramel skin, and I somehow knew she was more important than me. I told her to run."

His eyes were locked on Emma now and she broke his gaze, looking down and running a hand up each of her arms.

Michael caught the tension between them. "Did I miss something?" he asked.

"Do you remember?" Donovan asked.

She nodded and turned her gaze to Michael. "I was that little girl."

"What?" Michael asked, confused.

"Do you remember how I told you my sister, Donna, was murdered when I was eight?"

He nodded.

"It was here," she gently said. "She was going to a Halloween party with her boyfriend and a few other people. About ten minutes before she was supposed to leave, our parents got a call that our grandma had a stroke and was being taken to the hospital. They told her she'd have to watch me and left. She was so mad."

She smiled a grim smile and shook her head in disbelief. "She decided she didn't want to cancel the party, so instead of taking me trick or treating like she was supposed to, I was held captive in the back seat of the car. I remember I was excited because I was going to get to go to a big girl party. But when we got there, she told me to stay in the car. That kids weren't allowed. I sat there a while, but eventually I needed the bathroom. I got out and started walking to the house. I was almost there when the screaming started.

"I was eight years old and stupid and walked in anyway. This guy comes running at me. It was like it was out of nowhere because it was so dark. He picked me up and threw me over his shoulder. I thought he was crazy at first, that he was trying to kidnap me. Then I saw the crazy guy with the knife chasing us, getting closer and closer. I yelled at the guy to run faster, but the man tackled us, and I hit the ground hard. The next thing I saw was the guy that took me from the house wrestling the man and yelling at me to run. The look on his face as he screamed at me to run will always stick with me. He had to have known he was going to die to save me, a stupid kid he didn't even know."

Emma turned to face Donovan. "I knew you felt familiar, comfortable. I just couldn't remember why. I didn't even remember what happened. I was so young. After Donna's death, my family moved to New York. My parents just couldn't handle it. Too many memories. I met Claire during my first week at school there and we became instant best friends.

"I don't know if she ever mentioned it or not, probably not, but we survived a pretty horrific experience with a demon as kids. Claire became possessed just like my Bailey did. She needed an exorcism. She blocked it all out. When she was possessed, my mom was killed."

Donovan nodded, ready to let her continue, but Michael interrupted her.

"What made you start to remember, babe?" he asked.

"A little bit at a time but not fully until..." she broke off and looked at her watch again. 2:50. "When I started college, I decided to come back here. I always felt a piece of me was missing, but my d was so angry with me. We didn't talk until Grandma died. I felt panic and dread the very first time I drove past Blackwood Manor. My throat closed up, my chest hurt, and I felt drawn to it in a way that scared me. That feeling only increased more and more as I continued to drive past. It never registered that this was the place from my childhood. Then I started visiting Claire and felt like the place was really familiar. Still, it didn't hit until you showed me the yearbook photo." She squeezed her husband's hand. "Donna's photo popped off the page and it was like a slap in the face. She was in the Halloween Massacre at Blackwood Manor. I remembered she'd been killed on Halloween but that was about it. But it all hit me then."

She looked at Donovan with deep lines of regret lining her brow. "I remembered you talking about Blackwood Manor and Halloween, and I realized it had to have been the same party. That's when I remembered the boy who saved me. You. I guess I had convinced myself that you were fine since they didn't find your body. You look older. Guess it just never really clicked for me. But I am sorry that I never told anybody about you. Maybe your body would have been found and you wouldn't be trapped here."

Michael shook his head. "I'm so confused about so many things. How were you able to age if you died that night?" he asked Donovan.

"And how the hell did you and Claire get dragged back here?" he added to Emma.

"I can answer both," Donovan said, giving them a grim smile. "Because I committed the ultimate sacrifice to save Emma I have the unique ability to change my appearance at will. Nobody else can do that. I knew the easiest way to get on Claire's good side and hide in plain sight wasn't by being a scrawny, pimply faced teenager. I aged myself up to get 'hired' into the crew.

"I got the ability by pure luck. I happened to save someone very important."

It was Emma's turn to be confused. "How was I important? How am I important?"

"Because of who you are. You see, Josie's older brother, Isaiah, was the foreman and he ran off with a bunch of the other slaves. He tried to get Josie to go with him but she wouldn't leave Margaret. This was before Margaret lost it, of course."

"Of course!" Emma squealed with realization. "It's common knowledge in my family that we are descendants of an escaped slave named Isaiah."

"Okay, that's a weird enough coincidence," Michael said. "But how did you and Claire end up here now?"

"Because they aren't done with her. They see her existing on a plane where she should never have existed and then getting away before they were done with her. She slipped through their grasp twice. As for Claire, her previous brush with evil and its remaining mark on her drew her here like a moth to a flame. It's that very history that makes her exactly what the place needs. If they can get her and Emma at the same time, they will be absolutely giddy."

"Where is Claire?" Michael asked, looking over his shoulder as if he thought she would magically appear there. "I don't like this."

There was a loud bang from the second floor.

Emma looked at her watch again. "It's 3:00."

≈

Claire had followed the voice through the cellar door and down into the tunnel. Her breath caught as she saw that her theory had been correct. Sitting there, tucked up against the wall, was her father.

Her relationship with her parents had disintegrated horribly in her teenage years. When she went to college she had never spoken to them again. So, how could her father be sitting here before her? She didn't know but stranger things had happened.

He smiled at her, something he had not done often, but when he did, he had a smile that was light and bright and could move oceans and mountains. His blonde hair was streaked with dirt from the tunnel, along with his red flannel shirt.

"Dad?" she asked, trying to keep her voice even. Still, it faltered, and she sounded more like a guilty child who has to face their punishment.

"Hello, sweetheart," he answered, the smile never leaving his face.

"How are you here?"

"Mom and I died a while ago. I was granted special permission to come to warn you. You're in danger, Claire."

Her face went hot as she was flooded with anger towards her parents' neglect.

"I know that." She bit out harshly. "There's too much evil here, Dad. Children were killed needlessly. I can't just leave. I have to get to the bottom of it."

"You have to listen to your father, Claire Renee," his voice grew more stern.

She shrank back, feeling thirteen instead of thirty-eight. This man had always terrified her.

His face grew soft again, and he continued. "I think it's wonderful that you want to help these poor souls. I am glad you finally got some spirituality, but it's too dangerous. I hate to say it, sweetheart, but they're dead and you're not. I'd like to leave it that way."

"Why do you care?" she asked coldly, suddenly feeling a surge of courage that hadn't been there before. "You were horrible to me as a kid. Both of you. You always acted like I was a demon child. Nothing I did was right. When I went to college, I married the first man I met just so I'd never have to see you again. Guess what? You didn't even try! I never got a single fucking phone call!"

"Mom and I made mistakes," he agreed. "We didn't know how to handle what happened when you were little. We wanted to protect you from the truth of what happened, but it was difficult to see past what it, and we were always scared it would happen again. It was wrong. I can admit that. Your mother's heart was broken when you left. We wished we could've changed things, but it was just too late."

"Damn right," she nodded her head angrily, her eyes flaring in the shadows of the tunnel.

"Come here," he took her hand. "I want to show you something."

He led her further into the darkness, farther down the tunnel.

Her breath caught in her throat when her eyes adjusted to the dark and she saw what she was standing over.

The body was long and lanky. There was no odor, and the clothing didn't appear to be disintegrated in any way. The hair on the back of the skull revealed a slightly balding man. She forced up the courage to look at the face and found herself staring into Brock's glossy eyes.

Just as the realization hit her she heard a voice in her ear. Not the voice of her father, but the voice of Brock, cruel and cold. "You're next."

She turned and looked into his angry, menacing face and he rushed her.

She let out her suppressed scream just as the loud crash came from the second floor.

*The girl was thrashing in the water when Josie entered the room. Margaret had her blonde hair balled up in one fist with one hand and the other pressed into the small of her back, forcing her into the water.*

*"Margaret! Margaret, stop it!" Josie rushed forward, grabbing Margaret by the shoulders.*

*"She is evil! The devil's child!" she growled out.*

*Josie instinctively grabbed a soap dish and slammed it into Margaret's head, knocking her to the side. Her grip on the child loosened as she crumpled to the ground.*

*"Josie!" Margaret screamed out as Josie pulled the child out of the water.*

*She performed chest compressions until the child began to cough up the water and then pulled her tight to her chest.*

*"She is evil! She must be destroyed!" Margaret struggled to get back to her feet.*

*"She is a child! You are evil!" Josie scooped the girl up into her arms and backed out of the room, her eyes not leaving Margaret.*

*"You're right! I am evil! So are you! This is your fault! Our evil created her, and we both know it! Keep her away from me. Do you understand me? Keep her away!"*

## CHAPTER TWENTY-NINE

As Emma, Michael, and Donovan climbed the staircase to the second floor, they heard continuous bangs, as though heavy pieces of furniture were being ferociously thrown from one wall to the next. Emma reached out and grabbed Michael's hand and squeezed it tightly. They locked eyes with each other and then with Donovan. There was a collective nod of agreement and the three of them charged up the remainder of the steps as one.

They were met with the sight of torn boxes and debris scattered all down the hallway, doors of rooms ripped off their hinges and tossed at random areas of the hallway. A chest of drawers lay on its side in the middle of the hall, the wood split clear down the middle from the force of the throw from one of the rooms. The drawers were hanging out, their contents scattered about.

The hallway also had a standoff of spirits in various stages of period clothing, disintegration, and decay. Emma's jaw dropped. She couldn't remember ever seeing anything so bizarre looking. The spirits were fighting each other.

There were bursts of colored light flying in every direction, bouncing off walls, breaking anything solid they came into contact with. Spirits were being lifted off their feet and slammed into walls. Otherworldly growls echoed in the confined space.

"Why are they fighting each other?" Emma wondered out loud in awe.

Michael clasped a hand down over her mouth, but it was too late. Emma's pondering question had drawn the attention of the closest group of spirits. They disbanded and approached.

The closest one, a big man with impossibly big hands and skin so dark they didn't see him until he was right up on them, shot out a burst of red light and Emma was struck by a sudden need for air.

She was lifted off her feet, though he was not touching her. Her lungs were burning, her eyes were watering, and she felt as though her windpipe was being dangerously constricted. She had the fleeting thought race through her mind that the light was an extension of his hand, and he was choking the life out of her. She saw him constrict his fingers; the veins popping before her eyes. He was choking her without even touching her.

She felt tugging on her legs and realized that Michael was trying fruitlessly to drag her back down to the ground.

There came a scream of, "NOO!!" followed by another burst of red light, though brighter, that came streaking into her field of vision and collided with the man.

Donovan had tackled the man with his light and his concentration was broken, along with his hold on her. Emma crumpled to the floor and began gasping for breath.

Her lungs were burning almost unbearably as she drew air back into them.

Michael was patting her firmly on the back whispering, "Breathe, baby. Just breathe. It's going to be okay.

When Emma's vision began to regulate once more, she looked back up and saw Donovan fighting with the man who had attacked her. There were more of these standoffs than she could count going on up and down the halls. Groans and growls of exertion filled the space like the sound of gunfire. She wasn't sure which people she needed to be rooting for. She wasn't sure she would ever know.

≈

Bailey's head was pounding when she came to. Her skull felt like it weighed a hundred pounds and as she sat up, she cringed with the effort it took to hold her head up. Her vision was blurry, and it was dark.

"*Where am I?*" she asked herself. She scrunched up her nose as she became overwhelmed with a stale, musty, and damp smell.

She rubbed her neck and looked around as her eyes adjusted to the dark. When she looked down at the skull, she let out a scream and began scrambling to pull herself up. Thankfully, it wasn't deep, and she was able to pull herself up within a couple of minutes.

"*Why the hell did they put me in a grave?*" she asked herself as she struggled to slow her breathing. "*That is so sick. Who DOES that?*"

She whipped around at the sound of a very loud and heavy bang. The house was now in view. A hand grasped her wrist and she was hit with a feeling as though her arm had been plunged into ice water.

She looked up at Josie's blank face, but now she could see some of her features starting to show through. Josie didn't speak, but there was a tugging sensation just behind her navel and the world around her seemed to turn into a wave of purple smoke. Her feet left the ground, and a deafening roar filled her ears. She was beginning to feel nauseous just as her feet slammed onto solid ground again.

The air cleared before her eyes and her jaw dropped at the sight before her. She was on the second floor of Blackwood Manor and there were ghosts fighting in every direction. There were flashes of light in various colors going everywhere. Donovan was attacking one man, and he was glowing and shooting lights, just like the spirits were.

She looked down the hallway just as Claire exited a door. She was covered in dirt, her clothing was torn, and she looked extremely pale. They locked eyes.

Bailey felt a nudge on her arm and looked up at Josie, who jerked her head to one side and began to glide around the throng of ghosts, who seemed completely oblivious to their presence. Bailey followed her, and she saw Claire doing the same at the opposite end of the hallway. They came together in front of Emma and Michael who were huddled together at the top of the staircase.

Josie took Bailey's hand with one of hers, and Emma's with the other. They all joined hands, forming a circle. They were all hit with the sensation that Bailey had when being transported into the house. Then the sensation grew more intense. The smoke surrounding them turned a deep, blood red and the nausea was a painful clench. When their feet hit the solid ground once more and the smoke cleared, they were all standing in the entryway at another time.

The entryway was lit by the glow of a candle sitting on a long and skinny table that had long since been removed. There was a squeak and Margaret was descending the stairs. The train of her dress dragged on the steps.

She looked bedraggled and her eyes were ringed with dark shadows that indicated she hadn't slept in days. In one hand, she clasped a revolver so tightly that her knuckles were white. She rounded the corner, as though headed toward the door to the cellar. She stopped and then put her back to the wall, leaning her head back and letting out a deep sigh, then took a few deep breaths and slowly let them out, looking intermittently at the door.

The look on her face was a mixture of worry and fear. Lines furrowed her brow, making her appear much older than her years. She wiped one hand against her skirts as if wiping away sweat.

The silence was broken by the slight creak of the cellar door opening slowly and Margaret's head whipped around in that direction once more. The group had no way of knowing that her heart was beating viciously in her chest, that her breath had caught in her throat because, outwardly, she projected an unnatural calm. They felt the reaction in their own bodies, however.

A small child slipped through a crack in the door, turning as soon as she was out to quietly close it behind her. Her blonde hair tumbled softly against her shoulders and the white nightgown she wore trailed the floor.

The door to the cellar had no more than clicked shut when Margaret fired the revolver. The sound of the shot was deafening in the enclosed space.

The girl froze in place, the red stain of blood spreading over the white nightgown in a gory, obvious mess. The girl turned slightly, looking down at her front, which had even more blood pouring over it. Her skin was already ghostly white. She looked up at Margaret with big, surprised eyes.

"Mama," she squeaked in barely more than a whisper and she collapsed.

Margaret stood against the wall; her jaw was hanging open and her eyes were wide with shock. She stood there only a few seconds, though it felt like an eternity—to Margaret as well as the group watching on in stunned horror.

"Lucy," she spoke softly at first. When the young girl didn't move Margaret lunged forward, throwing herself over the girl's body and pulling her into her arms. She didn't notice that she was kneeling in her child's blood. She noticed nothing but the small, white, lifeless body in front of her. "Lucy! LUCY!"

Margaret began to shake the girl, whose eyes were already glossed over. "LUCY, NO!!!" Margaret had the sternness of a mother in her voice, as though ordering her daughter to stop playing such a silly game. Despite the sternness, there was a quavering panic as her voice continued to go higher.

"Lucy, you stop fooling now!!" she screamed at the girl.

The massive front door of the house was thrown open with so much force that it bounced off the wall and Josie ran into the house, wearing night clothes of her own. She ran right through the group standing in the entryway, sending a shocking feeling of ice through them all.

She paused at the sight before her, grabbing onto the door jamb of the parlor for balance. She could only look down helplessly at Margaret, covered in Lucy's blood, Lucy's lifeless body, and Margaret sobbing hysterically.

"Miss Margaret?" she managed to say and took one cautious step forward. She knelt and wrapped her fingers around Lucy's wrist. "Miss Margaret," she said more firmly. "She's gone."

She reached out and gently pulled Lucy out of Margaret's arms and laid her on the floor. She softly brushed her fingers across her eyelids, closing them, and returned her gaze to Margaret. It was then that she saw the gun, tossed on the floor, now against the wall.

"What did you do?" she asked, her voice quavering.

"I-I," Margaret stammered, her voice shaking, tears rolling down her face like a river when the dam breaks. "She—she wasn't supposed to be down there," she finally managed to get out.

Josie paused a moment, trying to keep her voice calm. "She wasn't supposed to be where?"

As if in answer to her question, the cellar door opened once more, and half of Gloria's small face was visible through the crack in the door. Her too-large eyes seemed to pop with an eerie glow in the shadowy candlelight. "Lucy?" her small voice creaked out in a whisper.

Josie tensed automatically as Margaret slowly turned her head towards the open door. The tears on her face seemed to dry almost instantly, and her eyes blazed with an infuriating hatred. "You," Margaret said simply with a biting edge to her voice.

Josie's eyes darted cautiously between Margaret and Gloria.

Margaret's arm shot out quickly and wrenched the cellar door open, seizing the rag that Gloria was wearing as a dress and pulling her forcefully through the door.

"Miss Margaret! No! She's just a child!" Josie cried out and reached out for Margaret's shoulder.

Margaret jerked away and pulled Gloria roughly into her lap, ignoring her cries. She had one arm around her neck and the other around her stomach, holding her still.

"Look! Look what you made me do!" she hissed in Gloria's ear.

Gloria was crying hysterically and turned her head away toward the wall.

Margaret grabbed a fistful of hair and jerked her head back towards Lucy's body, forcing her to look.

"Miss Margaret!" Josie cried out again. She leaned forward and grabbed hold of her shoulder, shaking her slightly. "Let her go!"

Margaret removed her arm from around Gloria's stomach and shoved Josie backward into the wall. When she turned back to put her arm back around Gloria's stomach, Gloria instinctively bit down hard on her arm, causing her to howl in pain and loosen her grip on the girl.

Margaret threw Gloria away from her and seized her injured arm with her good one.

"Little bitch!" she growled and made to rush at her.

"No!" Josie tackled Margaret to the ground and pinned her. "Gloria, run!" she yelled at the girl who ran for the stairs as she sobbed uncontrollably.

Margaret was struggling under Josie, unable to push up with her injured arm. "She killed my baby!" Margaret screamed. "Let me go! She killed my baby!"

"She didn't!" Josie shouted back, tears streaming down her face. "What happened to Miss Lucy is horrible, but it is not the girl's fault! Miss Lucy has been going down to visit her almost every night for a year!"

"No!"

"Yes! She wanted her sister."

"No!" Margaret screamed out again and spit in Josie's face. Josie's grip loosened and Margaret pushed her way, got to her feet, and ran into the parlor to grab a fireplace poker. "She killed her! She's the daughter of evil! She must be stopped!"

Claire noted with surprise that the fireplace was in a different location and the parlor was one giant room.

Margaret ran back out, clutching the poker in her hand, and made for the stairs.

Josie ran after her, gathering her nightgown in her hands, so as not to trip on it.

The group heard a struggle at the top of the stairs. Josie's screams of "no" intermingled with Margaret's declarations that Gloria was evil.

Then there was a loud scream of terror and Josie came flying over the banister at an alarming rate and hit the hardwood floor face-first. Blood began to pool out from under her as she lay still. Her face completely caved in.

There was silence for a moment and Margaret began bellowing for Gloria again.

They heard the high-pitched screams of a child, the sound of metal slashing into something solid, and then a disturbing silence.

Margaret reappeared at the top of the stairs and began to descend them, dragging a lifeless Gloria behind her by the arm. She dropped her arm at the foot of the stairs, and her body sank to the ground like a sack of potatoes and glanced around at the three dead bodies and the blood that covered everything. She was covered head to toe in Gloria's blood and brain matter.

There was a creak from above and the face of a boy, Percy, looking down at his mother from the rails of the staircase banister.

There was the lurching sensation in their stomachs again as they became engulfed in smoke.

When they settled again, they were in the entryway, modern day, the sounds of the fighting spirits going strong above them. Josie turned, her face starting to come back.

"You know what to do now."

Claire nodded. She certainly did.

## CHAPTER THIRTY

When Josie disappeared in a puff of red smoke, the members of the group stood in silence for a moment, looking to Claire for guidance. Bailey folded into her mother's arms, but her eyes never left Claire.

"Claire?" Emma was finally the one to break the silence. "What did she mean? You know what to do?"

Claire looked into the parlor before striding in and going right up to the fireplace. "Did any of you notice that the parlor was completely different in that memory?" she asked.

"So?" Michael's voice was shaky despite the outward calm that he was displaying for his family. "It's an old house. There is no telling how much it has been renovated."

"Yes, but the fireplace is now here in this corner." Claire rubbed her hand over the chipped brick where Donovan had been working. "This room was divided into three separate rooms with the fireplaces creating a column. Remember what Donovan said? That there was enough space in the middle for a small room?"

Michael's eyes went wide with realization as his own memories flooded him. "He told me he thought something was in there. He was going at that brick like a madman despite telling us before that it could cause the walls to collapse."

"That doesn't make sense," Emma shook her head. "Gloria is in that grave out there. You said her skull was smashed so you knew it was her. Josie wanted us to help Gloria. Gloria was buried."

"Em, think about it," Claire said with a slight edge to her voice. "Gloria was in *Lucy's* grave."

Bailey spoke up for the first time. "If Gloria was in Lucy's grave, then where is Lucy?"

The group turned, staring into the crumbling brick of the fireplace as though it were a deep abyss radiating with darkness and horror.

"She's in the wall?" Emma asked, horrified. "Why the hell would she put her in the wall?"

"It actually makes perfect sense," Claire answered as she ran the edge of her finger over the hole in the brick that Donovan had started. "Margaret had completely lost her mind. She'd want to keep Lucy close to her, and she wouldn't have known what to do about Gloria. A child that no one knew anything about."

She knelt and pressed her eye to the hole, though all she saw was a seemingly never-ending darkness. "It would have made perfect sense to her to put Gloria in Lucy's grave and keep Lucy close. Under the disguise of a home renovation for heat."

"There's no way she could have done this alone," Michael shook his head. "There must be some other explanation."

"Well, it's not exactly expertly done, is it?" Claire asked, turning to face the group. "Look, I know this is a gruesome theory, but it's time to face it. We have three people murdered by Margaret that night and only two bodies and a radically changed parlor. If anyone else has any theories I would love to hear them."

The group remained silent, looking anxiously toward Claire and the fireplace. Claire picked up the sledgehammer that Donovan had left abandoned on the hearth and swung it once, making contact with the brick and having it shift even more. Then she was thrown back with such force that the couch slid backward from the inertia of her making contact with it in the small of her back.

She let out a howl of pain, and Emma ran forward to try to help her up just as the air in the room began to thin and become hazy. It was filling with thick red smoke and from it, Margaret emerged, almost entirely transformed. All that was left of her human self was a nose that was slowly beginning to waste away to snakelike slits but was not quite there yet, leaving her nose as a bump in the center of her face. It was slit and had yet more smoke puffing out of it with each breath, with each demonic growl. She was standing before the fireplace, her red eyes blazing.

The sounds of the fighting continued above them, and the walls began to shake as a deafening sound filled the room.

The group watched in stunned silence as Bailey took one tentative step forward, straightening her spine as she approached Margaret. Michael tried to seize her arm as she walked past him, but she pulled it quickly from his grasp, never breaking eye contact with Margaret.

She stopped directly in front of her. "Step aside," she said with surprising confidence in her tone.

Margaret's claw-like arm shot out and grasped Bailey by the neck and began to squeeze, lifting her off her feet.

"NO!!" Emma charged forward and grabbed at Margaret, though she slid right through her as though she were nothing more than smoke.

Michael grabbed hold of Bailey's ankles and tried desperately to yank her down. The horrifying choking sounds that were coming from her had them both in tears, and Emma crawled over to grab Bailey's ankles as well, silently praying that their joint force would be enough to pull her from Margaret's grasp and back to safety. Their attempts were fruitless.

The claws that replaced Margaret's fingers dug into the soft tissue of Bailey's neck and blood began to ooze from the wounds, flowing freely down her neck and staining the collar of her shirt. Bailey was turning blue. Her eyes were bulging, and her entire body seemed to be on fire as it screamed for oxygen. She grasped at Margaret's claws with her hands. As her vision began to blur, blue electricity began to crackle from her fingertips.

Suddenly, a pulse of brilliant blue light emerged throughout the room and Margaret howled in pain. Her grip on Bailey loosened, and she dropped her to the floor and cowered against the wall, covering her face with her claws.

Bailey scrambled to her feet and looked around desperately, trying to see where the blue light was coming from. She looked at the faces of her parents, who were looking at her with shock. She looked at Claire, who was holding onto the arm of the couch and shakily making her way to her feet, though her eyes stayed locked on Bailey.

Bailey looked down and was shocked to see that the blue light was shining through her skin, making it almost entirely translucent.

There was a cracking sound and a swish of red smoke and the room was suddenly filled with angry-looking spirits, many of whom wedged themselves between Bailey and Margaret.

Emma rushed forward and grasped her daughter's hand. The moment that contact was made, Emma emitted a red light. Their lights mixed, creating a stunning, beautiful purple. Their eyes met, and Emma slowly nodded her head once. They raised their hands, and the light pulsed, tossing spirits aside and simultaneously shooting out tendrils of flame.

Brock emerged from the throng of spirits, coming at Claire with dark eyes, the beginnings of horns already growing out of his head, and his sick, twisted grin. She raised her hands and a white light shot out, and Brock screamed as it hit him square in the chest.

Claire then spun around the room, leaving her hands up, shooting the light like an automatic weapon, spirits howling in pain as it hit them.

The air had a burning smell as the effect of the sheer power coursing throughout the room now had a life of its own. As the spirits began to evaporate into nothing, Margaret was left exposed.

Bailey and Emma shot a blast at the fireplace that instantly exploded, and from the dirt within, Lucy pulled herself out. She was covered in soot, had rotten skin, dirty hair, blood-soaked rags of a nightgown hanging from her tiny frame, and black eyes. The blackest that any of them had seen at this point.

"Hello, Mother," Lucy growled out in a croaky voice.

"Lucy," Margaret gasped. "No! It was a mistake! You know that! You know that!"

But Lucy did not hesitate. Without warning, she shot forward, plunging her teeth into Margaret's throat. Margaret howled with pain and little by little she became more human-like, losing her appalling features. As she lost them, however, Lucy gained them. Lucy's skin turned scaly, horns shot from her forehead, growing at an alarming rate.

Her small hands became massive claws, and her bare feet became hooves.

When it seemed as though all of Margaret's power, her force, the very essence of her *being* was drained and her body grew limp, Lucy tossed her carelessly to the ground and turned to face the group. She let out an evil grin and the smoke that spilled out of the slits that now served as her nose revealed her delight. As one, Claire, Emma, and Bailey began to shoot their light toward her, and in turn, she shot the smoke at them.

The power in the room was suffocating for Michael, sitting in the corner and watching in stunned silence. He was immobile. Every nerve ending in his body was screaming at him to get up and get his family out, but he couldn't move. Realistically, his mind reasoned that this evil would never be over without them, and would eventually spill right out of Blackwood Manor, poisoning the land and everything it touched, dooming existence as they all knew it. So, he was powerless as he watched in silent horror the mix of the light and the smoke, the tendrils of flame that threw sparks onto the dry floorboards.

He tried his hardest to call out to the others, to warn them, as those sparks became a full-on flame, igniting the room, feeding on the furniture, the curtains. Hard as he screamed, no sound came from his mouth, despite the vibrations he could physically feel in his vocal cords. Still, he could not move. He was powerless to watch and feel the flames engulfing them.

## CHAPTER THIRTY-ONE

The smoke filled the air in the silence of Blackwood Manor. The burning smell was overwhelming, despite the fact that the brilliant fire had never left the parlor and had long since burned out, as though there was an invisible barrier keeping it under control. Only tiny embers remained scattered on the floor. Josie stood in the doorway to the parlor, her face entirely returned and a hand resting softly on Gloria's shoulder. "See there?" she said softly. She gently turned Gloria towards Margaret's body, crumpled on the floor, and very human.

She felt a tug of grief for the woman that had been her best friend for longer than she could honestly remember, but the grief melted away as she remembered that Margaret had become a monster like no other, killing her, killing her own children. Now she felt only pity and disgust. She wasn't proud of herself, but she had accomplished her mission. That was the most important thing of all.

"I told you she was just a person hiding behind a mask," she addressed Gloria again, "and now she's gone. You don't have to be frightened anymore. You can go."

Gloria twisted her head up and blinked at Josie. "What about Lucy?"

"Lucy is letting you go," she smiled down at the girl, but that smile didn't quite reach her eyes. "She knows it wasn't your fault. None of this was your fault. You set it in motion, but it was not your fault. All you did was be born."

A light appeared behind them, making everything behind it disappear, like a brilliant backdrop. She gently patted Gloria's shoulders. "Okay, love. Time to go."

Gloria took a step towards the light and then turned back. "What about them?" she nodded towards the pile of charred bodies in the parlor.

Josie sighed. "They're just sleeping, love. Go on now, or you'll miss your chance."

Gloria nodded and walked into the light, which immediately died once she stepped through. Josie walked to the spot where she had just been standing, hoping to feel her energy, but it was no longer there.

She turned towards Donovan who was sitting on the staircase watching and could no longer hold back the sobs. He rose from his spot, strode down the steps quickly, and pulled her into his arms.

"You did the right thing," he said gently, patting her back. "You had to get her out of here."

"What are we going to do now?" she sobbed into his chest. "This wasn't supposed to happen. It's going to be even worse now, isn't it?"

He didn't answer, just held her in his arms and looked over her shoulder into what was left of the parlor. He didn't want to voice it, but he had a sneaking suspicion that she was right.

≈

From the other side of the road across from Blackwood Manor, Sadie Collins peeked her head around the side of a large oak tree. She had watched silently as lights in various colors shone through the windows lightning quick, like whips. She had watched as the orange glow of fire had shown through the first-floor window of the parlor she spent many years cleaning. She watched as the fire burned down and now there had been no movement and darkness for at least an hour.

She felt the suffocating thickness of the air, even at this distance, and she let out a low, shallow breath before turning her back to the tree and sinking down to the earth, allowing herself to become absorbed in her thoughts.

She was afraid she knew what she would find if she were to waltz into the house right now, but she couldn't bring herself to do so. She had known the risks, of course. The energy of the two women and the young girl had been overwhelming when they visited her at the nursing home. Their auras had told a story of their own.

She wondered if she should have been more open about the risks. She had been completely open and honest about the auras, the transformation of evil, the devil-like creatures that these spirits would become the longer they hung around and the angrier they became. She was honest about what she had seen, and she was completely sure that the combination of Claire and Bailey's powers could be the answer. So, she had chosen to keep her mouth shut.

She hadn't been able to read Emma as well as the others, which was something that didn't happen to her often. There was one thing she was certain of; had she told Emma all the risks of her daughter's power, she never would have allowed her to go back to the house and fight the evil. There would have been no chance then. Despite the risks, there *was* a good chance that they could have ended it all. So, in the hope that all would be well, she had stayed silent.

Sadie closed her eyes, allowing a single tear to roll down her cheek as she remembered the girl's frightened persona as the power bubbled off her fingertips. That orange glow, though, was not normal. The air was ill heavy, suffocating. The hair on the back of her neck was standing on end. No, the evil was not gone. The evil was still here. Judging by the fire and the ceased lights, the fight was over. That could only mean one thing. The women were dead. That poor, sweet girl.

Should she have said something? She struggled with the question in her mind. She continued to tell herself that she had no choice. The positive outcome would have been incredible. There was no way she could chance that. But there had been risks. She still could have informed them. She could have told them that the amount of power in that house from the living and from the dead was more than she had ever seen in her lifetime. She could have told them that the more spirits they took out, and especially if they got Margaret, there was a chance another angry spirit could absorb the power and be more dangerous than any of the others had been. She could have told them that if that happened, the new spirit would also be able to take in their power, making them nearly invincible to the next talented person who came along. She could have told them that they could potentially take out hundreds of spirits but create a new, almighty one. Could have. Why didn't she?

The answer was simple. She had believed their combined power would be enough. She couldn't think of a spirit that would be so thirsty for revenge that it would all backfire. Now the real question was, would she ever forgive herself for her silence?

## *EPILOGUE*

### *TEN YEARS LATER—IN 2019*

On the hot summer day, Richard Price barely felt the heat. He didn't care how disheveled his appearance was or about the strong smell of whiskey that was coming out of his pores. He didn't care that he had stolen the bottle from a homeless man almost as soon as he had left the airport. He only cared that he needed courage. The courage to face the one thing that had consumed his mind for the past ten years. Blackwood Manor.

He gripped the steering wheel and ground his teeth unconsciously. How innocent and naive he had been when Aunt Claire had sat at the dinner table that day and told them she had bought Blackwood Manor. He and Bailey had been so fascinated. Ghost stories were fun after all, weren't they?

He shook his head and muttered, "Stupid." The next few months had gone by unnaturally fast, with one new thing after another happening. He would never get the image of the woman with the horns who had beat him mercilessly in the stairwell out of his mind. After the fire in their home, when they had been forced to move to Blackwood Manor, he had done his best to stay in the cottage out back where, surprisingly, nothing ever happened to him. Bailey hadn't been so lucky. Neither had Callie. Sweet Callie.

When their parents hadn't come to collect them after more than twenty-four hours and no phone call, which was completely unlike them, his friend's mom had become worried and began calling hospitals and the police, thinking they may have gotten into an accident. It was so much worse than she had thought.

A police officer had come to the house and told them that there had been a fire at Blackwood Manor and that his parents, Bailey, and even Aunt Claire had perished in the fire. They believed it to be faulty wiring and said that the rest of the house was fine. It had all been contained to the one room, though the four of them hadn't been able to get out. Faulty wiring. He knew the truth.

There wasn't much family to speak of. All his mom's family was gone and most of his dad's. He and Callie had been sent to live with a distant uncle on his father's side, whom he had met once at a family reunion. The uncle happened to be a racist bigot and had never treated him and Callie like family. They were merely an obligation; there because of the money set aside for their care.

Callie was tortured over the course of the next ten years. Torn apart by the emotional abuse and neglect of their uncle, of the memories of Bailey hurting her while possessed that plagued her every night when she went to sleep. She recounted it truthfully in therapy more than once, only to be locked away due to delusions and diagnosed with paranoid schizophrenia. Finally, last month, she had taken an entire bottle of pills and ended her pain. Now he was alone.

On his eighteenth birthday, Richard had received an ironic bit of correspondence. Aunt Claire had no family. In her will, she had left everything she owned to his mother, who had left everything to her children. He had been the owner of Blackwood Manor for ten years and had not even known it. The money had gone into a trust. Now that he was eighteen, he had access to it, as well as the keys.

He pulled the rental car to a stop on the road in front of the house and frowned at the overwhelming feeling in the air, the way his breathing slowed, the way the house still seemed to pull at him like a magnet. The driveway was once again completely overgrown and he would never get the car up it.

He got out of the car, pocketed his keys, and began the trek up to the house. As he got closer, he felt his lungs constricting, and he felt an uncontrollable need to run as if an outside force had taken control of his body. He felt the voice in his head echoing like surround sound, *"Hello, Richie. Come in. Kick off your shoes. It's been too long."*

"Stop it," he hissed between clenched teeth and found the inner power to slow his feet.

*"Welcome home,"* the voice said.

"Not today, you big bitch," he muttered. There it was. Now he found himself on the cracked steps of the porch and looked at the broken windows and the graffitied walls. He slipped the key from the Realtor into the lock and stepped through the door, closing it behind him.

What he didn't see was his mother banging on the upstairs window screaming at him to turn around. He didn't see Aunt Claire trying to force him away his entire walk up the path, and he didn't see his father screaming at him from the foot of the staircase. He didn't see Bailey leaning over the banister yelling at him to get the hell out.

Now the front windows of Blackwood Manor glowed, seeming to dance once again. Now the timeline would be corrected. Now she was complete.

## Acknowledgments

What a crazy and wild ride I've had writing this book! This has been a deep passion for me. There have been many sleepless nights and a few headaches along the way, but none of that overpowers the joys that I experienced.

I've had this one tumbling around in the back of my brain since I was child. I lived in an older part of town, full of old houses— (you know the type), and my best friend lived in one right down the street. Between our two houses, we had our fair share of spooks. Loud noises, shadows, things getting moved or lost. Everyone in both households shared stories of things they couldn't explain. Were we truly haunted? Who knows? Maybe we were just kids who got a rush out of being scared. Either way, those experiences always stuck with me. I always thought it would make a great book.

I'd like to thank everyone who has helped me shape this book into what it is today. For every critique partner who read those early pages, to the betas who let me know if they weren't understanding a plot point, I thank you from the bottom of my heart. My sister, fellow author Kat Bethel has been my biggest cheerleader, and I'm not sure I would have had the confidence without your support. Thank you and I love you.

Thank you to my editor Jenny Sliger with Owl Eyes Studios and cover designer Kelley York with Sleepy Fox Studios.

Then there's you, dear readers. You are the ones that make this art so enjoyable so don't stop reading! There's more Blackwood Manor to come so I hope you'll join me in the sequel!

www.ingramcontent.com/pod-product-compliance
Lightning Source LLC
Chambersburg PA
CBHW071355150726
48000CB00001B/29